BEATNIKKI'S CAFÉ

RENEE JAMES

AMBLE
PRESS

2023

Amble Press

Copyright © 2023 Renee James

Print ISBN: 978-1-61294-267-4

Amble Press First Edition: June 2023

Printed in the United States of America on acid-free paper.

Cover designer:
Ann McMan, TreeHouse Studio

Amble Press
PO Box 3671
Ann Arbor MI 48106-3671

www.amblepressbooks.com

To the Pioneers

We take them for granted today, but before I came out as trans, there was a generation of transgender people who blazed a trail for the rest of us to follow. They organized private events where trans people could express themselves. They found teachers to educate us on the things we didn't learn in childhood and adolescence. They created relationships with traditional groups and institutions, like the local police and retail store managers. And they demanded of themselves and those of us who came later that we get out and be seen, that we participate in the world as equals, that we take our place in American society as contributors and full citizens.

It's true, we have a long way to go to achieve full equality and acceptance, but without the pioneers, we'd still be hiding in dark places or, worse, in costumes and false faces.

The torch has been passed. Let us remember the pioneers and go forth with the same resolve and determination they brought to the challenge.

CHICAGO

No one paid any special attention to the guy when he came in. The staff was cleaning up after the morning coffee rush and getting the café ready for the lunch crowd. The few patrons in the place were sitting at the coffee bar.

The guy paused at the entrance to eyeball the layout. One side of the coffee bar was a game room, with tables that had chessboard tops and a dart board on one wall. The other side had regular tables and overstuffed chairs and a small stage at one end. The guy strolled over to a table by the window in the game room and sat down.

He was a big, hulking guy, a forty-year-old version of a lineman on a high school football team. He might have even played college, as big as he was. He had a shaved head underneath a red MAGA hat, and he wore a leather vest that bristled with steel studs and the symbols of the White Power movement, including an iron cross and a pin bearing the image of a swastika overlaying a green clover leaf. He wore a necklace with a swastika pendant, and swastika studs in his ear lobes. He was different from most BeatNikki customers, who were mostly Yuppies in the morning and arty types at night, and a blend of both during the rest of the day. But the neighborhood still had all types, and BeatNikki's pulled in all types, too, even the occasional biker.

The guy watched the staff as they mopped the floors, wiped the tables, and hustled food from the kitchen in back to the displays in the coffee bar. He smirked a little as he watched. They were a bizarre group. There was a twenty-ish girl with shocking red hair and piercings in her ears, nose, and lips. She flirted a lot with a twenty-ish guy with shocking blue hair and a headful of piercings. She cleaned tables while he mopped floors. There was a short, pudgy guy with facial hair and a beer belly mixing coffee drinks at the bar. He called the blue-haired guy to the bar to taste a drink, and at that moment a tall—really tall—woman in flared slacks and heels brought a tray of food out from the kitchen.

The blue-haired guy sampled the drink. "I give it a six," he said. "Maybe a seven for effort. It's nice you still work with us little people."

The red-haired woman joined the humor. "You're a born one-percenter, Little John. A pure capitalist pig."

Little John flushed a little. "Have your fun," he said.

The tall woman patted him on the back. "I told you, the life of a rich business owner isn't easy."

"It's not exactly ten percent of Amazon," Little John said.

"Ten percent of this place is way cooler than Amazon," said the blue-haired guy.

The new customer heard the banter, but his attention was focused on the woman. She was a good six feet tall and slim, but she was also buxom and had unusually wide shoulders. She had long, curly hair and her face was an exotic blend of strong bone structure, almond-shaped eyes and puffy lips. She wore a silk blouse cut low enough to show off her cleavage. She moved with a dignified grace—perfect posture, gliding steps, quiet footfalls—and she spoke to the others with quiet authority. She was obviously the "Nikki" of BeatNikki's Café, and she was pretty hot for a mature woman, maybe mid-thirties, maybe forty. And the other thing about her, the bigger thing, was the fact she was obviously a transgender woman. Her large hands and feet, the thick bones in her wrists, and her muscular calves were all dead giveaways if you knew what to look for, and the guy did.

The guy smirked as the red-haired girl grabbed an order pad and came to his table.

"First time here?" she asked with the youthful exuberance of a tip-hunter.

"It sure is, honey," he said.

She welcomed him, then took his order. When she came back with his coffee and roll, he said, "Can I ask you a question?"

"Sure." She said it with that same youthful enthusiasm.

The guy smiled, but it wasn't a friendly smile. "Are you a lesbo or a twink, like everyone else in here?"

The girl blinked and froze, like a deer caught in the headlights of a car. Then her face registered fear and sadness. "Enjoy your coffee," she said, and spun away.

The girl with shocking red hair went to the coffee bar where the tall woman was stocking display shelves with sandwiches and pastries.

"Nikki," she said, "that guy in the MAGA hat has Nazi shit all over his body and he just asked me if I'm a lesbo or a twink like everyone else in here." Her voice trembled a little as she said it. The guy had really gotten to her.

Nikki glanced at the guy who leered back at them. Nikki's face clouded. "I'll take care of it," she said. Her voice was calm, but there was an edge to it.

"Nikki, please leave it alone," said Little John. "He'll be gone pretty soon."

Nikki smiled. "He'll be gone sooner than that. It's bad

enough we have a Nazi for a president. We don't have to serve them here."

Nikki walked to the man's table. "Good news," she said, "your tab's on the house. Leave."

The guy grinned. "You're kicking me out?"

"Not yet," said Nikki.

"How's a faggot like you going to throw me out?" The guy's grin turned to a sneer.

Nikki smiled at him coolly. "It doesn't matter, because you're leaving."

"I didn't do anything."

Nikki's face got serious. "Keep it that way."

The guy stood. "I've never been thrown out of a place by a tranny before. Wait'll I tell the guys."

Nikki gestured to the exit. "Don't come back."

The guy sneered again and pointed at Nikki's chest like his finger was the barrel of a pistol. He used his thumb to pantomime the pistol being shot. He rounded his eyebrows for emphasis, then left, laughing out loud.

1

His meaty fist looms inches from my face. It's as big as a ham and as hard as a sledgehammer. It can flatten my nose or shatter my jaw or crush my skull. He's trying to intimidate me and it's working. If I had anything in my bladder right now, I'd pee in my pants.

Just beyond his fist, at the other end of his outstretched arm, his smile comes slowly into focus, a curious blend of dull-wittedness and pure malice. Light glints from a chrome-plated swastika on his necklace. I saw these things when I kicked him out of the café, but he didn't seem so shocking then. Seeing him now, like this, realization floods over me. This is the face of evil. I'm an atheist. I don't believe in supernatural gods and devils, but I've seen enough evil in my life to understand that it exists in abundance.

"I'll say this for you, queenie," he says. His brows lift, making his face seem more intelligent but no less cruel. "You got more balls than this *guy*." He says "guy" ironically, as if my business partner isn't really a man. Little John is a man, one of the best I've ever known, but he started life with a female body. We have star-crossed body parts in common. I was born with a male body and a female mind. If we could have swapped bodies, life would have been a lot easier for both of us, and this Nazi hooligan would be terrorizing someone else.

We're standing in the service alley behind BeatNikki's, my café, which sits just beyond the leafy streets of Chicago's prestigious Lincoln Park neighborhood. This used to be a so-called "marginal" neighborhood where crime was more common than in the "nice" areas of the city like Lincoln Park. But gentrification has taken place in recent years, and situations like this have ceased to occur. Until now.

Mr. Swastika attacked Little John when he took trash out to the dumpster in the alley. I saw it from a window in the kitchen and came running. I probably should have called the police instead. I'm not exactly striking terror in this man's heart. I'm tall and have unusually broad shoulders for a woman, but years of hormone therapy have feminized my body, and whatever strength I had as a male is long gone. Plus, I'm wearing heels, which is insane, but it's one of the things I do to make myself feel like a woman.

Mr. Swastika is massive. At least six-four, maybe two-seventy. He continues to impugn Little John's testicles then asks me if I've had my dick cut off yet. He holds Little John by his shirtfront with one hand and drags him along as he reaches for me with the other. Little John is barely five-four and looks like a teddy bear being held at arm's length by an upland gorilla.

"Let's see if the pussy has a pussy," he smirks, his free hand groping for my crotch.

I step back beyond his reach. I should run for the café, lock the door, and call the police, but if I do, he'll pulverize Little John before the cops even start their engines. So, I remain here, waiting for Mr. Swastika to beat both of us into submission.

Unless, of course, he's here to kill us. That's a real possibility in this, the summer of 2017, the first summer of the Trump presidency. Right-wing crazies all over the country have taken his election as a signal that it's open season on minorities, and transgender people are a favorite target of theirs. So far, in Chicago's white-ish middle-class neighborhoods, it's been mostly verbal harassment, but that's bound to change. These people feel entitled to shoot, maim, and kill as they wish.

"Oh, playing hard to get," he says, that horrid grin spreading across his face like a flesh-eating disease. His teeth are curiously white, like a toothpaste commercial, but misplaced on his sagging, lantern-jawed face, like a tuxedo on a flophouse wino. He scuttles another step closer, dragging Little John like a rag doll, his quickness so startling I don't respond fast enough. He seizes one of my breasts. I try to pull away but he squeezes as hard as he can, and he's very strong. The pain brings tears to my eyes and my mind goes red with rage. He giggles about my "big titties." I try to push his hand away. He giggles again, a taunting giggle. He yanks me toward him. I raise one hand to claw at his face, scratching for his eyes with my nails. Just as I feel soft tissue, his huge hand engulfs my wrist and pulls my hand away as easily as a parent stops a child from grabbing candy at a grocery store. He giggles again. This is fun for him. But he's also arrogant and his arrogance is blinding him, and that's my chance.

He's still sneering and giggling as I cock my right leg, and he's still oblivious as my foot thunders downward. But when my spike heel shatters the small bones in his foot, his world explodes in pain and suffering. Even though I'm a middle-aged woman, I stay in shape, and I take self-defense classes, and I'm heavy enough to make a spike heel feel like Thor's hammer slamming onto his foot.

Mr. Swastika howls. He releases me and Little John and bends forward, eyes closed, all his weight on one leg. His ear-splitting curses echo down the alley, and his face goes scarlet with rage and pain. His fury should frighten me, but I have my own anger issues. When people try to intimidate me, I can get crazy. And unlike Mr. Swastika, when I go into attack mode, I don't play with my prey.

I reach for his face again, both hands this time. He grabs one hand, but the other finds its target. I push the long pink nail of my thumb as deep into his eye socket as it will go. At some depth, it could kill him. That would be okay with me. He shrieks, falls to the ground covering his wounded eye with both hands, blood oozing from between his fingers. He'll never see a swastika with that eye again. I raise my right foot above him and look for targets. A couple broken ribs would slow him down for a few days. A hard shot to his temple or the vertebrae at the base of his neck could kill him and he'd never bother another civilized person again.

Little John wraps his arms around me and walks me back a step.

"You could kill him," Little John admonishes me.

"What's your point?" I'm shaking with adrenaline and I'm fueled by a fire this Nazi never imagined. When I was transitioning, a knuckle-dragger like him beat me to within an inch of my life because he didn't like my looks, and when the kicks and punches stopped, he peed on me. That's why I started self-defense classes and regular workouts. That's why I worked on my attitude. I'm fully prepared to kill this thug and take my chances. Whatever comes next, it won't be a guilty conscience.

Little John gets in my face.

"If you kill him, you're no better than they are." He lets that sink in for a minute, but I don't give a tinker's damn about morality right now. He sees I'm not convinced.

"And the lawsuits," he says. "You could lose everything. These morons all belong to groups that have money and lawyers and sympathetic cops and judges. Our café could become one of their profit centers."

That works.

I nod slowly and step around Little John to kneel beside the writing goon. I speak directly into his ear.

"If you ever come here again, I'll tear your limbs out of their sockets." I say it in a half-whisper. My body is still trembling with adrenaline rush, but my voice is as steady as a psychopath's.

He scoffs. I'm a fairy, after all, and he's a big tough guy who preys on people like me.

"We'll get you," he rasps. "You'll beg us to kill you." His words are barely audible because of his pain.

"Okay," I say to Little John. "Go call the cops. If he doesn't try to get up, I won't kill him."

Little John shakes his head. "Listen to you, Nikki."

He peels off his shirt. His upper torso is what he imagined a male body to be all the years he was in a female body—a hairy chest, a tattoo of a crucifix over his heart, and a beer belly. He crouches beside our horizontal Nazi and binds the man's hands with his shirt.

"I'll stay. You call the cops," he commands. It's his alpha-male voice, which works for him even though we both know he doesn't have an aggressive bone in his body.

"Kill that bastard if he moves."

"Sure," says Little John, as if I'd told him to steal a Rolls Royce.

"I mean it," I say. "Don't let him get away."

"Call the police," he says. "I'll take care of this."

I stop at the door and look back. Little John is standing at the goon's head, bending at the waist, saying something to him. If I were a ventriloquist, Mr. Swastika would be hearing that if he so much as twitches we're going to cut open his abdomen and stuff his intestines down his throat. But Little John is probably reciting Scripture to him. I take a deep breath. He's right, but our arrogant Nazi still deserves every bit of what I wanted to give him.

As I enter the café, Mr. Swastika's threat plays again in my mind. I laugh to myself, imagining the kind of friends he would have. The America-First Lobotomy Clinic All-Stars.

Detective Sergeant Brooks gives me the stink-eye, a condescending blend of I-know-you're-queer and I-can't-bear-to-look-at-you. He glances away from me frequently, eyeballing other people at the scene, checking his notebook, shifting his gaze to Little John, as if he couldn't stand to look at me. We've given our accounts of what happened twice already, once with Little John talking to Brooks and me to a different cop, the second time, together, to Brooks.

"So you kicked him out of your café, then you assaulted him?" Brooks asks, as they load the ailing Nazi into an ambulance.

"After I asked him to leave, he attacked Little John, then me, back here. I disabled him," I say, keeping my answers as short as possible. He's almost as hostile to us as the goon was.

"You claim he made an unwanted advance on you?"

"I said he squeezed my breast to disable me, and tried to fondle my crotch to see if I had a pussy." I offer to show him the bruises on my breast. My forthrightness about body parts makes Brooks wince and look away. "He was assaulting my business partner and he made it clear he intended to do harm to both of us."

"What kind of harm?" Brooks looks me in the eye.

"He was going to beat us bloody," I say. "Our lives were in danger."

"But all he said was, you have more balls than Mister—" He pauses deliberately to look up Little John's name in his notes. "Mister McGee, here, and he said he wanted to see if you had female genitalia. Just words, right?"

I don't bother to respond, and neither does Little John. It's obvious where this is going.

Brooks continues, "Did he ever say he was going to beat you

10

up or kill you?"

"I told you what he said," I snap. "And I described how he assaulted us."

Little John inserts himself between Brooks and me before I say something I regret.

"We were both assaulted by that man," says Little John. "He attacked me without provocation on our property," Little John continues, his voice quiet, but with a little edge to it. "He walked up to me and began pushing me around and telling me I didn't belong here. When Nikki came, he assaulted her, too."

Brooks glances from Little John to his notebook, not writing anything down. He flashes a phony smile at Little John.

"Right," he says. He slaps the notebook closed and pockets it. "We'll get back to you if we have any questions." He finishes the sentence walking away.

"You're arresting him, right?" Little John calls after Brooks.

Brooks stops, turns, flashes his sarcastic smile again.

"We'll charge him," he says, "but it's not like he committed the crime of the century. The guy will probably bail out as soon as he can walk, and then I'd bet he'll sue you for assault."

Little John and I look at each other in shock.

"Can you believe that?" Little John asks me, watching Brooks leave.

"A year ago, I'd have said that was crazy," I answer.

I don't complete the rest of the thought, but we're both thinking it. We are well into the Age of Insanity. Every day in Trump's America is an anything-can-happen day.

JUNE 2017

2

Blythe's house is a verdant, three-block stroll from the Winnetka train station. This is millionaire country, and I stick out like a panhandler at a debutante ball, but it's a gorgeous walk through a veritable forest of old hardwoods now in full leaf, drenching the narrow streets and sidewalks in lush shade. Beneath the trees are manicured lawns and beyond the lawns are cavernous houses that shout "old money" the way urine-scented L-station stairways scream "Saturday morning" in my neighborhood.

I pass a woman walking her golden retriever. She smiles and greets me. If she's startled to see a tall transgender woman in this aristocratic neighborhood, she doesn't show it. Maybe it's poise that comes with good breeding, or maybe she's the neighborhood communist—she's walking her own dog, after all.

May has come and gone and we survived the Nazi incident without any further repercussions, but now I face what may be an even greater test of my will to live: I'm picking up my daughter for a week of visitation. It will be the first time since her childhood we've spent more than a day together. She's almost sixteen and she hates me, so this will probably be a week of mud wrestling.

I try to push these thoughts from my head as I walk up to the imposing front door of the castle-like house my daughter and ex-wife share with my ex-mother-in-law. I pause before ringing the doorbell. I fear it will bring my ex-wife's frowning visage to the fore. She will swing open the door and stand at the threshold while her eyes survey the face and body of the woman who was once the man she loved and married and with whom she produced a child. Her sense of loss still makes me feel like a cheat and a fraud, not really a woman, and not a man, either. It's an irrational fear—I haven't seen Blythe in months. My daughter has been answering the door on visitation days for the past year, always greeting me in sullen silence, which is no picnic either.

The doorbell chimes a tune from some classical music piece. I position myself to be in the center of the security camera image. Clicks and rattles announce the release of locks and deadbolts. The door opens to reveal my daughter, Morgan, and behind her, Blythe's mother, a prune-faced bitch of a woman who's too mean to get into hell when she dies. They're posed in the grand foyer, a huge, sundrenched room rendered in earth tones. At its center is a wide, curving staircase that leads majestically to a second floor of lavish bedrooms and bathrooms.

Blythe's mother looks like she's got a flagpole up her ass, as usual, and Morgan also has the sour look on her face that's been there so long I can't remember what she looks like when she smiles. She opens the door wide enough for me to come in, but says nothing. Her attitude towards me is all about my transition. Having a dad who became a woman is the source of constant embarrassment for her, and her mother and grandmother have reinforced the idea that I'm a subhuman species. I've consulted a couple of professionals and learned there's not a lot I can do about Morgan's anger except to keep reaching out to her and not giving her other reasons to hate me. My time with her is

16

always tortured and often leaves me doubting my worth, but I'm not giving up on being her parent. It's like walking into a social gathering where I know people are going to see me as a freak—but if I don't go, I'm admitting they're right. Plus, kids need to know who their parents are, and they need to know they're loved, even if they can't love you back.

"Blythe wants to see you." The wicked grandmother forms the words with thin lips and she pivots simultaneously, marching up the stairs without looking back. I hug Morgan, who allows me to embrace her but keeps her own arms at her sides. I end the hug with a kiss on her cheek which she accepts with rigid stillness. I begin my ascent to Blythe's room alone, Morgan remaining on the first floor.

It's a grand staircase, curving through the immense foyer to a U-shaped landing marked by doors to four bedrooms and one bathroom and a door to the stairs leading to the third floor. Each bedroom has its own bath; the "public" bathroom is for anyone staying in one of the attic bedrooms. Original art lines the walls in between doors, all of it expensive, though I don't understand the attractiveness of any of it. Blythe's father, now deceased, had always wanted to be a starving artist in Paris but settled for being a millionaire financier who supported a number of starving artists by buying their works.

The house belongs to Blythe's parents, but as their only child, she will inherit it when her mother dies. When we divorced, Blythe moved in with her widowed mom, partly to recover from the shock of the divorce, and mostly to help the old battle-ax take care of things. She could have stayed in our condo, or sold it and bought something else, but she chose the Winnetka castle and gave me the condo as a kind of dowry to start my new life. Both attorneys thought she was crazy, but I understood. As much as she hated me for shattering her life by transitioning, some part of her still loved the part of me who was the same person she married.

Blythe's door is open, the tawny colors of the landing giving way to lilac walls and hardwood floors set off with plush throw rugs. The walls are dotted with impressionistic oils from Paris, mostly street scenes, mostly purchased on our trips there. As I step into the room, Blythe is lying in bed, her mother fussing over her, hiding her from my view. Blythe is a high-energy woman, always on the move, not one to be in bed at ten o'clock in the morning. I had expected to find her at her desk, at work on her latest project.

Her mother steps away and I see Blythe. She is almost gray, her eyes sunken, her hair pulled back into a stringy ponytail. She gestures with a rubbery arm for me to come to her bedside. Her mother moves away. I'm shocked and have to will myself not to cry.

"Mom," she says, her voice low and weak, "give us a moment."

Blythe surveys me. I'm wearing hippy-style flared jeans and a cotton peasant top. My hair is up in a messy, high ponytail, the mass of curls well off my neck to help me stay cool on a hot day. I'm wearing light makeup that only a cosmetics pro would detect. Lots of people make me as trans, but I look good. I have good bone structure and I've had some plastic surgery to feminize my face.

Blythe grimaces and her lips form a tight line of disapproval. "Congratulations, Nick; you have bigger boobs than me."

I don't know what to say. My boobs have been bigger than hers for many years. I invested in implants as soon as I could afford them because I associate my breasts with femininity. They're not porn-star huge, but my cleavage crowds the line where immodesty starts.

"It was never a competition," I say.

"It was for me."

"Well," I say, "I have bigger feet, too."

She ignores my humor and looks away. The sight of me still pains her, even though she's fine with other transwomen, and everyone else for that matter. This reality is unbelievably painful for me. I still love her. I'll always love her.

She ignores my humor. "I need you to keep Morgan for the rest of the summer," she says. She glances at me, her face filled with defeat.

"What's going on?" I can barely get out the words. I had to threaten court action to get a week with Morgan.

"My cancer's back."

"What cancer?"

"I had breast cancer a couple years ago. It's back."

She looks away from me. The news hits me like a bus.

"You never mentioned it..." I stop. This isn't the time or place.

"Can you imagine what it would be like to tell your ex-husband you've had a double mastectomy when he's out there shaking his double-Ds?" Her bitterness makes me recoil.

"If I don't make it, you'll be her legal parent. I can't do anything about that." She looks at me again. "You should let Mother raise her. All her friends are here."

"You're that sick?"

"Look at me, Nick!" Her voice rises. The one thing that energizes her is her anger toward me.

I sit in the chair at her bedside and listen. She's going to a special clinic in New York. Her mother is coming with her. The odds are awful, but it's her last shot. I thank her for entrusting me with Morgan.

"I don't like it, Nick," she says. "But you were a decent father to her and I'd rather she was with family than a camp somewhere. Besides, you deserve what she's handing out these days." Blythe says this with a "gotcha" smile that comes across as ghoulish in her diminished physical condition.

"What's she handing out?"

"Sass. Anger. She's sneaking alcohol. She says she wants to do drugs this summer because all her friends are getting high. And she wants to get laid." Blythe grimaces.

I'm caught completely off balance emotionally. The daughter I still see as a toddler and a first-grader in my dreams is perched on the perilous cliffs of adolescent rebellion, all her instincts herding her toward the worst decisions an almost-sixteen-year-old can make.

"Well," I say, "I guess we won't be playing Barbies this summer."

"You can afford to make jokes," she says. "You haven't been there for her." She doesn't finish the full thought, but we both know what she's implying: I've been focused on my business and my body all these years, while she raised Morgan. Of course, my attempts to be involved in Morgan's life were harshly rebuffed at every turn. I had to get a court order to see Morgan again after the divorce. It took a year to get a hearing, and another year to get Blythe in compliance. And for several years after that she produced one excuse after another to cancel visitations. Not to mention the propagandizing about what a perverted person I was.

"I wanted to be there," I say.

"Well, congratulations," she says, acidly. "You're getting your chance. Do you think you can keep her from getting addicted and pregnant for a couple months?"

I flush with anger and lock eyes with her.

"Do you know for a fact she's not an addict now?" I snap. "Or pregnant?"

"No," she says. "You'll have to figure that out for yourself."

My head throbs as I descend the stairs. The reality of Blythe's condition has slammed into me like a bullet. I want to release the pain that's welling up inside, but not here in enemy territory.

Blythe's mother ascends the staircase as I go down. She

20

stares daggers at me as we pass each other, as if Blythe's cancer is my fault somehow.

Morgan is sitting on a decorative bench beside the front door, her backpack and a duffel bag at her feet and a hundred pounds of attitude on her face. She's not the surliest teenager in the state, but she could make the all-star team. The hell of it is, she's not just a rich kid. She's also beautiful—long beach-blonde hair, wide brown eyes, perfect lips, an athletic five-six or so with a cute figure. And she's smart. Brilliant, even. Straight As at one of the best high schools in Illinois.

She stands as I approach, a sneer on her face. I've always been a pushover for her little shitstorms, letting my guilt make excuses for her, but she's picked the wrong time to press my buttons. Her petulance arouses nothing in me so much as disgust. My wife, her mother, is dying. Her petty adolescent angst belongs in a closet.

"Will that get you through the summer?" I ask, nodding to her duffel.

"I'm just staying a week."

"Really?" I give her attitude back. "Where will you go then?"

"Back here."

"No one will be here."

"I'll stay with a friend."

I stand directly in front of her and make her look me in the eye.

"Get a grip, kid. You're a miserable, ill-mannered teenage girl who brings gloom wherever she goes. You don't have any friends whose parents will take you."

As I vent, I'm aware that this is not good parenting. I'm supposed to reason with my child and never waver in my respect and love for her.

"If I'm so miserable, why are *you* taking me?" Triumph floats across her face. She has bitch-slapped me with flawless teen logic.

"Because I'm partly responsible for bringing you into this world," I counter. "I deserve you."

"That's not a very nice thing to say." Morgan pulls an indignant face. I have no patience for this. I'm already wondering how either of us will survive two-plus months together.

"I can do worse, and so can you," I say. "Let's try to get along and make it through the summer."

Morgan makes a face. She'd projectile hurl if she could summon the power. So would I. I wait for her as she packs a large suitcase and bounces it down the stairs. She rolls it to the door, and I wait some more as she says goodbye to her mother and grandmother. She returns to me, finally, clad in store-bought holey jeans and a low-cut tank top that reveals a startling amount of cleavage. Her face is a mask of pain, suffering, and superiority. I pick up her duffel bag and let myself out. I'm halfway to the sidewalk when I hear her come out the door.

"We're walking?" she screams.

I turn. She's standing at the front door, backpack over one shoulder, the suitcase in tow, her face turning to and fro looking for some form of modern transportation.

"I can't believe we're fucking walking!" she shrieks.

"I loaned the Rolls to a friend," I yell back. "My Jag's not worthy of you."

I don't wait for a response. I head down the sidewalk in the direction of the train station and don't look back. She'll come or she won't. If she stays with Blythe, well, that's Blythe's payoff for brainwashing the kid to think of me as a creep. Maybe she'll spend the summer giving her grandmother the same crap she always gives me, which would be some kind of proof that there's a God worth worshipping.

3

Morgan arrives at the train platform several minutes after me. For the first block, I was afraid she had stayed home, forever severing any connection between us, and probably between Blythe and me, too. By the time I got to the station, I was even more afraid she'd come. I don't have a clue about what to do with her. Now, I watch her dragging her suitcase awkwardly, letting it flop on its side every ten steps or so, making sure I know how powerfully humiliating it is for her, a royal child of Winnetka, to be forced to walk several blocks hauling heavy objects.

If I weren't so worried, I'd laugh. I vaguely recall being pretty good at adolescent histrionics myself, though I couldn't sustain it indefinitely the way she can. As I watch her wrestle her suitcase onto the platform, I think of all the ways she can torpedo her stay with me. I'm going to have to put her to work in the café, a place she's never deigned to even visit. There's no way I can watch her all summer, and if I leave her on her own, she'll end up shooting drugs, getting pregnant, and burning down my apartment building. Or running away to live with her friends or stay with her wicked grandmother in New York—a somewhat attractive option, compared with the others.

There's not much chance this hostile, spiteful child will do a lick of work, let alone help sustain the ambience and morale at BeatNikki's. Given her attitude, half the staff will hate her on sight, and the other half, the next day. I don't even want to think about the impression she's going to make on customers.

We take the train to the Ogilvie Transportation Center in the Loop, and I lead her out the Madison Street exit. It's a quiet moment in late morning. I stop before we cross the bridge over the Chicago River and take another shot at human communication with my lemon-faced daughter.

"Would you prefer to take an Uber to my place or the L?" I ask.

She looks at me as if I'm the village idiot and strikes that precious pose where all her weight is on one leg, the other sticks out to the side, and she puts one hand on her cocked hip.

"Well, duh," she says. "Like, what's the L? Some kind of stinking bus?"

"I'm talking about the elevated train lines that get you around the city at about ten times the speed of your fucking Mercedes," I say. "You do have a Mercedes, right? You wouldn't be giving me this much shit if you were a Chevy girl."

She tries to glower, but my rejoinder was pretty funny and she's trying hard not to smile.

"If you ever want to be an independent woman of the city, you have to know your way around the L. You might as well start learning about it now."

She snarls back that she doesn't want to lug all these bags on public transportation. I choke back the adolescent urge to say something nasty and call an Uber instead.

Morgan exhales an exasperated sigh as we enter my flat, a

spacious three-bedroom in a modern four-story building that I own. Like my café, it's near Lincoln Park, but on the other side of it. It's a nice neighborhood, safe enough for Republicans if Chicago had any. The rents are reasonable and the people are down to earth, but it's slowly becoming an extension of Lincoln Park because there aren't enough homes in Lincoln Park to accommodate all those nice rich people looking for a safe place to live in the evil city.

I bought here in 2012, three years after I bought the building that houses BeatNikki's. The first real estate purchase was an act of desperation—no one would rent commercial space to me, a transgender woman with a plan for a start-up business. Fortunately, the real estate market had hit bottom after the financial crisis so I got a private loan from my friend and mentor, Ophelia, who had parlayed a career in finance into great wealth before she transitioned. She was actually pushing me to take a flyer on the place and get on with my life. It worked out pretty well. By 2015, the building had appreciated so much in value I used it to secure a conventional mortgage on my apartment building, and I make the payments on them both with the rents from the apartments in both buildings.

Ironically, my apartment building and the BeatNikki's building combined may be worth more than Blythe's Winnetka castle, but Morgan feels like she's slumming in the loud, dirty city and it pisses her off. Which doesn't do much for my disposition, either.

Morgan pauses at the entrance to the living room to look about and shake her head in disapproval. I lead her to her room; she follows behind, dragging her suitcase like it was packed with lead. I place her duffel on her bed. She drops the handle to her suitcase, throws her backpack on the bed, and looks around the room like it's a jail cell. She looks like she's going to cry. It melts my heart. I put my arms around her.

"What?" she says. Hostile, cold.

"Your mother is going to be fine," I say, ignoring the hostility. I try to convince myself she wants to be hugged.

"Of course she is." Morgan's body is rigid, her arms at her sides. I feel like I'm hugging a totem pole. I release her and stand back.

"Look kid," I say, willing myself to stay cool. "You'll get out of this what you put into it. If you want to be miserable all summer, you'll be miserable. I can't help you with that. If you give it a chance, this is a very cool city and you'll get to see a lot of it and you'll have great stories to tell your friends when you go back home."

She's still fuming, her face red, her lips drawn in two thin lines, a perfect imitation of her grandmother's face whenever she looks at me.

"Oh, goody," she says.

I shrug. I tried. I wish I could give up, but we're about sixty minutes into a relationship that has to last all summer, so I have to keep trying.

"I'll give you some time to unpack and settle in," I say, "then I thought we might get some lunch and head for the café. I can introduce you around to the staff."

"Why would I want to meet those people?" She says "those people" like they are criminals or dope addicts.

"Because you're going to be spending a lot of time with them, Morgan." I ignore her tortured sigh. "I can take a couple days off, but I have to work and I can't leave you here alone. So, like it or not, you're coming to the café with me."

"Oh God!" she groans.

"You can work and get paid, or you can read and play computer games, but you're going to be there."

"What if I don't want to?" she snarls. "What if I just take off?"

"Got me," I shrug. I've been thinking about this, too, and I really don't see any viable punishment I can dole out to prevent her from running away.

She blinks. She wasn't expecting that answer. Which makes us even. I wasn't expecting to say it. She regains her poise.

"Interesting," she says.

She looks around the room again, like she's never seen it before. She has stayed overnight in my apartment exactly once since I bought the place, and that was when she was still a child. It's her choice. She doesn't like being with me. She doesn't even like being seen with me.

I tell her to come out when she's ready. She doesn't answer. I can hear her talking to her mother on her phone before I even leave the room. I close the door, but I can still hear her pleading to come home, like a homesick child at summer camp. This is going to be the summer from hell, and there's nothing I can do about it.

Twenty minutes later, Morgan enters the living room and sits in a chair. She doesn't speak. Her eyes are red from crying. She takes a deep breath, then pulls out her phone and focuses on it, mainly to avoid acknowledging me.

A few minutes pass. "Shall we go?" I say, finally.

She stands and gets into her waiting pose, one hip cocked, one foot to the side. I lead her to the door. She follows in sullen obedience.

As we walk to the L station, I ask her what kind of food she has an appetite for. Halfway into the question I bitch-slap myself mentally for giving her the setup for more sarcasm and vitriol. But if I don't treat her like a normal person, she'll never be able to become a normal person with me. She announces that she's not hungry and wouldn't eat in a Chicago restaurant even if she was. Then she gives me a three-sentence rant about Chicago corruption and how all the restaurants are overrun by rats and cockroaches. It's highly bigoted fiction undoubtedly authored by her grandmother. I amuse myself with the thought her grandmother may be the one person in all creation with nothing to fear from such creatures because not even waste-eating vermin would find her appetizing.

"We'll get something at BeatNikki's then," I say. "You can inspect the building first for rats and roaches. You won't find either."

"I said I'm not hungry," Morgan snaps.

"Then don't eat. You can inspect the premises and watch me eat and meet the staff."

We don't say another word to each other on the L or as we walk to BeatNikki's Café. She deliberately positions herself a little behind me as we make our way through the busy commercial area. Obviously, she doesn't like to be seen with me. Her mother and her grandmother and probably her friends have convinced her I'm an embarrassment or worse. Before I transitioned, we were really close. We went for walks and played hide-and-seek and had tea parties in the backyard. She laughed at my silly jokes and we hugged a lot. My transition and the divorce changed everything.

When we get near the café, she steps up to my side.

"Should I call you Dad in there?" she asks, all insolence and cruelty.

"Sure," I say. "You call me Dad and I'll call you Snot."

"Deal," she says, with a grim, jack-o-lantern smile that creeps me out.

4

Despite herself, Morgan is a little dazzled by the neighborhood as we approach the café. Eclectic shops have sprouted up on both sides of the street over the past decade. First to catch her eye are the several trendy boutiques with flashy women's fashions in the window, then an art gallery, its window festooned in colorful oils, abstract images, and a series of male and female nudes. Two doors down, a photography studio's window is filled with portraits, still lifes, and a couple more nudes. Closer to BeatNikki's, Morgan stares at the posters of gorgeous models wearing outrageous hairstyles and wild colors that fill the window of an ultra-hip beauty salon. Elsewhere, the neighborhood includes restaurants and cafes serving up ethnic and vegan specialties, a head shop, two gourmet bakeries, a nail salon, an LGBT bookstore, and the usual assortment of service businesses.

"I get my hair done in there," I tell Morgan, nodding at the salon. "I'll introduce you to the owner if you're interested."

Morgan sniffs. "I have a stylist at home, thanks."

"You'd look good in hot pink with purple lowlights."

She looks at me to see if I'm joking. I kind of am, but I'm

also half serious. I'd like to see my daughter have a little fun with her life. She might be more fun to be around.

BeatNikki's Café sits on the corner, its windows facing two streets. A small but colorful sign carries the name of the place in neon, just above the entry door, which faces the corner where the two streets meet. The windows display vintage images of beret-clad beatniks, and black-and-white portraits of Lawrence Ferlinghetti, Jack Kerouac and some lesser-known stalwarts of the Beat Generation. It's my best attempt to recreate the last beatnik coffee shop in the area. I discovered it when I was in high school and it was love at first sight. I didn't like espresso coffee and I didn't understand a word Ferlinghetti was saying, but The No Exit was the coolest place I had ever seen, with people playing chess and reciting poetry and singing folk songs and playing darts, the aroma of coffee in the air, the men with beards and women with long straight hair, the low buzz of intellectual and pseudo-intellectual conversations. It was hopelessly out of step with the times, of course, and transitioned to a hard-rock club before I went away to college, but I never forgot it and when it came time for me to start a business, that's where my heart was.

Morgan barely notices the images.

Inside, the café is settling into its quiet period between the morning rush of commuter coffee drinkers and the noon lunch trade. The interior is flooded with natural light in the morning, but in late afternoon we darken the place to the shadowy levels of an old-time espresso house. Our lunches are a limited menu of gourmet sandwiches and salads, along with coffee and tea drinks and a selection of old-time phosphates—hand-mixed blends of carbonated water and sweet syrups. Our dinner menu is the same, plus an assortment of gourmet desserts from the local bakery.

Morgan glances about the main room as we enter, her face showing no emotion. She's undoubtedly viewing it as her prison for the summer. There are worse places to be confined. BeatNikki's Café is pretty large for a coffee house. From the entrance, it splits into two areas on either side of a V-shaped coffee bar. One area is the size of a large living room, decked out in small tables and chairs with a small stage at the far end. The stage is barely big enough for two musicians and sits a foot above the rest of the room. This is where we have our live entertainment—poetry and literature readings, folk singers, guitarists and other stringed instruments. We even had a harpist a couple years ago who was very popular, but she graduated from her university and moved out of town.

The other area is a little smaller. It's given to comfortable chairs, conversation areas, chess tables, and, against the far wall, an area set aside for dart throwing competitions. The floorplans are flexible. Staff and clientele alike are used to moving furniture according to need—adding seating space in the game room for a dart tournament, or to the entertainment room for a popular entertainer.

Little John is the only staff member in sight as we enter. The others are flying around the café, getting ready for the lunch crowd. He sees us and almost runs to greet us, his gait still somewhat feminine, a warm smile on his face.

"Morgan!" he exclaims. He steps past me to throw his arms around Morgan and give her a welcoming hug. She's taken aback, but accepts the hug and even returns it, albeit uncertainly.

"I can't believe how gorgeous you are," he exclaims, standing back to take a closer look at her. "Nikki talks about you all the time, but she never mentioned what a doll you are."

Like I say, Little John is a guy, but, like me, there are still bits of his former identity that define him now, and one is relating to young people like a mom. Morgan seems confused by him, like she's not sure whether to smile or recoil, but Little John's effusive personality pulls her out of herself and she decides on a smile. She's really pretty when she does that.

"Let me show you around the place," Little John says, lacing his arm through hers and leading her off. "Your mom's name is on the door, but I'm the real power here."

"He's not my mom. He's my dad," says Morgan. She tries to insert a nasty tone into the sentences, but Little John doesn't take the bait.

"Oh, we don't get hung up on gender around here, gorgeous," he says merrily. "It gets needlessly confusing. Mom, Dad, Aunt, Uncle. Who cares? Call her Nikki like the rest of us do. She's not a bad boss. We just have to keep her in her place."

As they walk off, Ophelia Francis Langston rises from her stool at the coffee bar and approaches me, her arms open for a hug. The sight of her brings a smile to my face and gladness in my heart.

"Congratulations," she says. "You actually got her here."

Ophelia is my best friend and mentor. She's a statuesque transwoman pushing sixty, and a longtime stalwart in the Chicago trans community. When I came out, she was the only person in the world I could talk to, really talk to. She was my role model, my guide, and my mother confessor. She was a pioneer in the effort to bring trans people out of the closet in the nineties, when polite society assumed we were all an especially perverted and obnoxious branch of the gay community. Restaurants would refuse to seat us, often with overt hostility. Doctors would refuse to treat us, often with humiliating remarks. On the street, transwomen who ventured out alone lived with the threat of beatings and rapes, and even in groups, they were often the victims of acts of humiliation. Police invested little effort in tracking down our assailants, and many judges didn't take us seriously when we appeared in court.

Ophelia challenged all that, and convinced people like me to stand up for ourselves, too. She took me under her wing after I was beaten and urinated on and we've been like sisters ever since. She was one of the few people who knew I was picking up Morgan today, and what that meant in terms of emotional wear and tear.

"Getting her here was easy," I say. "I just led her by her cell phone."

Ophelia kisses my cheek and gives me a motherly smile. "Maybe this will be the week when everything changes."

"It already has. It turns out, I have her all summer. Blythe is dying. Cancer."

Ophelia hugs me again. She knows how much I love Blythe. "Well, use the time to patch things up with Morgan," she says. Ophelia always looks on the bright side.

"If I don't kill her first."

Janet, one of our baristas, interrupts us.

"There's a Mr. Campbell who came to see you at ten," she says. "He said he had an appointment." She gestures toward a man sitting at a far table, studying his cell phone. He looks like a middle-aged model from the pages of GQ.

I groan. I forgot. A real estate guy who wouldn't take no for an answer.

"Damn," I say.

"I told him something had come up and you'd be here at noon," says Janet.

I nod to her appreciatively. Ophelia studies Campbell with a smile. "Wow, Nikki, your ship's come in. I'll leave you to it."

Alan Campbell is one of those middle-aged men who, when you see him, you immediately know has always been a charmer and you should be careful. He rises to greet me as I approach. He's a tall man, taller than me in heels, reddish blond hair, a tad on the shaggy side and just tousled enough to suggest he's coming from a midday assignation with a beautiful woman. He's strikingly handsome, with white teeth and a ready smile and bright blue

33

eyes. He was undoubtedly a heartbreaker as a young man, and middle age has only added to his allure by softening the angles of his face to make him seem warm and trustworthy.

"I'm so glad to meet you at last, Nikki." He's as enthusiastic as a lottery winner. I'm supposed to feel like the prize. I don't, but I can see where it might be fun. I keep my expression professional—a friendly, business smile—and extend my hand to his. Unlike many men I meet, he shakes hands with me like I'm a woman—soft pressure, his hand surrounding my fingertips, rather than the full-grip, firm handshake between males. His hand is also huge, my hand disappearing into his as we shake. I don't know if he treats me like this because I'm simply a woman to him, or if he knows I'm trans, and treating me the same way he'd treat any other woman is part of his pitch. Either way, it feels good.

I apologize for missing the earlier time. We order decaf coffee drinks and chat socially until they come. Alan Campbell is a real estate developer who has built some of the city's most acclaimed buildings. He loves the arts, and he loves Chicago, and he jogs on the lakefront several times a week. We're just getting to him running his first Chicago Marathon when the coffees and scones arrive. As soon as the waitress leaves, he gets down to business. The transition is so abrupt I find myself blinking.

"I know you're busy," he says. "You've got a business to run and so do I. So, I'll get right to the point. I want to build in this area."

He launches into a smooth spiel about how successful his company has been, and rattles off several conspicuously successful developments he's undertaken, including a site in the Loop and another in the very tony River North area. I know enough about Chicago real estate to know these were developments involving hundreds of millions of dollars. He's trying to impress me with what a big player he is and how cool it would be to do business with him. I'm impressed, all right, but not because of his business acumen. The man's physical aura is overpowering me. I look into his eyes and feel little tremors in my nervous system. He makes me keenly aware of my body, my skin, my breasts, my womanhood. I'm not panting or plunging into a teenage episode, but I'm aware of a tingling sensation all over my body, and my mind wants to picture us in bed.

I try to focus on business. It's not like I'm some sex-obsessed flirt. I knew when I transitioned that desirable men weren't going to be attracted to a six-foot-tall woman, especially one who still looked like a man in some ways. Many transwomen far more beautiful and petite than me had shared how hinky men got when they found out they were with a transgender woman, even a cute one. So when the desires started, I skipped the heart-breaking rejection phase and made a practical adjustment. I employed—and continue to employ—the services of a very nice escort. I call him every couple of weeks for a romp in the hay. It's not love, but he's artful and respectful and it gets the job done for me. I'll need to call him when Campbell leaves.

"I want to develop this block," Campbell is saying. He's arrived at the point of his visit and it's no surprise. Developers and real estate speculators have been all over this commercial strip for months. They sense that this will be like the west Loop was in the previous decade, and River North was the decade before that.

"You and the other pioneers here have done a great job of showing the potential for upscale housing and commercial development," he says. "Now it's time to cash in. Your investments are worth a fortune now, yours especially, Nikki."

Campbell has reached the closing part of his pitch. "I know you've got all kinds of people like me calling on you, Nikki, but I'd like you to consider me different. Someone you'd like to work with. I can guarantee you'll end up with a lot of money, and you'll always be proud of what we do with the property." He pauses for a moment and fixes his pure, honest blue eyes on mine. I feel the sexual tingle again as he speaks. "What do you think?" he asks. "Can we work together?"

I flash an automatic smile. As much as I'm aware of my arousal, I'm also aware that he's playing me. He read me somewhere in his pitch. He figured out I'm an oversized transgender woman who has trouble getting laid and I'm crushing on him.

"Adam," I begin, deliberately calling him by the wrong name. "Alan, I mean, please forgive me. I spoke to one of your associates last week and I told him BeatNikki's isn't for sale. Nothing has changed."

"But with the money you make from the sale of the building you could start up again anywhere," he reasons. "You could locate next to the Old Town School of Folk Music, or Lincoln Square . . ." He rattles off several more areas where artists and intellectuals gather.

"I couldn't afford those areas," I say. "Whatever you offered for this place, a similar building in one of those areas would cost twice as much—if I could find one at all."

"You don't need to buy, Nikki," he says, his eyes shining with excitement. "You've arrived. You'll have enough money in the bank to secure any lease, and a loan to build out, too. You don't need rental income because your real estate profits will be earning money for you hand over fist in stocks and bonds. This is your ticket to freedom."

He's really good at this. If I had any desire to sell, I'd sell to him in a heartbeat. And if he had any desire to seduce me, I'd want to throw my arms around him and whisper "Take me" in his ear. But I don't want to sell, and he doesn't want to seduce me, so my answer to him is a simple repeat of previous answers: "Thanks, Alan, but no."

His response is so smooth it's obvious that he expected me to say no.

"Let's leave it this way, Nikki," he says. He keeps using my name to emphasize how familiar we are with one another, and how completely he accepts me as a woman. "Let's leave it at no for now, but let's keep in touch, okay? I like you, as a person, I mean, apart from business. I feel like we have a sort of connection, so I'd like to get to know you better. No pressure. Maybe a friendly lunch or dinner sometime? No business, just getting to know each other. Can we do that?"

I was an up-and-comer in the business world before I decided to transition, so I recognize great salesmanship when I see it, and I also understand the difference between salesmanship and courtship. This is salesmanship, so I should say no, as nicely as a I can. But I don't.

"Of course, Alan," I say.

5

Moments after Campbell leaves, Little John bursts in the back door with Morgan right behind him. He's shouting my name, and yelling breathlessly to blue-haired Marvin to call the police and an ambulance. Marvin freezes for a moment.

"Call now!" Little John says, his face flushed and his eyes troubled. "Tell them the service alley. Two doors down."

Little John grabs my hand. "Come on, Nikki. You need to see this."

Little John, Morgan and I rush to the back door. Little John stops before opening the door.

"You stay here, precious," Little John instructs Morgan.

She starts to object, but I raise a hand.

"Let me make sure it's safe, Morgan," I say. She obeys, though with a sour expression on her face.

The alley runs like an asphalt river flowing between low-rise buildings on either side. Our side is mostly three- and four-story buildings with commercial businesses on the ground floor and apartments above. The other side is apartment buildings between three and eight stories, the taller, newer ones signaling the gentrification of the neighborhood. The alley is as neat and clean as a suburban subdivision, with its scrubbed pavement, neatly tucked-away trash containers, freshly painted buildings, and tasteful security fences—all signs of the mushrooming affluence of the area.

As we trot down the alley, Little John fills me in. He was showing Morgan where to dump trash when first he, then Morgan, saw someone stagger into the alley from the hair salon, two doors down. He recognized the person as one of the stylists, clad in the shop's traditional dark clothes. As he and Morgan watched, the man collapsed.

"I tried to keep her away," Little John apologizes breathlessly, "but she followed me. The guy's a mess, Nikki."

Seconds later we're kneeling beside the prostrate form of Billy, a pretty young man in his mid-twenties who is just starting to get a following in the hair styling business.

"Can you hear me, Billy?"

I put my lips near his ear to ask the question, and I ask it loudly. He doesn't move. I can't tell if he's breathing.

Little John is checking his pulse. I glance at him and ask, "Anything?"

"It's weak," says Little John.

I'm worried that if we leave him face down until the paramedics arrive he might die of injuries we can't see. I say as much to Little John. He looks dubious.

"They say not to move them," Little John says. But there's doubt in his voice. He's thinking what I'm thinking, which happens a lot.

I run my hands over the parts of Billy's body I can touch, checking for broken bones and blood. Nothing.

"Let's try rolling him over," I say. "We'll stop if he cries out."

We turn him over. His face is covered in blood and bruises. One eye is swollen shut, the other has a cut on the brow that's bleeding profusely. His nose is severely broken, almost sideways on his face and gushing blood. Fifteen minutes ago, he was pretty enough to be a model. Now he looks like a monster from a horror movie.

Little John opens Billy's mouth and looks for obstructions in his throat. I open his shirt and check his ribs and collarbones for breakage. I can feel his heart beating, and he's breathing shallow breaths.

"He's alive," I say. Little John nods, his face relaxing a little.

"The ambulance is almost here." Morgan's voice comes from behind us. I swivel my gaze back to her, angry that she disobeyed orders. But the sight of her makes my anger evaporate in a trice. Her surly, know-it-all demeanor has vanished. What's left is a horrified youngster with her arms crossed, hugging her body, tears streaming down her cheeks.

"He's going to recover," I tell her, as gently as I can. We hear the ambulance siren echoing through the canyons of the city less than a block away.

"You people are going to have to start taking precautions," Detective Sergeant Brooks says, warm and charming as ever. We're still standing in the service alley where Billy was beaten. By "you people" he clearly means gay and trans people.

"What are you people going to be doing?" asks Little John.

"We can't prevent crime, son," he says. The "son" is deliberately condescending, but at least he got Little John's gender right. "We can only enforce the law when it's broken."

"That would be a pleasant change of pace," I chime in, letting my temper get the best of me. I immediately regret it. I should let Little John handle this—he needs the practice and he was doing well.

"What's that supposed to mean?" Brooks puts his face in mine when he says it, like a playground bully. I'd love to twist his balls into a pretzel and drop him with a solar plexus shot but that would only land me in jail and wouldn't do a thing for Billy.

"Are you trying to kiss me, Detective?" I ask. "Is that in the department's standards of conduct, or are you just hot for trans women?"

That works better than a punch in the gut. He flushes and steps back.

"If you want our protection, you ought to show a little respect." There's anger in his voice. He'd like to curse me and maybe even belt me, but he can't because this is Chicago where LGBTQ people have some political power and the rights that come with it. So Brooks has to rein it in. So do I. The police have lots of power, too.

"We have lots of respect for the police," says Little John, trying to defuse the situation. "You just don't seem to be all that interested in what happened here."

"I took the statements," says Brooks. "No one saw it happen. I'll talk to the victim when he's able to talk."

He's right. The police have deduced that Billy was jumped when he took trash out to the dumpster in back of the salon, just like Little John a couple of weeks ago, but this time, there were no witnesses. The owner came looking for him just as the ambulance rolled in. She's still shocked, standing at the salon's back door, watching the police finish up. The plastic bag of trash still lies upside down beside the dumpster, telling us that Billy was attacked before he could complete his chore.

"If he's able to talk." Little John puts an emphasis on "if." Billy was still unconscious when the ambulance left. We wondered if the kid might be in a coma, and I'm wondering if he might die or have permanent brain damage. Which calls to mind the last time a thug tried to terrorize someone in the area. My favorite white supremacist.

"You might find the Nazi who assaulted Little John and me," I tell Brooks. "This looks like his work, wouldn't you say?"

Brooks breaks into an ugly smile. "He's still in the hospital and word is, he'll never see out of that eye again. I'm still betting he sues you when he gets out. And if he comes back to this neighborhood, he'll be looking for payback from you, sweetheart."

I stare at him. "You'd like that, wouldn't you?'

He shrugs. "Just giving you the facts."

I turn to Little John. "Somehow, I don't think Detective Brooks is here to serve and protect us."

"You're getting more protection than you deserve, *ma'am*." He uses the feminine noun ironically, like I'm not actually a woman.

"That's your answer?" Morgan's angry voice erupts behind me. Her face is flushed and her hands are clenched in angry fists. "Somebody gets beaten senseless, and all you can do is insult the people who called it in?"

Brooks stares at her, stunned. I know exactly how he feels, having tasted the whip of her teenage tongue often in our short time together. It feels good to see someone else get a few lashes from her, especially someone as deserving of it as Brooks. I wonder if her inability to stay silent in the presence of assholes is something she inherited from me. At least she got her mother's brains and good looks.

Little John inserts himself between Morgan and Brooks and gently herds her away. I can hear him telling her to let me handle it. Brooks is babbling, but I don't hear him. My mind is filled with the realization that I've exposed my daughter to murderous violence on her first day with me. Blythe will be horrified when she learns of this, and all I can think is, she's right. I'm a terrible parent. This would have never happened under Blythe's watch. Maybe it's been for the best that I've been denied contact with Morgan for most of the past ten years.

I turn abruptly and follow Little John and Morgan back to the café, leaving Brooks flapping his big mouth. I catch up to them and put my arm around Morgan.

"I'm sorry you had to see that," I tell her. I pull her close. She doesn't resist, which feels like a full body hug compared to what I expected. It's just for a few seconds, but the connection I feel with her ignites a spark of hope in my soul.

Inside, Little John makes Morgan one of his concoctions that combines tea and fresh fruit juices and his secret sweetener. She grimaces when he puts the glass in front of her but once she tastes it, she likes it, just like everyone else who's tried one of his potions. His genius with this stuff took BeatNikki's from a retro coffee shop to a very successful cafe, and won him equity in the business.

When Morgan's shock wears off, she looks at Little John, then me, ready to ask a question. For once, she isn't snarling. In fact, it's striking how beautiful she is with her perfect skin a tawny, just-enough-sun color, and those soft brown eyes and long, dark lashes. She has a lot of structure in her face, but it's subtle, like her mother's, just enough angles and shadows to project a seriousness about her, an aura that tells you she's pretty enough to be a Barbie, but she's also a strong-willed, assertive woman who's going to have her own agenda in life, assuming she survives her forays into sex, drugs, and alcohol.

"Why would someone beat up that man?" she asks. She tries to swallow the tremor in her voice and mostly succeeds.

"We don't know, angel," I tell her. "Since the election, hate groups have been targeting gays and trans people along with a lot of other people they don't like. Billy's gay and out, so it might have been because of that."

"That's just wrong," says Morgan.

Little John nods.

"You won't get an argument from any of us or our customers," I tell her. "Even the people who aren't gay or trans love someone who is."

After a moment of thoughtful silence, Morgan looks at me

and squints her eyes in question. "You and that detective were talking about someone attacking you and Little John. What was that about?"

I cough a little, trying to think how to tell her about it. "Well, we had an incident a couple weeks ago when some demented moron tried to assault a staff person in back, and we, uh, prevented him from, uh, inflicting injury on our people."

Morgan looks at me like I'm a babbling idiot, which is a reasonable assessment of my statement. I shrug. She looks to Little John.

"What's she talking about?" Morgan asks.

"She called me 'she,'" I smile.

Morgan gives me a token grin, like I'm an immature twit who's not worth answering, and turns to Little John again.

"Like she said, a man assaulted me in the alley, " says Little John. "Nikki came out to try to talk him down. One thing led to another."

"And the guy ends up in the hospital, blind in one eye?" Morgan's eyes widen. "What did you do to him?"

"I pacified him," I say, glaring at Little John to keep him from saying anything more. I glance at Morgan. She's puzzling over the meaning of my words.

"You beat him up?" she asks. "You blinded him in one eye?"

"It was self-defense." I say it weakly. This isn't a part of me I want to share with her. It's the part of me that was supposed to disappear with testosterone. Every once in a while, I release my inner militancy on villains like the Nazi, and it leaves me with doubts about my legitimacy as a woman. This is a doubt Morgan already shares and I don't want it to solidify into some kind of certainty.

"So, you still fight like a man?" Morgan says.

"No, Morgan. I fought like a woman who's had years of self-defense training."

For a moment, I expect a snarky response, but all she does

is nod. She sips her drink, looks me in the eye, and says, "Well, if I have to live in this ghetto, I better get some self-defense training, too."

6

In the aftermath of the alley violence, talking quietly with Morgan and Little John in the comfort of BeatNikki's Café, I realize that I'm just starting to learn who my daughter is, other than she's an angry kid who doesn't like me very much.

The first revelation is, she's surprisingly poised. Even though the gruesome injuries inflicted on Billy upset her terribly, she was never hysterical and has recovered her equilibrium in a relatively short time. Now, we're all talking normally and she's shown an interest in the things we're talking about and even smiled once or twice. The smiles and her ability to converse intelligently with adults are not qualities that were readily apparent when she was scowling and complaining about everything. Seeing her now as a bright, engaging person is like watching a new life emerge from an egg.

Eventually, Little John steers the conversation to work. "If you're going to be with Nikki all summer, we should put you to work here. Have you ever waited tables or made coffee and tea?"

Morgan says no, but in a way that suggests she's interested. Compared to the puke face I got from her when I brought up working here, it's like the kid has been exorcised or something. I'm sure it's because she's talking to Little John and she likes him, which makes me jealous, but also gives me hope. Maybe if we can get past her resentment of me, there's a real person in there, someone easier to love.

Little John and I explain the work our staff performs, from waiting on tables to running the cash register. Afterwards, Little John demonstrates how to draw coffee and tea during the morning rush, and mix his refreshing drinks in the afternoon and evening. Morgan is willing to wait tables, but what excites her is learning how to mix drinks like the one she's sipping now.

I ask her if she was serious about doing self-defense classes.

"Of course." She says it flippantly.

"I need to know if you're really interested or just kind of, because it's a serious commitment of time and money."

She reverts back to her prune face. "Of course I'm serious," she says. "I wouldn't have said so otherwise."

It's striking how much respect she shows to Little John and how little to me. I swallow my pride and ask her what kind of athletic equipment she packed. About what I thought: designer clothing that would shrivel and melt if stained by perspiration.

"We need to get you some clothes to sweat in," I say, thinking: this is where she'll get off the self-defense train, probably with a sarcastic comment.

"Okay," she says, without a trace of attitude.

We say our farewells and head for the L station. As soon as we get outside, Morgan pulls out her phone and ignores me, giving me time to think about my next move before we get to the train. My first thought was to take her to the high-end stores on Michigan Avenue so she can experience the city version of the snooty shopping malls in the north suburbs. Then it occurs to me that she's probably already seen the so-called Miracle Mile, and besides, I have a better idea.

We get on the Red Line going north, headed for a family-owned sports store in the Lakeview area that I'd rather patronize than a national chain on Michigan Avenue where people like Morgan's grandmother shop.

The Red Line train is hot and loud. The crowd is midday light, most passengers seated. I lead Morgan to a pole a few steps from the door. She starts to sit but I gesture for her to remain standing. We both grasp the pole. As the doors close, I direct her attention to a map of the Red Line on the wall and bend my lips to Morgan's ear so she can hear me above the clatter and grind of the train.

"If you're going to be a woman of the city, you have to learn how to get around," I start. "The L is the fastest way to cover distances in the city. This is the Red Line . . ." For the fifteen minutes it takes to get to our Lakeview stop, I lecture Morgan on the neighborhoods around the Red Line stops between the Loop to the south and Andersonville to the north. Her eyes glaze over, but at least her phone stays in her pocket while I speak.

We walk to the sports store wordlessly but Morgan still manages to communicate that she's unimpressed with the neighborhoods, even though they're pricey and prestigious by Chicago standards. By Winnetka standards, the architecture is ordinary—older, low-rise buildings, for the most part—and the street-level shops are dominated by service businesses with boring window displays. For all that, the in-store shopping experience goes quickly and successfully. Morgan is civil, even charming, to the young woman who waits on us, and she's satisfied with the outfits she found.

The store sits on the edge of Boystown, Chicago's officially designated LGBTQ neighborhood. When I was transitioning, Boystown was a second home to me because it's a safe and accepting place and has been ever since gay men began congregating there back in the sixties and seventies. In a moment of sheer insanity, I decide to give Morgan a tour of the place.

Maybe the sight of same-sex couples walking hand in hand and transgender men and women strolling about like real people will soften her attitude about being related to a trans woman.

We head east to Halsted Street, which forms one side of the triangle that creates the Boystown area. As we walk north on Halsted, I stop at a plaque mounted on a pedestal in the sidewalk that formally acknowledges Boystown as an LGBTQ neighborhood. Morgan reads the inscription; then we resume walking.

"I want you to know about this neighborhood, even if you don't approve of me," I tell her. "This place was a refuge for people like Little John and me back in the day. As trans people we were easy targets for abuse but this was the one place we could walk safely on the street and find stores and services that would treat us like regular human beings."

Morgan shows no signs of paying attention to me. Her face is turned toward the display windows of the shops we're passing. Most of them are colorful and some are wildly alluring. She stops at one of the several sex shops in the neighborhood. I groan. The focal point of the display window is an impressive array of dildos that range in size from what I consider the average male dimension to colossal lengths and thicknesses, and in color from white to black and everything in between. She stares at them.

"Is this what they're like?" Morgan asks. She means male erections.

"I'd say the ones on the left are pretty representative," I answer. I refuse to be embarrassed by sex talk. "The ones on the right might be more fantasy than real life."

Morgan continues to stare at them, deep in thought. "So, size matters."

I shrug. "I think it's different for different people."

"The jumbos look like they'd hurt," she says. Then she turns to me with a smug smile and asks, "What's the biggest one you've had?"

She's really good at baiting me. "That's not a conversation we're ever going to have," I tell her.

"Well, do you have one of these I can try?" As she asks, she looks up at me impishly, being deliberately provocative.

I calm myself. "Do you enjoy masturbating?" I ask her.

She blushes. I've finally gotten past her supercilious wall. "Like guys, you mean?" she asks.

"Women masturbate, too," I say. "Some women use tools like these, and some just use their fingers. And some just hold off until they can get the real thing."

Morgan stares at the window. Her lips are pursing and her eyebrows are slightly raised. She's deep in thought. "Which are you?" she asks, finally.

I take a deep breath and look at her. I stay silent until she looks at me and we make eye contact.

"If you really want to have that conversation, we'll have it, but not right now," I say. "I want us to get better acquainted first and I want to make sure I'm not scarring you for life by speaking candidly about sex."

"My father has boobs and a vagina; how much more scarred can I get?" She smirks.

"Who told you I have a vagina?" I ask.

She jerks her head toward me, shocked. "You don't?"

"We're in the one place in the universe where you don't make assumptions about someone's gender or their sexuality or their body parts," I say. "Instead of judging people you don't really know, maybe you should ask questions and listen to their answers."

We head back to the L station.

"I understand that for some reason you feel the need to hurt me," I say to Morgan as we walk. "And just so you know, it does hurt, but not in the way you want it to. I've heard all the insults you can possibly come up with. That's not what hurts, not any more. What hurts is knowing my beautiful, brilliant daughter who has so many advantages in life is a common, ordinary bigot who takes pleasure in demeaning people who have done nothing to her."

After several tense moments, Morgan speaks in a vehement, angry tone.

"But you have done something to me, *Dad*!" She spits out the word "dad" with special disdain. "You turned into a freak."

This time her words hit the mark.

"I've got news for you, you little snot," I reply. "My transition is none of your goddamn business. The only thing I owe you is love and support, and I've provided both."

The last few blocks to the L station feature us in an angry exchange, Morgan accusing me of abandoning her and her mother, and me accusing them of excommunicating me, each in her own way. These are old arguments and nothing is resolved. The train ride home passes in silence, Morgan's face clouded and stressed, mine probably more so.

Much to Morgan's righteous dismay, we make one more stop on the way home. I duck into a local hardware store and purchase ten cannisters of pepper spray. I can see that Morgan is dying to ask what they're for, but she doesn't want to lose her anger to a normal conversation so she just stews. I'm impressed. I could never hold back my curiosity like that.

As we approach my apartment building, she delivers the message she's been working on since I snapped at her. "I can't believe anyone would call their own daughter a little snot," she says, her teeth clenched, tears coming from her eyes. "I'm going to pack my bags and go back home. I never want to see you again."

"This isn't fun for me, either," I tell her. "I've been treated with more respect in a pie fight." I say it in anger, but as I hear the words spill from my mouth, I see the humor in them. I try to hold it back, but a snicker escapes my tightly closed lips. I glance at Morgan. She's trying to stay mad but her lips tremble with an almost-smile.

"Want to stop somewhere and pick up a couple pies for later?" I ask her. I burst into laughter, just as she does too, her lips making a kind of sputtering sound at first as she tries to hold back the laugh. After all the tension, my lame joke seems so funny I'm breathless with laughter. I stop and hold up a hand, asking Morgan to wait a moment. She does. She doesn't laugh as hard as I do, but she watches me with a smile on her face.

When I recover my breath, I say, "Well, at least we can still laugh a little."

"It doesn't change anything, though," she says, the smile fading. "I don't like you. I don't respect you. I don't want to stay with you."

We resume walking. "Believe me when I say this," I tell her, "I don't like having you here against your will, but the fact of the matter is, neither of us has a choice. You have nowhere else to go. I'm the house of last refuge for you. The good news is, it's just for a couple of months." I ramble on for another minute or two, about how the city is a cool place and she can explore it this summer, and about how she can learn some things from me if she opens her mind.

"Learn things?" she echoes. "Like how to make sandwiches and sugary coffee drinks?"

"Is that beneath you?" I ask.

"If I was home this summer, I could be taking trigonometry or calculus."

"I'll teach you to cook," I say. "Think of it as a survival course so you don't starve to death when you're learning brain surgery."

"How exciting." Her voice drips with sarcasm, the way only adolescents can do it.

"We'll start tonight on the most important part."

"Let me guess." Morgan's face gets that prunish look she favors. "Peeling potatoes? Slicing onions?"

"No." I smile at her slyly. "Washing dishes. You can work

your way up to peeling potatoes."

Morgan gives me the finger.

We make dinner together. Simple fare—broiled fish and asparagus, and sushi-grade Japanese rice. She tries to claim she's a vegan, but I remind her I saw her eat a chicken sandwich. She shrugs and waits for orders from me. I have her brush a little oil on the asparagus and apply seasonings to the fish as I patter softly about how to make fast, healthy meals quickly. She pretends to ignore me, but my sense is, she's hearing every word.

She watches me critically when we sit down to eat. I cut my fish and asparagus into small chunks and mix it into my rice, explaining how this way I avoid the extra calories of a sauce or butter or some other flavoring for my starch. She rolls her eyes. She eats the asparagus and most of the fish and pushes the pile of unflavored rice around on her plate for a while, hoping to get a rise out of me, I'm sure. It doesn't work. I'm responsible for giving her access to good food; she's responsible for eating it.

At the end of the meal, I ask her if she'd rather load the dishwasher or hand-wash the broiler pan.

"Neither," she says. I'm so impressed with how articulately her body language communicates utter disdain for either task that I feel like applauding. My own adolescent rebellion was played out in much cruder, ruder ways, but then, I was a testosterone-driven male.

"Okay," I say cheerfully. "I'll show you how to do both and tomorrow night you can make a decision."

I show her how to fill the dishpan with soapy water, and how to put her hands in it, and how to scrub. When we finish, she says she'll do the dishwasher from now on. My daughter may be hard to live with, but she's not stupid.

The next morning at the café, Morgan gets her first lesson in self-defense. So does the rest of the staff. I gather everyone and start with a short speech about the recent incidents in the area involving neo-Nazi types, then distribute pepper spray cannisters to everyone and demonstrate how they're used. There's an aura of disbelief in the group, and several people say they can't resort to such violence.

"Fine," I say. "All I ask is that you carry it with you, and know how to use it. Then, when someone attacks you, you can make a choice. You can let them crush your skull, or you can nail them with a chemical spray and get away. If you don't have the spray, you don't have a choice."

7

We make it through the first week without killing each other, a milestone I decide to celebrate by taking us out to dinner. I ask Morgan if she has a preferred restaurant or cuisine, but she replies with a shrug and goes to her room. That's how the week has passed. Sullen silence and muffled words, carefully uttered so as not to be heard, interrupted by the occasional smile so labored as to suggest the next one will come only by caesarean section.

At the café, it's completely different. She comes alive talking to Little John and other staff, and she's sunny and bright with customers. That's a relief—I don't know what I'd do with her if she didn't work at BeatNikki's—but it's also a carefully orchestrated put-down of me. My daughter is whip smart and thinks strategically and she wants to remind me every moment of every day that she despises me. At times, I'm able to be mature and philosophical about it. At other times, I think of her loathing of me as my punishment for not having changed genders earlier in life, before involving Blythe and Morgan in my curse.

Our celebration dinner passes like an all-day root canal.

When she speaks at all, it's one-word answers accompanied by eye rolls or facial grimaces. She doesn't utter a complete sentence until I'm paying the tab and we're getting ready to go. That's when she says, "I met the man I'm going to have sex with."

My head snaps to attention, which delights her.

"I have to thank you for that," she continues. "I never would have met him if you hadn't made me work in the café."

If smugness was a disease, she'd be on her deathbed right now. I swallow and try to collect my thoughts. I've actually thought about how to handle this kind of conversation with her, but now that she's thrown it in my face, the only fragment of sanity I can dredge up is to not make this about me. I'm not the one risking pregnancy or venereal disease or loss of self-esteem. This thought seemed much more reasonable when I was thinking in the abstract but now that it's upon me, I'm in full-fledged panic mode and can't think of anything to say. I manage a weak, "Oh." I picture Blythe's furious face in my mind, her beautiful lips forming the words, "Do something!" followed by an obscenity I probably deserve because I'm completely at a loss.

"Don't you want to know who it is?" she asks. Her voice is playful, but she doesn't mean to be lighthearted. She's trying to punish me.

"Sure," I say.

She describes one of our regulars, a thirty-ish man whose name I don't know.

The power of speech returns to me slowly. "Next time I see him I'll fill him in on the facts about statutory rape in this state."

"I can sleep with anyone I want to," Morgan snaps.

"You can," I say, "but he can't. And don't doubt for a minute I'll have his ass slapped in jail."

"Go to hell, *Dad*." Her voice is deeply sarcastic. She stands abruptly and leaves the restaurant. I trail behind, dreading the hostile cab ride home.

At home, she goes directly to her room and closes the door.

I try to unwind, but I can't. The silent apartment, the snotty teenager sitting in her room, simmering in angst, the tension, it all gets to me. I have absolutely no control over this situation. If she wants to have sex, she'll do it, whether with an older man or someone in her own age group. If she wants to get high, she'll find a way. I can't stop any of this from happening. Nor can I run from it. If it was a business problem making my mind grind and my stomach turn, I could go out for drinks with a friend or catch a movie or take in a set at a jazz club or engage in a night of cheap, uncommitted sex. But this is Morgan and she's living with me and I have to be here, even if she hates me and even though I have absolutely no influence on her actions.

I put some classic jazz on the CD player and pace, trying to focus on the rhythms of Oscar Peterson and the riffs of Sonny Rollins. It doesn't work. I'm so wrought with tension I feel like I could throw up. Finally, I decide to exercise the nuclear option: I find the terse note Blythe sent me with her contact information in New York, and punch the numbers into the phone.

"Yes?" The voice is clipped and unfriendly. It's Blythe's mother, of course. She will be hovering over Blythe like a mother hen for as long as Blythe can stand being treated like an egg.

"I'd like to speak with Blythe, please," I say.

"Who is this?" She knows who it is. This is just a dominance game.

"I'm calling about Morgan," I say. "Please put her on. She needs to know what's happening here."

"What does she need to know?" Her tone is imperious.

"None of your business," I say. "Please put her on."

It's all I can do not to swear at her. Instead, I try to think what to do if she refuses to let me talk to Blythe. I can't really afford to take time off to go to New York, plus, spending hours in a car or airplane with Morgan would bring me to the brink of suicide.

After a pause, there is a muffling sound. She's putting her

hand over the receiver so I won't hear her highly confidential exchange of state secrets with Blythe, but I can hear her anyway.

"It's Nick," she says. I can picture what her face looks like, crinkled in the haughty sneer of the elite. Several choice obscenities pop into my mind, begging to be shared with her. I bury them. This isn't the time.

A moment later, I hear "Hello?"

Blythe's voice is raspy and not much louder than a whisper. I can picture her frail, shrunken condition. I start to speak but my voice catches. My emotions well up.

"Nick?" Her voice is still weak, but insistent.

"Blythe." I get her name out. I swallow. I can't think of how to start the conversation. It seems insensitive to ask her how she is.

"We were talking about you at dinner and I thought I'd call and see how you're doing," I lie.

"You talked about me?" Her voice is disbelieving.

"She misses you," I say, shifting out of the lie to something I know is true.

"She's called me twice already, Nick." Blythe is telling me I'm stupid and out of touch.

"She's planning on having sex with a middle-aged man," I say.

"So? What are you going to do about it?"

The question rocks me. "What would you do about it?"

"It doesn't matter what I'd do, Nick," she says. "You're not me and I have one foot in the grave right now. And to tell you the truth, you two deserve each other."

"You don't mean that."

"Oh, but I do."

"You don't mean that about Morgan," I correct myself.

"She's a self-centered, quarrelsome little snot," says Blythe. "It's your fault, Nick. I'm glad you two have each other."

"She's mourning for you." My voice rises. I'm angry. I can

feel my face getting flushed. "I'm sorry you're not feeling well, but don't take it out on Morgan. And my name is Nikki. I'm a woman, whether you like it or not."

The receiver clicks as she hangs up. I get a tissue and wipe tears from my face and berate myself for how badly I handled the conversation. I sit back in my overstuffed easy chair, close my eyes, and conjure images of my simpler past. I want to remember when I was single and carefree and I could get away from my worldly cares by going out to bars or calling my lover for a tryst, but what I remember is spending a lot of nights sitting in this room and mourning the loss of Blythe and Morgan until I fell into a fitful sleep. The irony doesn't escape me.

After a while, I go to Morgan's room and knock. At first she ignores me, but the third time I knock and call her name she responds and I enter. She's lying on the bed, her face buried in a pillow.

"You're right," I say, skipping the throat-clearing niceties. "I can't stop you from destroying yourself. If you want to be a druggie or some sleazebag's easy punch, that's your decision. You'll live with it and I won't."

She keeps her face buried in the pillow and doesn't acknowledge me.

"What I owe you is information," I continue. "My responsibility to you is to make sure you know what you're getting into, and the only thing you have to do is to pay attention. You don't have to believe me or take my advice, but you have to listen. I'll be as brief as possible."

She remains inert, her body moving only to breathe.

"Tonight's lesson will be about sex," I say. I leave her for a moment, ducking into my own room to fetch my teaching tools. When I return, I make her sit up.

"This is a dildo," I start, holding up my soft plastic sex tool. It's about the size and girth of an average male penis, flesh-colored, with a lifelike knob on one end and a reasonable facsimile of a scrotum on the other. "This is more or less what a man's penis looks like when he gets aroused."

She sighs, exasperated, a woman of the world who knows all this.

"This is the end that goes inside you when you have sex," I continue. "It's the most sensitive part of his penis. As it rubs up and down in your vagina, he gets more and more aroused. If you wait to do this until you're in love with a decent guy, you'll get aroused too. Either way, when he reaches climax, his head emits a white, viscous fluid—science calls it *semen*, you and your friends will call it *cum*."

Another dramatic sigh, this one to cover her embarrassment.

"Everyone knows this shit, *Dad*," she sneers, but her blush suggests some of it is new to her or maybe finally confirmed a rumor going around the girls' bathroom at school.

"Call me Nikki," I say. "And pay attention."

"Semen carries sperm, the microscopic organisms that can get you pregnant," I continue. "But it can also introduce things like gonorrhea, syphilis, chlamydia, and HIV into your body. These diseases can cause long-term misery for you." I talk a little about how sexually transmitted diseases can impact a life.

She doesn't say anything but she's listening.

"That's why, even if you want to get knocked up, or even if you're on the pill, you should use a condom," I continue. I pass her a wrapped condom and open a second one as she watches. "If you're going to start fucking strangers, you need to carry your own condoms and you need to know how to put them on the one you're going to make it with."

I demonstrate how to roll the condom on the dildo. She no longer tries to feign disinterest.

"I'm not showing you this because I want you to start screwing men," I say while I work. "I'm doing this because the kind of males who want to have sex with a sixteen-year-old girl aren't likely to bring their own equipment. When it comes to sex, they aren't that considerate. They're ruled by animal instincts that make them focus on orgasm and pretty much nothing else."

"You'd know," Morgan mutters, her eyes still fixed on the dildo in my hands.

"You're damn right I know," I snap.

"Do you have sex with men?" she asks. "Or are you—?" she nods toward my crotch. She doesn't know what words to use, but she wants to know if I have female genitalia.

"I've had male lovers," I say.

"More than one?"

"I've had several relationships."

She tries to pin me down on whether or not I have a lover. I tell her no, but we're not going to talk about my personal life.

"Why not?" She's boldly insistent.

"Because it's none of your business," I say. "I'm not going to talk about my personal life with someone who doesn't know me and hates me, to boot."

"But you're intruding into my personal life," she argues.

"No, I'm not," I reply. "I'm showing you how to protect yourself if you decide to start having sex. I'm not asking you any personal questions. Frankly, I don't care. All I owe you is the information you need to make intelligent decisions."

She gets a smirk on her face. "You're fine if I get knocked up?"

"It's your life." I say it like I mean it, because right now, I do.

It would be poetic justice to return Morgan to Blythe and her mother with a bun in the oven. They deserve each other, though I'd feel terrible for the unborn child. I keep these thoughts to myself and leave Morgan's room, but a plan is forming in my mind.

On Thursday, after the lunch rush, Little John takes Morgan to a corner table where they sit down with one of Little John's pals, a cisgender gay man who is an AIDs activist and has been living with HIV for years. The conversation lasts about twenty minutes. Morgan's eyes are wide open the whole time and I can see pain on her face from across the room. More than I expected. She's not only getting an education, she's showing empathy, a quality I didn't think she had. Maybe she's human after all, just not with me.

8

Our second week together passes quietly. Morgan still barely tolerates my presence, but she gets along well with everyone at work and even seems to enjoy the business. Our time together boils down to the walks to and from the L station and preparing our evening meal. The walks are mostly silent, other than the occasional grunt or one-word answer to the occasional question I pose to her. Meal preparation produces something closer to conversation. Her prior knowledge of cooking was telling her grandmother what she wanted for supper and knowing how to microwave frozen dinners.

Meal preparation started out like a rugby scrum, just like everything else with Morgan. At first, she tried to act as though cooking was boring and stupid and not worthy of her class and upbringing. I managed not to blow up at her sighs and martyred poses, and by the end of the week, she started to show some interest. She was working with food and beverages at the café and beginning to understand the art and creativity of it, I think. The evening meals introduced her to different foods, seasonings, and preparations, and the opportunity to experiment.

When we focus on the food, it's easy to communicate. Not that we say much, but she has no inhibition about asking me a question or answering one of mine, and she does so without histrionics or put-downs of my gender or my worth as a human being. Lately, the conversation has extended to the meal itself as we critique our work and ponder other ways to make the fish or flavor the salad. Again, it's not much, but at least there's no hostility.

After dinner, we clear the table in silence. Morgan knows how to wrap leftovers, so we share that duty, then one of us loads the dishwasher and the other one washes the sharps and pans. We alternate those duties and she silently accepts her chores. When the chores are done, she goes to her room and I usually don't see her again until morning.

It's not what I'd like to have with my daughter, but it could be worse. For that reason, I've resisted the urge to try to start personal conversations. I've seen her flirting with the middle-aged customer she told me she's going to sleep with, and I'd love to ask her what she sees in him. He seems very ordinary to me, not even close to someone I'd expect a young woman to have sexual fantasies about. On the other hand, he seems like a decent enough person and his byplay with Morgan seems more like standard customer-waitress fun than a lecherous lothario hitting on a ripe young virgin.

I'd also like to ask her why she loves Little John and hates me. We're both trans. We're both good to everyone. I do a little more of the discipline than Little John, but neither one of us is a bully. I mean, I know the answer to my question, but I'd like to hear it in her own words.

But none of my questions are urgent enough to risk the tentative truce we've reached.

Week three is ending on a high note. Morgan has been almost civil to me and has even smiled several times, though in response to text messages on her phone, not in reaction to me or anything I said. Still, I feel like we're getting there. I don't know what she's saying to her friends, but two of them are joining her in the city today for a girls' day on the town—led by Morgan, who I'm certain has been touting her vast knowledge of the city to them. Of course, the outing is carefully arranged so her friends never see me. They're meeting in the Loop at the train station, where her friends will arrive from the wilds of Winnetka. Morgan will sweep them away to parts of Chicago they haven't seen. I wanted to suggest she include Boystown in the tour, but if I said it, she'd probably gag. On the other hand, Little John might have suggested it—not because it's gay, but because it's cool— in which case, they'll probably do it. I can envision Morgan huddling her friends in front of the window of the dildo shop and explaining that things are a little different in the city.

It's a nice break for me, too. I have the afternoon off. I've been home long enough to enjoy a refreshing bath and get into soft cotton short-shorts and a tight, low-cut tank top. I'm barefoot, my pink toenails glistening in the sunlight seeping into the apartment. I check myself in the mirror. My hair hangs in damp curls, still thick and girly despite my advancing age. My breasts bulge in the tank top, unrestrained by a bra, still shapely thanks in part to the miracles of modern cosmetic surgery. I don't have as much butt and hips as I'd like, but I have enough to look feminine in this garb, and the shorts show off my shapely legs.

William's soft knock sounds as I'm examining my butt in the mirror. I hurry to the door. As I open it, I wonder what I'd do if it isn't William standing there. What if I find myself flashing all this skin at one of my neighbors who just wanted to borrow a cup of sugar, or a couple of Mormons spreading the gospel? It adds a bit of a rush as I swing open the door.

But it is William, tall and lanky, his Afro adding a couple more inches to his height. He wears cutoff jeans and a Windy City Bulls T-shirt. His arms and legs are leanly muscled, his skin a beautiful chocolate brown. What my eyes can't see my mind fills in from memory: slim, hard torso, muscular chest, an athlete's thighs, and male genitalia befitting a porn star.

"You look gorgeous," he says.

"I was just thinking that of you."

He steps into the apartment and I embrace him. William smells of Dove soap, freshly washed cotton, and a shampoo aroma I can't quite place but love. His lips are full and soft and he embraces me gently, his hands running up and down my back, one of them coming to rest on my butt. I'm already purring inside.

We sit on the couch and sip ice water and chat like old friends, William telling me about his new job and his roommate. I tell him about Morgan and BeatNikki's and why I haven't called in more than a month. While I talk, he begins seducing me with his hands, which are amazingly large and soft and make my body do flip-flops wherever he touches me. As my libido comes alive, he kisses me softly on my lips, my face, my neck, my breasts. I express the emotion I'm feeling in groans and gasps. Finally, he leads me into my bedroom and makes love to me.

Much later, when we emerge from the bedroom, I bring iced tea and snacks from the kitchen. As we sit on the couch, I hand William his envelope.

"Thank you," I say, like I do every time. "That was wonderful."

He offers the envelope back to me. "You don't have to do this," he says. But I do have to do this. I pay William for sex and we're both better off for it.

He's not actually a sex worker by profession. He's a very

genial, loving guy who has a day job and loves to pleasure women. We met at a party years ago and ended up in bed. I had been through a run of one-night stands and brief affairs, enough to realize that an oversized woman like me was never going to score a stay-the-night lover, let alone a live-in lover or husband. So I asked him if we could hook up again at my place. When we did, I asked if I could pay him. At first, he was insulted, but when I explained, he felt bad for me. Now, I think he understands. Me paying for his sexual favors gives us both a lot of freedom, enough to keep this relationship going for a long time. If he's involved with a prettier, younger woman, coming to me is just his job and doesn't have to take him away from his love interest. And, we're friends. We actually like each other, so there's an informality here that makes it laid-back and easy. If he has a conflict, he can say so and we come up with a different time. If I were ever to have a headache—not that I ever would, mind you—he'd understand.

The other thing is, William can use the money. He works construction, but the work's not steady and his employers have a way of going out of business. I hope, for his sake, that a great job and maybe a great woman come along for him. I'd hate to lose him, but we're not dependent on each other. I only call every few weeks or so. It's like getting my hair done at the salon—every week would be too much, but every three or four weeks is a trip to paradise.

I'm lucky to have found William. While so many men have weird hang-ups about sex, especially with trans women, William is completely accepting. He's also tireless and joyful. I'm guessing he's around thirty, about ten years younger than me, but that doesn't bother him either. And it's not always just sex. Every once in a while, we go out to dinner or catch a show.

We head back into the bedroom. Our lovemaking segues into postcoital cuddling and kissing and we fall asleep. I wake up first and go to the bathroom, then to the kitchen for refreshments.

The sun pours through my west-facing windows and I realize it's early evening. Morgan should be home any minute and here I am walking through the apartment stark naked. As that thought forms, I hear a key scratching the door and freeze in horror. I should be running for the bedroom, but my mind locks on the sound of a key trying to find a lock. It shouldn't be that hard. I hear at least two voices, laughter, people trying to be quiet but being too loud.

The door swings open and Morgan staggers in. Her legs are rubbery and her eyes unfocused. She's being held upright by a teenage boy with blue hair and a nose ring. They're snickering and laughing and quite drunk. I'm sober, but stark naked, in the middle of the living room, holding a beer in one hand and a glass of wine in the other. I can't make my body move. After a few beats, they notice me. My nudity stuns them. The blue-haired boy's eyes widen and his mouth hangs open. Morgan stares, her eyes watery. She seems to have trouble focusing. She staggers a little, grabs the blue-haired boy for stability, then nods with the solemnity of a village elder.

"Well, that answers that question," she slurs, her eyes fixated on my crotch. She looks me in the eye, a smirk on her face. She has trouble focusing, but her put-down is clear, not that I care much, given that she's reeling drunk and quite possibly in the first hours of pregnancy.

Then there's the question of what to do about my exposed body. My first instinct is to run for the bedroom in mortal embarrassment, but my second instinct is, it's my body, my apartment, and I won't be ashamed. I put down the drinks and drape myself in a throw blanket on the couch and speak as though I'm dressed for tea with the queen.

"Who's your friend?" I ask.

Morgan turns her head to look at the blue-haired boy, staggering a little.

"Yes," she says, "who are you?"

He smiles, showing white teeth and preppy charm.

"Dave," he says, bracing Morgan with one arm and extending the other in my direction. I shake his hand. "Wow did you really used to be a man?" he asks with an inebriated grin. Obviously, Morgan has been sharing my story with her friends.

"Dave, please sit down a moment," I tell him, gesturing to the sofa. "Morgan, go to your room and wait for me."

Morgan makes a mocking face for Dave's benefit but complies. I duck into my bedroom, give William his beer, don a robe, and come back out. Dave is sitting zombie-like staring into space. I fetch a notepad and pen and ask Dave to jot down his phone number and address.

"Why?" he asks.

"I'll need to call you if you've gotten Morgan pregnant."

His eyes round again. "Oh no, ma'am, we didn't do it. Honest. I'm just making sure she got home okay."

"Write," I tell him. He does.

I go to the kitchen to boil water for instant coffee. While I'm there, Morgan barrels out of her room into the bathroom and vomits. I follow her in and do what my mother used to do for me when I threw up: I kneel next to her and put one arm gently under her middle, and the other hand on her forehead. I used to take great comfort from both gestures. I don't know how Morgan feels about it, but she doesn't reject my parental gesture.

When she's done heaving, I tell her I'm making coffee and offer to bring her some. Her pallor is green. She shakes her head no and goes back to her room.

I bring a cup of coffee into the living room for Dave. William is sitting opposite him, telling a story. I interrupt, handing Dave his coffee.

"Please tell me you're not driving," I say.

He laughs. "No. The L."

I make him talk so I can assess how messed up he is. He's from Oak Park. He has to get to the Blue Line. His speech isn't horribly slurred, but he seems to be talking slower than normal and concentrating on forming his words. His eyes are opened too wide, like he's being constantly attacked by visions of ghosts or maybe irate parents, but he seems to be able to focus. He sips the coffee. I ask him to walk toward me and away from me a few times. He's fairly steady, much more so than Morgan.

I ask William if he'll get Dave to the Blue Line and just as he nods, Morgan comes out of her room again. She goes to the kitchen, then joins us with a cup of coffee in hand. She stares at William.

I introduce everyone, acting like we've all just run into each other at a church social. Morgan continues to stare at William whom I introduce as my friend. She's not being impolite. I think it's half alcohol stupor and half shock at realizing her strange parent has a sex life.

"When you're ready to go, William will make sure you get to the Blue Line transfer," I tell Dave. He assures me he's city wise and needs no help and I assure him he can either accept William's company or call his parents right now and make arrangements with them. He opts for William.

Before they leave, Morgan bolts for the bathroom again. We can hear her vomiting. I excuse myself and tend to her again. This episode ends with several dry heaves, bringing back memories of my own early experiences with getting shit-faced. The dry heaves came with the second drinking binge for me and helped convince me not to engage in a third one.

I help Morgan to bed. She's weak and still unbalanced. I help her peel off her blue jeans and top, then put her under the covers. She curls into a prenatal ball and falls asleep.

The guys are waiting for me when I return to the living room. I'm not quite ready to say goodbye, though.

"How did you run into Morgan?" I ask Dave.

"Uh, there was this party in Wrigleyville," he starts. He and his friends had heard about it on social media. While they were there, Morgan and her friends rolled in. Dave happened to be leaving when she left and he could see she was in trouble, so he helped her home.

"Who gave her the booze?" I ask.

Dave shakes his head. "There was a lot of alcohol there," he says. "Lots of people brought beer, wine, vodka, you name it."

"Drugs?" I ask.

"I'm sure," he says.

"Did Morgan imbibe?"

"I don't know," Dave says.

"Sex?"

"I don't think so," he says. "Not with me, for sure, but when I saw her, she was dancing and drinking." He shrugs, like that's all he knows.

I thank him for helping Morgan and give him my phone number, in case he runs into any problems on his way home. They leave, William's farewell kiss a brief reminder of how wonderful the afternoon had been, before reality interceded again.

9

I awaken Morgan after an hour, to get her back on a normal sleep schedule and head off a morning hangover. When I enter her room, the sight of her stops me with a jolt. My worldly, spiteful, mean-spirited daughter is curled up in a ball, clutching a doll to her bosom as if it were a fairy saving her from the horrors of life. Her position brings memories of her infancy into my mind. I remember standing at her crib, watching her sleep, thinking that no life-form this sweet and this vulnerable can possibly survive. She did, of course, though until this moment I would have said her innocence perished in adolescence. Now, instead of insolence and cruelty on her face, I see pain and torment. I realize she's mourning for her mother, and her sense of loss has added sharp edges to her rebellion and to her feelings about me.

I have no idea what to do with these realizations, or the feelings I have for her, the love I feel, and the fear of her rejection and scorn. I wonder what Blythe would do, but I know the answer even as the question occurs to me. I go to Morgan's bedside and sit beside her, then lean down to kiss her cheek. She remains still. Her skin is soft and warm and the contact brings back memories of us hugging when she was a toddler. Warmth flows through me. I kiss her softly again, then lay my cheek against hers. She stirs. I sit up so I don't frighten her when she awakens, but I take one of her hands in mine and hold it.

Morgan's eyes open and close several times. This was how she woke up as a child, too. The first couple of times her eyes open, she's still asleep, but by the third or fourth time she's conscious and awakening. She blinks and her eyes stay open. She feels her hand in mine, then sees it. She frowns a little, then follows the trail of my arm to my person. She pulls her hand away and uses it to help her roll onto her back. She grimaces as she moves, but she positions her hands above the covers, where I can reach them. She looks at me, her expression a blend of curiosity and confusion. She's getting her bearings now that she's back in the world.

"I saw you naked," she murmurs, her voice full of sleep and her mouth moving slowly.

"And I saw you drunk." I smile a little when I say it. My voice is soft.

"I suppose that means a leash and collar for me."

"We'll talk about that when you're feeling better," I say. "How do you feel?"

"Like someone hit me in the head with a hammer. And sick." She closes her eyes, brows furrowing in pain.

I take her hands in mine. She doesn't fight me.

"Welcome to the glamorous world of binge drinking," I say. I keep my voice soft and I try to smile a mom smile when I say it. Her face puckers up to cry, but the tears don't come. I leave her briefly and return with water and two tablets of ibuprofen.

Thirty minutes later I offer to help her get dressed.

"Why would I get dressed? This is as good a place to die as any."

"You need to get up and move around a little," I say. "We're going for a walk and then we'll have a light dinner. Otherwise, you'll feel terrible tomorrow."

She flashes her sarcastic grimace-face at me. "I already feel terrible tomorrow. Besides, it's raining."

A summer squall has blown in since our latest battle started.

"There's nothing like a walk in the rain to clear your head," I say.

After several more objections, she gets dressed, dons rain gear, and braves the great outdoors. Morgan looks comically cute in one of my raincoats. It comes down nearly to her knees and has enough room inside for two of her. The gusting winds make our rain gear flap like flags. When we walk into the wind we have to lean forward and squint to keep rain out of our eyes. When the wind sails in from the side we have to scramble to keep our balance. The streets are dark and deserted. It is a gloriously miserable night.

"I feel like one of those squatty little gnomes in this coat," Morgan grumbles. "It's humiliating."

"You're comfortable. You're dry. And you're less interesting to rapists. Rejoice, and enjoy the moment."

"The rapist would take you instead?" She poses the question as if it could never happen. "Just because you have big tits?"

That dig manages to get under my skin. I'm still trying to think of a suitable response when she interrupts my thoughts. "I was just kidding, Dad."

I put one of my oversized hands on Morgan's arm and stop us in the middle of the sidewalk.

"I wouldn't mind you calling me Dad if you weren't doing it to make me feel bad," I say. Our faces are a few inches apart and I don't disguise my anger. "But you are trying to make me feel bad and I'm sick of it. You can call me Nikki or Aunt Nikki. You can even call me Mom. But don't call me Dad."

"What are you going to do about it?" She challenges me with an ugly sneer. Her eyes are slits, her lips thin bands of contempt. If insolence could be painted, it would look like this.

"I have no idea," I tell her. I resume walking. I don't look back to see if Morgan's coming. She will or she won't. Actually, she probably will. She doesn't have a house key or money with her. We walk in silence for another fifteen minutes and stop at a deli. I invite Morgan to order something if she's hungry.

"What's good for a hangover?" she asks. I can't tell if she's being sarcastic or seeking advice. Nor do I care. I'm so sick of her abuse and attitude I'm ready to help her pack her bag to run away.

"Abstinence," I say. "It works for pregnancy and venereal disease, too."

"Like you with William." Her blue eyes meet mine and she widens them, like an exclamation point. "I bet he has a big one. Is that what you like? Dad."

The world stops for me. The only thing I can see is Morgan's sneering face, and the red veil of anger that colors my vision. She is begging for a good hard slap across her face—literally, she wants me to hit her. And part of me would like to give her a good smack for being a bully and for being cruel and inappropriate. But I could never hit my daughter.

"Shut up," I tell her. "Shut up and order, or just shut up."

The man at the counter is staring at us. Morgan glances at him, then me. She smiles triumphantly and marches to the exit. She waits in the wind and rain until I have my food in hand. We say nothing else on the walk home but when we enter the apartment, I tell Morgan to join me at the dining table. I hand her a bag with a tuna sandwich and chips in it. She pretends to disdain it, but by the time I have my sandwich ready to eat, she's picking at hers.

"I've taken enough abuse from you," I say. "Let's get to your real issues."

"Let's talk about William," Morgan says. She has a wise-ass grin on her face.

"Let's do both. What do you want to know about William?"

"First, I want to know why it's okay for you to screw him but not for me to have sex." She smirks.

I shake my head a little, trying to form a coherent thought.

"One thing has nothing to do with the other," I say, finally. "You can sleep with anyone you want to, but the fact is, right now, you're not in love with anyone. Just sleeping around with strangers has a lot of dangers—"

"Ooooh, HIV." She says the words in a spooky voice and raises her arms in mock horror.

"Yes, HIV, gonorrhea, several others. Not to mention low self-esteem. I'm sure there are other issues but those are the ones I know about."

"How long have you been with William?" she asks.

I have to think for a minute. "About eight years," I answer.

"Why haven't I met him before?" she asks.

"Because you've never shown the slightest interest in me or my life."

"Does he usually stay here, or do you stay at his place?"

"It's not that kind of relationship," I tell her.

Morgan's surprise is genuine. "What kind of relationship is it?"

This is where I should tell her to mind her own business, but I'm aggravated and when I get like this I tend to blurt things out.

"I pay him for sex," I say. "He sees other women and I could see other men, if any were interested in me. We enjoy sex together on occasion and I pay him for it."

"He's a prostitute?" Morgan's eyes round. "I thought that was just a guy fantasy."

"I don't think he's a sex worker," I correct her. "Paying him was my idea. I've always had a hard time attracting decent men. He likes me, we get along well. The arrangement takes sex off my list of urgent needs so I can pursue other things."

"He's Black." Morgan says it in a leading way, like a

white woman with a Black man is a statement that demands explanation.

"African-American," I say.

"They have bigger things, right?" Morgan smiles but it's not a friendly smile. "Is that what you were after?"

I flush with anger. "Let's talk about you now. I think the reason you're so cruel and belligerent is because you're mourning your mother's illness."

"That's none of your business," she snaps.

I clean off the table and gesture for Morgan to put our few dishes in the dishwasher. "It is my business," I tell her. "Aside from being your parent, you've made it my business by making my life hell. Do you resent me for being healthy while the parent you love is sick?"

Morgan steps in front of me and tilts her face up to confront me. Even though I'm five inches taller than her, our faces are so close together I can smell the tuna fish on her breath as she speaks and I can see the fury in her eyes. "Don't talk about my mother. You have no right to talk about her. You abandoned us. She's the only person who loves me in the whole world."

She doesn't cry, she doesn't back down. She glowers. I can feel hate radiating from her the way heat waves shimmer from the desert floor.

"I didn't abandon you," I say, quietly. "You both rejected me. It broke my heart."

"Bullshit," she says. "You didn't love us." She makes the accusation for the second time: If I had loved them I would have remained male.

I reach out to put a hand on hers, but she snatches her hand away and turns her back on me. I put my hand on her shoulder. She lets me, but her body is rigid.

"I used to accuse myself of betraying you and your mom, especially in those first few years, when you were learning to hate me. I thought I should have been braver and I thought I should have overcome my feelings. But Morgan, I couldn't. I was at a point where I had to be a woman or I had to die. I couldn't pretend I was a man anymore."

"Grandmother says you just wanted to have boyfriends." She spits out the words.

"Grandmother is a crabby old lady who was supposed to be a dumb woman with big tits, but she didn't get the big tits."

As soon as I say it, I regret it. I sound just like Virginia. I take a deep breath and calm myself. "I'm sorry. That's a terrible thing to say about anybody. I take it back. But Morgan, try to understand this much: being transgender isn't a choice. It's the way a person's brain develops. Most people get a sense of gender identity that agrees with their body, but some of us don't. I tried to deny it, then I tried to hide it, but it was all a fake. I was pretending to be someone I wasn't. Every day, I had to be this made-up person. The real me didn't exist. Until I just couldn't take it anymore. I had to transition, I had to be the real me, or I had to die."

There's so much more to the story, of course, but it's impossible to tell in a way a cisgender person can comprehend. Seeing the wrong face in the mirror each morning. Being repulsed by my body hair. Getting male haircuts when my inner self cried out for long hair with waves and highlights. Trembling with euphoria when I could wiggle my body into a dress in a private moment. Dreaming of what it must be like to have breasts and a vagina and smooth, soft skin. And yet, engaging in trash talk and macho insults with my male colleagues as if I was a model hetero male, maybe even a Republican. Never backing down from a confrontation on the field of play in sports. Presenting myself as the all-American guy, even when my mind was playing movies of me in a dress and makeup and heels. I was lying to everyone, especially myself.

Morgan turns to face me and I try to hug her, but she holds me off. We lock eyes, mine moist, hers glaring.

"She's going to die." Morgan's words are angry. Her lips quiver a little. I can feel her pain, and I know what she's thinking. She's thinking it should be her perverted father who is dying and her beloved mother should be in the prime of life.

10

I can't trade places with Blythe, but I'm hoping Morgan can relieve some of her grief and anger at my self-defense class. Working to exhaustion and hitting things—especially hitting things—has always worked for me.

The class meets in a private gym that was unique in my coming out days in its acceptance of all types of minorities, including trans and gay people. They all do, now, but I've stayed with Sloan's out of loyalty. But it's also a great gym, with separate rooms for strength training, aerobics, and indoor sports. The sports gym is primarily for basketball and volleyball, but twice a week, for two hours, it's given over to self-defense and martial arts training. One end of the basketball court extends twenty or thirty feet under a track that circles the gym. The extra space is mostly multiuse for things like stretching or chairs for people watching games on the court. But part of it includes a couple heavy bags and a speed bag for martial arts people. The heavy bags have played an important role in my life, serving as surrogate villains for me in the most intense and violent moments of my workouts.

Morgan and I go through a forty-minute workout together, practicing forms and kicks and punches. Morgan gets into it. She's athletic and shows an aggressiveness in this setting. She's quick to pick up the kicking and punching and graduates from tentative, girly movements to solid, thud-inducing blows rapidly. I see a hint of a smile of grim satisfaction on her face as she pummels the dummy held by her partner and wonder who the dummy represents to her. Probably me, but I'm not discouraged.

The instructor, a man named Ted Otari, invites me to join Morgan and the novices when he takes them aside to teach basic street defenses. I decline. Morgan would prefer to be on her own anyway, and I have another segment of my workout to complete. I move to one of the heavy bags at the far end of the gym. I flail at it with my fists first, trying to maintain straight-punch form for three two-minute bursts. It's exhausting, but I know my life could depend on my power, form, and endurance someday. Transitioning, especially when I did, taught me harsh lessons about the society we live in. After the punching workout, I focus on kicks—power shots to the mid-section, and speed kicks to the head. I'll never use the head shots—I'm too slow and lack power at that angle—but the workout is good for maintaining my agility.

After the kicks, I fetch a baseball bat from my gym bag and begin a choreographed workout in which I swing the bat violently into the heavy bag, rapid-fire, from different angles, moving all the time. The impact of each blow sounds like the muffled roar of a distant cannon, or maybe a rapist's head splattering. I take five swings from the left, five from the right, and then perform a series of pugil stick moves, using the bat like a rifle with a bayonet affixed to it—straight thrusts to the midsection and head. I rest for thirty seconds, then repeat everything. For an intense fifteen or twenty minutes, it sounds like a shooting gallery in my corner, my swings and thrusts powered by leverage and strength and bad intentions. As I tire, the noise levels recede. I finish barely able to swing the bat, my body cloaked in sweat-soaked workout gear.

Morgan and one of the other novices are watching me, their faces filled with awe and horror. Ted Otari passes by and pats my back. "Wet T-shirt contest?" he cracks. My cotton tank top clings to my body like a second skin. As Morgan and I walk to the locker room, I brace myself for some kind of bruising quip about my body or my gender, but she has moved on, at least for the moment.

"Is that how you beat up that guy at the café?" she asks. She nods her head in the direction of the bat, which is attached to my gym bag.

"No," I answer. "I did him without a weapon." We take several more steps. "I was lucky. The bat's in case he comes back."

"You could kill someone." Morgan's tone is disapproving.

"Yes," I say. "That's the idea."

Morgan glances at me. Her expression is a blend of disapproval and disgust.

At nine o'clock, I knock on Morgan's bedroom door for our evening walk which has become a ritual. I let her sulk and mourn and do whatever she does in her room after dinner, but at nine we go out for thirty minutes. Usually, she's as taciturn as ever, but I feel like I'm making it possible for her to talk to me if she wants to.

Tonight, she emerges almost immediately and has a cheerful expression on her face. I choke back the temptation to ask her why she's so happy. She'll tell me, if she wants me to know, and if she doesn't want me to know, asking her would just put her in her usual snit.

It's a dark, overcast night. The air is wet and the wind is gusting, portents of a coming storm. The streets are deserted and gloomy, even within the glow of the street lamps which emit an unnatural, eerie radiance. I see a furtive movement in the shadows up ahead. A tremor passes through me, my fear impulse. I keep my eyes trained on the spot where I sensed movement. Nothing. A few steps later I realize the movement was the shadow cast by a tree branch blowing in the wind. The anxiety remains; I've had bad experiences with dark, deserted streets.

A clanging noise erupts behind us. I whirl around. A metal garbage can has blown onto the street. Morgan looks at me like I'm crazy. I take a deep breath and smile at her. As we begin walking again, I finger the can of pepper spray in my pocket and ask Morgan if she remembered to bring hers. She didn't. I admonish her that the pepper spray is more important than money for a woman walking city streets at night.

"Right," she says, but she says it without her usual wise-ass attitude when I bring up safety. She's saying she heard me.

"I have some news," she says, a few steps later.

"Oh?" I say, cuing her to continue.

"David asked me out Friday night." I can hear the smile in her voice. She's almost giddy. This surprises me. Dave is a pretty average-looking boy. When I was in high school, girls as attractive as Morgan ruled the roost, or at least, I thought they did. I'd have thought a girl as pretty as Morgan would have received longing gazes and prayerful overtures from boys like Dave so often it would be passé for her.

"And what did you say?"

"I said I'd love to," answers Morgan. "You don't object, do you? You keep telling me to go to bed with boys my own age."

I start to issue an indignant rebuttal, but Morgan is laughing. "Gotcha, Nikki," she says.

I smile good-naturedly. Our mood is light, for the first time I can remember. I guide us toward the commercial strip, thinking a cup of tea will prolong the evening and the good cheer. I try to keep the friendly banter alive.

"Why do you think I would give my consent to you seeing Dave again?"

"Well, you'd be rid of me for a little while," she laughs. "Long enough to have William come calling."

We're still exchanging lighthearted barbs as we turn the corner to Chaya's Tea House, but the quiet little shop that should be getting ready to close is lit up in the flashing red lights of a police car. A cluster of eight or ten people huddles on the sidewalk, peering in through the picture window. An ambulance arrives as we join the crowd. Inside, two cops kneel beside a prone body and Chaya, a tiny, elderly woman, stands just beyond them, her face shocked and tearful, her arms folded and clutching her sides. Two EMTs emerge from the ambulance and wheel a gurney into the tearoom. The cops give way, the techs check the patient and ask questions we can't hear. The person on the floor seems to be moving. When they lift the injured party to the gurney, I can see it's an older man. They wheel him rapidly to the ambulance.

"What happened?" Morgan asks the woman next to her.

"That man was having tea and reading when a hooligan came in and smashed him in the face with his tea pot," says the woman. She's older, sixties, maybe seventies, and as tiny and frail as Chaya. She wears a Star of David on a fine gold chain around her neck. Her face is angry, her lips set in a thin line of determination. "It's those Nazis," she says. "They keep doing things like this to Jews."

Another woman nods her head in agreement and tells us about a recent street crime in another neighborhood also targeting a Jew. Morgan shares the story about Billy being beaten in the alley by our café. The ambulance leaves. The cops finish up with Chaya and come outside, looking for witnesses. An older man comes forward. They take him aside to get his statement. Two of Chaya's friends go into the tea house to offer condolences. Morgan and I follow them inside. After the friends share hugs and concerns, I ask Chaya if she'd like Morgan and me to escort her home. I don't know her that well—I'm just a patron of her shop—but she appreciates the offer, even as she says there's no need.

"She'll have an army escorting her home," says the woman Morgan was talking to. "Never again!"

Damn right, I think to myself. Never again!

On the way home, I say to Morgan, "That's why you need to carry your pepper spray at all times." I glance at Morgan and recall her disapproval of my violent workout in the gym.

"And if you ever have to use it," I continue, "don't be timid. If you can't run away, crush his fucking skull while he's down."

Morgan looks at me like I'm an axe murderer. "Really, Nikki," she scolds.

"Think about Billy," I say.

11

I read an article once about how road crews in Alaska are required to have a person with a high-powered rifle posted as a guard while they work to protect the crew against the state's many huge, aggressive bears. It's not just black bears and grizzlies, it's also brown, like Kodiaks and grizzlies, and farther north, polar bears. The bears are everywhere and wherever they go, they're in charge.

This thought raced through my mind as I thought about the attacks on Chaya's customer, Billy, and Little John and me. It's not that the attacks are organized or even the work of a single, sick group. It's that we live in a new environment. Every hate-filled screwball in America has been licensed to exorcise his demons on the targets of his choice. Like Alaska's bears, our psychotic alphas are everywhere. No minority is safe, and no one patronizing or working for a minority business is safe, either.

So, on the Tuesday morning after the attack at Chaya's, I gather the staff after the coffee rush hour and make a few announcements. I tell them I've purchased a baseball bat that now hangs by the back door. It's a Little League model that even our smallest staff person can handle. Henceforth, when anyone goes out back to take out the garbage, or take a break, or have a private phone conversation, or anything else, they must be accompanied by another crew member and carry the bat for protection. I make sure everyone has the police emergency number on their phone's fast-dial setting. And I make sure everyone is carrying their pepper spray, including the guys, even Jermell, the waiter who pumps iron and looks like he could whip a grizzly in an arm-wrestling contest. Jermell, an African-American man in his early twenties, grinned and said he'd love to kick some white supremacist ass, with or without pepper spray. To which I said, great, but blind the bastard first. Our repartee produced some nervous giggles. None of us are comfortable with the prospect of violence, including me, but I understand it happens, and when it happens to you, it's better to give than to receive.

I spend the rest of the week making sure my rules are obeyed. It's a pain. No one wants to have someone else watch over them when they take the garbage out, and no one wants to stand at the back door with a baseball bat in hand. It feels stupid. But I insist, and I make Little John enforce the rules, too. He hates it. He's a pacifist at heart. But he also understands the problem. He keeps an eye on the back door and he makes sure the people on his shift have their pepper spray at hand.

We're nearing Morgan's one-month performance review, so I've taken a little more time to watch her work. We're very serious about performance reviews at BeatNikki's, even though most of our jobs are entry-level, low-wage positions and we have a lot of staff turnover. People appreciate the feedback, and they like being treated like professionals, and when management does that, good things happen.

Little John was my first employee at BeatNikki's Café. I

hired him because he seemed honest and conscientious, and because he was in the early, nervous stages of gender transition and desperate for work. I hoped his desperation was enough to keep him at BeatNikki's long enough for me to figure out what I was doing. I knew he had more experience than me in food service when I hired him, but I didn't appreciate his passion for food and beverage creations until we sat down for his first performance review. After praising his work, I asked him if he had any ideas for the business. It turned out he had a lot of ideas for menu offerings that could expand our clientele.

When we hired our next employee, we were smart enough to not only watch how she interacted with customers, but also to get her thoughts about the business and give her constructive feedback on her performance. She stayed with us for several years, until she finished college. Even then she said it was the best job she ever had and she hated to leave. So, we learned that making sure everyone knew they were appreciated and keeping everyone engaged in the business was a good business practice. It was also good sociology—when everyone's happy, it's a lot easier to come to work in the morning.

Morgan fits in well with the staff. She's also surprisingly good with customers. She's friendly, chatty, and efficient, and she adds just the right amount of youthful effervescence to engage even the grumpiest customer without being too saccharine for our feminist clientele. Who knew an American royal, a literal one-percenter, would find happiness serving inner-city riffraff.

She especially loves working with Little John. Her face lights up whenever he talks to her and she hangs on his every word when he guides her on mixing our special drinks. He's getting the love and acceptance I crave from Morgan and I've had to fight back a sense of jealousy. I understand she's not choosing him over me—she just genuinely likes him—but it hurts anyway. Little John is a special kind of man with a gentleness you rarely find in men. He makes you feel warm and fuzzy inside, and safe and loved. If he was in his teens, Morgan would be in love with him. If he was in his forties, I would be.

As for Morgan and me, we've reached a kind of equilibrium in our relationship. She treats me with respect and obeys the few commandments I lay down at home. I treat her like an adult and don't overload her with rules and warnings. She doesn't love me and I can still feel an undercurrent of resentment in her, but we should be able to survive the summer together.

"Why isn't Little John doing my performance evaluation?" Morgan asks. We've just sat down at a quiet table and I've barely uttered my standard opening remarks. She's not being deliberately insulting, but the question has the same effect. "I mean, I work with him all the time and hardly ever with you."

"I do the formal evaluation because I'm the boss," I tell her. I keep my temper under control. She's not the first millennial to get under my skin with an outsized sense of worldly knowledge.

"But Little John sees me work."

"So do I. So do our customers. So do other members of the staff." I lean forward a little to make my point. "We've collected input from a full range of people, and Little John and I have talked about you privately. This will be the most thorough performance evaluation you'll ever get," I say. "Unless you decide to work here full time." I throw out the last bit as a joke to lighten the mood.

Morgan makes a face. "Not in this lifetime."

She's delivering a message to me. This is a café, not a Fortune 500 corporation, and the job is an hourly wage position, not something that comes with a castle in the suburbs.

I set aside my annoyance and work through the review. It's very positive. She's doing an excellent job. She's smart and efficient and everyone likes her, except me, I suppose. I love her, but it's not the same thing. When I finish I ask if she has any questions.

"No," she says. "Can I get back to work now?"

I keep her just long enough to explain that she has now qualified for a ten percent raise. She is the first employee of BeatNikki's to ever receive this news with complete indifference. I've had employees get teary-eyed with joy at this news, and everyone smiles, but all Morgan does is shrug, say thanks and go back to work.

Dave comes to pick up Morgan for their date promptly at seven o'clock. I announce his arrival to Morgan who is still in her room. She says she'll be a minute. I tell Dave I have a gift for him and take him into the living room where I give him a can of pepper spray, like the ones I distributed at the café.

"Hopefully you won't need this," I say, "but it's an effective way to get out of a violent situation."

I show him how it works and advise him to go for the eyes, then run like mad. He looks at me, confused, as Morgan promenades from her room. She's wearing denim short-shorts and a thin, tight-fitting tank top that falls well short of her navel and shows enough cleavage to draw a second look. Her hair is partly up, with a few curls framing her face and dangling down the back of her neck. She's wearing strappy sandals with three-inch heels. If I was dressed like that, I'd be hoping to get laid tonight. I'm guessing she's hoping that, too, but I have no idea what I can do about it.

She wants to whisk him out the door before I can ruin her night with parental advice, but the sight of us standing in the living room, discussing a can of pepper spray that he holds in his hand, stops her short.

"My God, Nikki," she groans. "Not here, too."

"We've had some incidents with right-wing crazies," I explain to Dave. "They're targeting minorities, and they might go after Morgan to get at me."

He nods like he understands. Morgan strikes a martyred pose. I ask if she has her pepper spray. She says yes, but she's utterly insincere. I make her show it to me. She does. She has it in one of her pockets. Her identification, credit card and cash are in the other pocket.

"Okay?" She says the word thick with insolence.

I look at her for a moment, letting the image of her as a toddler creep into my mind, just long enough to wonder how humans go from that to this, then I come back to the here and now.

"Okay," I say. "Have fun."

There's really nothing more I can say or do, and I hate the feeling.

12

"He's nice, but boring." Morgan shares this assessment of Dave like a debutante describing the gardener's apprentice.

I took her to breakfast this morning to start what I hoped would be a happy day together, maybe even the start of a new normal in our relationship. We'll shop for clothes for her later, and take in a play tonight.

My hopes soared when she came home clear-eyed and sober last night and she seemed to be in a good mood which means she smiled when she came in the door and engaged in a few bars of pleasant conversation with me before retiring to her room. I thought she might enliven our breakfast with some details of her night on the town with Dave, but in just four words, she's piled him onto the same rubbish heap where I exist in her life.

"You seemed upbeat when you got home last night."

"Well." She says "well" like a towering intellectual starting a long answer to a question about the meaning of life. "I did get out, for once, thank God. And we danced at a club. That was fun. And I met a guy."

She makes me draw the story out of her, even though she's

eager to tell it. They went to a dance club that served non-alcoholic drinks and mostly enjoyed it, though the techno music was weird and Dave was a geeky dancer. The atmosphere was open and friendly and they had conversations with lots of other revelers, including Ralph, a college guy home for the summer. Ralph was handsome and cool and a great dancer. They exchanged phone numbers and he said he'd be calling soon.

"I think he's going to be the one to deflower me," she says. She smirks at me in that way she does when she's baiting me.

I make myself act noncommittal, lowering my eyes to my coffee and checking my phone for messages.

"No great moral pronouncements, Nikki?" she asks, mockingly.

"I've said what I have to say," I reply. "It's your life."

"Maybe I should hire a prostitute, like you," she says. "A Black one with a big cock. Maybe William has a friend." She's using vulgar language and bigoted insults to pick a fight with me. For the life of me, I don't know what brought this on.

"You'll need another pay raise," I say, flipping through text messages.

"Does he do real women, too, or just trannies?"

She has finally succeeded in hitting my rage button, though I manage to control my voice and my language when I respond.

"That word, for people like me, is like the n-word for Black people," I say. "It is deeply insulting and disrespectful. By using it, you're telling me I'm a lesser life form."

I pause and rap on the table to get her attention, and make her look me in the eye.

"I understand that you're doing this to get even with me, somehow, for something, and I'm willing to tolerate a lot of your angst because I was a teenager once, too, and I was pretty snotty at times. But Morgan, I will not tolerate expressions of bigotry from you. Save your crude remarks about Black men and transgender women for somewhere far from my ears. If I hear

93

any more of that crap I'm going to kick your bitchy ass out."

"Really?" She says it with equal parts doubt and spite.

"Really." I hold her eyes with mine. This is one of the ways I'm not like a mom. I have a low tolerance for bullshit. I thought it might change with my body chemistry, but it didn't.

"You'd just throw me out on the street?" Same tone.

"No, I'm going to put you on the next plane to New York and let your mother and grandmother deal with you. They made you into a bigot."

I shouldn't have said the last part, but it's what I believe and it slips out.

"Go ahead, tranny." Morgan juts her chin out. She's daring me.

"You got it, kid."

I pull a wad of bills from my purse, slap them on the table, then stand and leave. I don't look back to see if she's coming. She catches up to me on the street and walks beside me in angry silence. When we get back to the flat, I point to her room and tell her, "Go pack. You've got fifteen minutes."

She gives me the finger and goes into her room. I get on the Internet and book a one-way ticket for her to LaGuardia. As soon as fifteen minutes has elapsed, I knock on her door.

"Ready?" I call.

"I can't get everything in one suitcase," she says.

I walk in. Her suitcase is open on her bed. She has thrown unfolded clothes and toiletries into it, probably in a rage. She's crying. Her face is angry. I throw the excess clothing on the bed, then bunch the rest to fit. I slap the suitcase closed and stand it on the floor. My hands are still trembling with rage.

"Time's up," I say. "You can go shopping with Granny."

I leave, towing the suitcase behind me and wait for her at the door. She dallies, sobbing, expecting me to relent. I don't.

"Come on," I snap. "Airlines don't wait for petulant teen queens."

Morgan sobs and sniffles all the way to the L station, but she doesn't apologize and I'm not bluffing. By the time we get on the Blue Line train to O'Hare she has dried her tears. Her eyes are still puffy, but she's arranged her face into that leering, angry, know-it-all sneer she does so well. At O'Hare, I grab her suitcase with one hand and her hand with the other and drag her into the American terminal. I print her boarding pass and baggage check at a kiosk and show her how to check her bag. I walk her to the security line.

"I'm going to call that nasty old bitch you call grandmother and tell her to meet you at LaGuardia," I say. "She probably won't because she'd have to mingle with so many common people, so here." I count out a hundred and forty dollars for her. "The cab will probably be around seventy dollars. That leaves you with enough cash to eat and some walking around money."

When I slap the cash in her palm she looks at me, finally, and her expression melts. Suddenly her eyes are wide and misty brown and her face is vulnerable and she looks like the toddler who used to run into my arms and cuddle. I can see tears starting. Shit.

"You're really going to do it?" She says it in a kind of disbelief that only the young and innocent can muster. Her lips quiver.

"You leave me no choice, Morgan." I'm selecting my words carefully, more for myself than her. My heart's melting. My anger is evaporating. I'm not on the planet to hurt people.

"Mom can't take care of me," she says. "And I can't stand Grandmother." The tears flow freely now.

"You should have thought of that before you started calling me vile names and insulting my lover." I say the words softly, thinking, if she apologizes, I'll take her back. She doesn't.

We're frozen in place. Morgan turns her head slowly from side to side, like she's feeling shock and grief at the same time, like someone mourning the loss of a of a loved one. I try to think of a way to defuse the situation, but it's out of my hands. If I invite her back without her apology, she has license to continue spewing her anger and bigotry.

"Time's getting short," I say.

She glances at me and I gesture toward the security line. She sniffles, then cries in earnest. I put my arms around her and hug. My heart is breaking.

"I love you," I whisper to her.

She pushes herself away from me and runs through the maze of poles and straps that delineate the security line. When she reaches the end of the line she stares straight ahead at the back of the man in front of her. She bends her head to sob once in a while, but never looks back. When they check her boarding pass and identification and let her in the screening area, I turn to leave, but stop when I reach the exit for the Blue Line station. I turn and look back at the security area, hoping to see my daughter coming away from there, looking for me in the crowd.

Of course, no one comes out. I feel weak and weepy. I sit on a metal bench and bury my face in my hands and let the tears flow. I mentally curse myself for being a terrible parent and worse human being.

In the midst of my bereavement, I realize my name is being paged on the public address system. I go to the service desk. A tight-lipped TSA officer verifies my identity then leads me to a small room. Morgan sits at a metal table, her face buried in her arms on the table. She doesn't look up when I come in.

"She had a can of pepper spray in her belongings," says the officer. "When we pulled her out of the line she fell apart. She was crying so hard we couldn't get her to talk. We brought her in here and she finally gave us your name. She's not ready to fly today, ma'am."

The officer is being somewhat kind, but it's also clear she wouldn't allow Morgan on an airplane if I threw in a thousand-dollar bribe. I nod to the officer and go sit across from Morgan. I put a hand on her arm. She sobs. I stroke her hair and try to think of something to say. Amazingly, she tolerates my touch.

"We need to find a way to get along," I say quietly, still stroking her hair with one hand and holding her arm with the other. "Do you think we can do that? Meet each other halfway?"

I don't expect an answer, but her head moves and I hear a tiny, squeaky voice coming from her. I lean closer to hear what she's saying.

"I talked to my mom this morning. She's dying," she sobs. "She loves me and she's dying. She's the only person in the world who loves me and she's dying."

I stroke her head. "We don't know that for sure," I whisper. "She might get better. But know this, Morgan. I love you too."

"No you don't," she wails. "You called me a bitch and a bigot." More sobs.

What to say? I did call her those things, and I meant them. But her heartbreak is tearing me apart.

"I did say those things about you and they were true, but I still love you. I've always loved you and I always will."

It's as if I'm talking to a rock. She doesn't move. Her only signs of life are the rise and fall of her chest as she breathes, and the occasional muffled sob. I wait. Nothing changes. I glance at the officer. She's twitching impatiently, stuck here until we leave, I suppose.

I put a hand on Morgan's arm and rub. She remains inert.

"We have to go," I say in a low voice. "You can't fly today. We're stuck with each other. Let's get your bag and see if I can get a refund on the ticket." I stand up and lift her arm gently. Morgan complies, her eyes downcast, her face red with emotion. She follows me from the room like a bereaved zombie. I nod a thank you to the officer who scowls.

When we return to the apartment Morgan runs to her room, me floating behind, just quick enough to keep the bedroom door from closing. She throws herself on her bed. I stay in the doorway.

"We need to talk, Morgan," I say. "Any time you're ready, just come on out and we'll figure out where to go from here."

I'd love to launch into a lecture about respectfulness and decency and getting along in the world, but I have no credibility with her anyway and, besides, if there's a decent person in there, a little quiet time might help it emerge.

After lingering in the living room for a few minutes in case Morgan wants to talk, I take a few deep, calming breaths and go in my bedroom. I close the door and go into my closet. It's the farthest point from Morgan's room and filled with clothes and soft surfaces that will absorb sounds I don't want Morgan to hear. I call Blythe.

"She's not available," Blythe's mother snaps when I ask for Blythe. "What's your message?"

It's not, *can I take a message?* or, *can I have her call you back?* or any other concession to civility. It's a command, from a superior human being to a lesser one.

"The message is, call me at once. Our daughter is in crisis."

"What's the crisis?" she demands.

"It's none of your goddamn business," I hiss. I've carefully avoided swearing in my dealings with the old battle axe, but civility has proven ineffective.

She sputters. "It most certainly is my business. She's my granddaughter. I helped raise her while you were out playing with your transvestite friends."

"You're a warped, nasty old lady," I say. "You have no parental rights over my daughter. Blythe and I have huge decisions to make about her and I'll make them myself if I don't hear from Blythe."

I hear a short squeak emitted in an indignant exhale, then the click of the receiver. I've been hung up on, which, all things considered, is probably the only honest way to end the conversation, and perhaps the most civil. Granny would curse Jesus for curing the lepers. I don't know if she'll convey my message to Blythe or not. I take a moment to send Blythe a text message. Maybe it will get through to her, but if it doesn't, it will at least document my attempts at communication.

13

Blythe calls back five minutes later.

"How dare you talk to my mother like that!" she starts. She rambles for a minute, but it's obvious she doesn't have the energy or volume to get where she wants to be on the moral outrage scale.

"Let's not waste time talking about your mother," I say. "You know what she is as well as I do. We need to talk about Morgan." I give her a condensed version of Morgan's drinking escapade, her being intent on getting laid by a college guy, and her unmitigated bigotry towards me.

"I had her all but aboard an airplane coming to stay with you," I say. "She had a problem in the security line then went on a crying jag so bad they wouldn't let her fly. So she's still here and I'm still not willing to accommodate anyone who calls me 'tranny.' What would you like me to do? I can send her to you or maybe you know some friend of hers whose family would keep her for a month."

"You should be more adult than that," she chides me. "Can't you take a little name-calling?"

"Not that name."

"Would you throw her out on the street?"

"I'll put her in the hands of whatever oligarchical family you make arrangements with," I say. "Or we can send her to a summer camp for kids who want to do drugs and have sex. Or I'll send her to you. What's your choice?"

"She can't come here, Nick—"

"It's Nikki," I interrupt. "I'm done with your put-downs, too."

"She can't come here, Nikki." Blythe's voice is so weak I immediately feel ashamed for my outburst. "I can barely get to the bathroom under my own power."

"I'm sorry." I remember her haggard appearance and fatigue from a month ago. "It's not going well?"

"No." She doesn't elaborate.

"Will you still be back in Chicago in a month?"

"Maybe in a casket." Her voice is tinged with anger and bitterness.

"Oh my God." The words just slip out of my mouth.

"So here's the most important thing to know about parenting," Blythe says. "Sometimes there's no right answer."

"It's that bad?" I'm having trouble forming complete sentences.

"Yes, it's that bad." She whispers it. "So maybe you could get off your high horse and take a little shit from your daughter for a week or two. I've been taking it for sixteen years." She stops, but I don't respond. I'm still reeling.

"If I die, when I die, she's going to be an orphan if you don't take her in," Blythe continues.

"What about your mother?"

There's a long pause before she speaks. "Like you said, we both know what she is. They'd destroy each other."

"You've told Morgan? What kind of shape you're in?"

"I think Mother's told her. I call when I can, but I don't last

101

long. Work it out with Morgan," she says, her voice fading.

Before I can respond she hangs up. I dimly realize that she's not being impolite. She just can't talk any more.

A midday squall blew through Chicago while Morgan was in her room, coming out of the northeast and across Lake Michigan instead of from the southwest, like most of our summer weather. I watched the hardwoods out front bend low in the gusting winds, and the rain blowing horizontally, and over the lake there were flashes of lightning in the sky. Under different circumstances, it would be exciting, but today I can't get past my Morgan problem. I can't think of a solution other than putting up with her vile disrespect and self-destructive impulses for another month and hoping to hell Blythe somehow recovers.

The squall clears off before four. I knock on Morgan's door.

"Is it dinner time?" she asks, her voice weak and a bit hoarse.

"Close," I say, cracking the door open a few inches so I don't have to yell to be heard. "Let's go for a walk and we'll find a place to eat when we're ready."

I expect an adolescent tantrum or at least a squawk, but there's a rustling noise in the room and then Morgan is standing at the door. She's wearing the same clothes she started the day in and she's holding her raincoat. She doesn't say anything, but she looks at me expectantly, like she's looking for direction.

"You won't need that," I tell her, pointing to the raincoat. She starts to object. I shrug. "Suit yourself."

We take an Uber to Navy Pier and pick up the Lakefront Trail, walking north. It's so spectacular even Morgan notices. The sky is bright with sunshine and the air is comfortably warm. The trail is alive with skateboarders and strollers and joggers and rollerbladers; Morgan's eyes move constantly, people-watching. That's the difference between the suburbs and the city. Here, you don't need a television set to be entertained. When we get to Oak Street Beach, I ask her if she's hungry.

"Not much. A little." She's not being indifferent or snotty. She's just not hungry yet. Maybe we're getting somewhere.

We walk a little further to an empty bench and sit. The sound of the waves roaring ashore in front of us, the dull rumble of traffic on Lake Shore Drive behind us, and the rush of the wind around us create a bubble where we can talk but not be overheard.

"I talked to your mother this afternoon," I start. I take one of her hands in mine and hold it. She lets me, though she doesn't squeeze my hand or make any other sign of affection. "She says she's not doing well."

Morgan looks out on the lake, to the horizon, blinks a few times, nods her head. "That's what Granny says."

"Does she really let you call her Granny?" It's a silly aside, but I've wondered about it since the first time I heard Morgan use the term. Blythe's mother is the most status-conscious pseudo-aristocrat I've ever met. It's hard to imagine her accepting such a common, down-home expression of endearment.

Morgan laughs softly. "No. I'm supposed to call her Grand-mere. Grumpy Granny is my little secret."

"Is she claiming to be French?"

Morgan laughs again. "No. I think she just likes the sound of it."

"Have you talked to your mom lately?" I ask.

"Not much. Mostly she's too weak. Mostly I get Granny." Morgan is still staring out at the lake, but her voice falters.

"That's what I was getting," I say. "I pushed through and got her on the phone today. At least 'Grand-mere' likes you."

"She doesn't like anyone," says Morgan.

"She dotes on you."

"That's only when you're around," says Morgan. "She hates you so I look pretty good when you're there. The rest of the time

103

she just lectures and gives orders."

After a moment, I work up the courage to say, "Your mom thinks there's a chance she's may not make it."

Morgan continues to stare out at the lake, but silent tears streak her face.

"She wants us to make peace," I continue. "Not just for the summer, for always."

Morgan doesn't move except to blink away tears.

"If your mom dies, do you want to stay with your grandmother?"

Morgan sobs and gulps for air.

"We need to have this conversation, Morgan," I say. "I need you to look at me when you're ready, so I know you're hearing me."

Slowly, she turns to me. Her face is so sad it breaks my heart not to be able to hug her, but she wouldn't take comfort in my gesture and this is a conversation we need to have.

"If you want to stay with your grandmother and tolerate visits from me, we can work with that. I can send you to a camp for the rest of the summer until your grandmother comes home. But if you want to live with me, we need to reach an understanding."

I raise my eyebrows to elicit a response from her.

"Okay," she says.

"Okay what?" I ask. "You do or don't want a relationship with me?"

She purses her lips. "Do. I think."

"I want that, too," I say. "I love you with all my heart. But if we're going to go on together, there has to be respect between us."

"You have to respect me?" Her eyes widen, like that has never happened in the history of the world.

"Of course," I answer. "That doesn't mean I have to agree with everything you say and do, but it means I respect you as an intelligent human being and someone with her own ideas about her life and who she is and what's right and wrong."

"That would be refreshing," she says, her voice dripping in sarcasm.

I bite back the impulse to point out how respectful I've been, even in the face of her abusive behavior.

"Well," I say, "you can coach me. If I say or do something that seems disrespectful, say so and we'll talk about it."

She does one of those *I'll bet* facial tics and nods dubiously. "Okay," she says.

"And I expect respect back," I say. "I don't ever want to hear the word *tranny* again, or racist comments about Black men, or any other kind of slur." I pause to let it sink in. After a moment, she nods.

"Do I have to respect you for hiring prostitutes?" she asks. She's challenging me, but not in a snide way. More like, she's trying to see how far our mutual respect goes when it comes to talking about sensitive issues in my life.

"No," I say. "But you do have to respect the fact that it's my choice and I have a right to make that choice because I'm an independent woman who fulfills every responsibility she's ever been given. You might also respect the fact that I'm up-front about it. I don't pretend to be someone else."

Morgan doesn't react, but I think I'm getting through to her because she doesn't look away or pull her hand from mine.

"Do I have to love you?" she asks. There's a trace of venom in her voice, but mostly I think it's an honest question. Which makes it hurt all the more.

"No. Of course not," I say. "No one can make you love someone you don't love."

"Okay," she says. "Good." She smiles a brief, tiny smile, just this side of a grimace. She wipes the tear streaks from her face and sits up, like the conversation's over and starts to stand up.

I pull her back down. I want to clarify everything. No, she

doesn't want to go to a camp. Yes, she wants to work at the café. Yes, a relationship based on mutual respect will be fine. It's not exactly the happy ending I hoped for, but it's a thousand miles better than this morning.

JULY 2017

14

As we near the end of my first month as Morgan's full-time parent, we seem to be settling into a vague semblance of normalcy. Our conversations are civil, if not deep, her work at the café continues to be excellent, and business is very good. Life is as easy as it can be with the specter of Blythe's illness hanging over us, and the daily churn of right-wing hate-mongering from the White House and its echo chambers.

I suggested to Morgan that we celebrate our first month together by going out for a fancy dinner tonight, but she already has plans. The college boy she hoped would seduce her—Ralph is his name—has finally asked her out and she was afraid if she cancelled it wouldn't happen again. I don't have to tell her my thoughts on the subject, so I don't repeat them.

Ralph arrives a fashionable thirty minutes late and by the looks of him, fashion is what he's about. He's a tall blond kid with an adult bearing—erect posture, lean body, permanent smile on his face, like a politician working a crowd. His eyes twinkle with a blend of different vibes. The one I'm supposed to see is the easy sociability and self-confidence—again, so like the way politicians are in a crowd. But there's this other, darker undercurrent, too. Something about the way his lips curl into a smile conveys more duplicity than mirth. I associate this look with people whose sense of self-worth allows them to lie, cheat, or steal because they're above the rules. Like Trump.

I want to plead with Morgan not to sleep with this man. Nothing good can come of it for her. My instinct is, he's not someone who takes pleasure from lovemaking. I'd bet he engages in sex as a form of domination, not pleasure. But of course, I don't have the credibility with Morgan to make such an assertion and, even if I did, she's at an age where she wants to make her own decisions.

I seat Ralph in the living room and go to Morgan's room to let her know he's here. I knock softly on her door and enter when she responds.

"Ralph's here," I say.

"Isn't he gorgeous?" Morgan gushes.

"I'm not the one he needs to impress," I say. "Do you have your key and your condoms?"

She gives me a sort of double take, then smiles. "Yes."

"Your pepper spray?"

"Yes."

"If you tell him 'no' and he doesn't stop, what are you going to do?" I ask her.

"Make him stop," she says, picking up her purse.

"How? What moves will you use?" I want her to have her tactics ready. People who don't think about defending themselves ahead of time don't resist effectively when they have to. To me, screaming and crying aren't a form of resistance, they're just a servile form of acceptance. Resistance should leave scars on the attacker. Ideally, it should discourage him from ever trying to assault another woman. And if you happen to kill the bastard? Well, that's not ideal, but it's not the worst possible outcome either.

"Whatever I need to use," Morgan says breezily. She angles past me and opens the bedroom door. "It's not going to be a problem, Nikki."

I give serious consideration to counseling Ralph about the consequences if he forces himself on Morgan tonight, but choke back the impulse. I don't have grounds for such a vile accusation. I've spoken my piece to Morgan. That's all I can do. I wish them well as they disappear out the door, Morgan whisking Ralph away without pausing for a hug.

I go to my room to prepare for my own date night, sliding into a summery long dress and doing my hair and makeup. It's not really a date, more an infomercial with Alan Campbell, the handsome real estate tycoon who wants to buy the BeatNikki building. He's taken to stopping in for coffee now and then, and corralling me to chat with him. I have no interest in selling, but he's so charming it's hard to ignore him. I tried to convince myself he was a sort of local version of Donald Trump, but the analogy didn't work. Alan is intelligent and amiable and the projects he builds are financially successful and aesthetically pleasing. I've known him for a month and he hasn't told me a lie yet, whereas our esteemed president spins almost a hundred whoppers a month by official tally. Alan is also head-spinningly sexy if I let myself think about him that way. I don't, but if I were a young, cisgender woman with any sort of chance of attracting the affections of Mr. Campbell, I would dream of melting into his arms and perhaps someday welcoming him to my bed. But, of course, I'm not a genetic woman, and the rare male who is attracted to me isn't interested in spending the night, let alone a lifetime. So I will enjoy his company, but at an emotional distance.

I take an Uber to the posh Gold Coast eatery near one of Alan's developments where we're meeting. I'm a few minutes early, but when I enter the restaurant, the woman at the hostess station seems to be waiting for me.

"Ms. Finch?" the woman asks. She's an elegant platinum blonde in a formal dress, conservative makeup and understated jewelry, and she moves with the grace of a model.

"I guess that means Mr. Campbell is here already and I'm the only six-foot woman in the place tonight," I respond.

"Mr. Campbell told me to watch for a tall, beautiful woman with curly blonde hair," the hostess says. Her smile is as white as a snowstorm and she says the line so gracefully, I almost believe she and Alan see me as a beautiful woman.

"You should both be in politics," I say.

Alan's table is tucked into a quiet back corner away from the noisy main dining room. He's obviously someone special here. He rises to greet me as we approach, his movements precise, smooth, and sure. I ready myself to shake hands, but when I reach him, he opens his arms and I walk into a hug. It's a full hug, not one of those faux hugs where people don't actually touch because they really don't like each other that much. Still, it's mostly a friend hug, except that our cheeks touch and he holds me a beat or two longer than a pal would hold a pal. I have to rise on my toes a little to fit my chin over his shoulder, a rare treat for a woman as tall as I am. It's one of several very sensuous characteristics of William, who is also taller than me. When he and I occasionally go out, I can wear heels, another treat, and when we embrace I have to stand on my toes to reach his lips with mine. Standing on my toes to hug Alan sends a charge of femininity through my body. I block the emotional rush before I make a fool of myself. Mr. Campbell is interested in my building, not my affections.

Alan holds my chair as I sit down. The table already bears a bottle of wine and two Bordeaux glasses with two inches of red wine in them. Alan sits across from me and picks up his glass for a toast. I follow his lead.

"To friends," he says. "Thank you for sharing your evening with me, Nikki." He adds a couple of lines about how much he appreciates me taking the time to be with him tonight. He does it artfully, finishing up just before it would get saccharine, leaving me with a glow I don't want to have but do anyway. Flattery from handsome, intelligent men—even false flattery—is as unlikely for a woman like me as a winning lottery ticket.

We clink and sip. I'm not a wine connoisseur, but I don't need to be to recognize that this wine is extraordinary. By force of habit, I inhale the vapors of the wine before sipping and find a rush of wine snob metaphors coursing into my brain. I sense crushed grapes and a musty cellar, and a forest floor in autumn, and other fruits and oak. Most of all, there's a velvety elegance to the vapors beyond anything I've sensed in a wine before. The first sip is another sensory adventure, sweetness, dryness, fruit, cherry, smoky oak, earthiness, and flavors I can't identify. I let it linger on my palette for several long beats.

"My goodness," I say, "that's extraordinary."

Alan beams. "Aha, I knew you were more than just another beautiful face. A wine aficionado, too!"

"Hardly." I'm blushing. Morgan would have more poise than I do at this moment. "This just tastes exceptional to me."

He swivels the bottle so I can see the label. "I think so, too. Stags Leap Cask 23. Year in, year out one of the top California cabs. Are you familiar with it?"

I smile and try to suppress a blush. "No," I say. "This is way more expensive than the wines I drink."

He launches into a lighthearted narrative on expensive wines from all over the world. "I favor Yank wines because I'm nouveau riche," he says. "I don't want to lose track of who I am."

I look at him quizzically. "What do you mean?"

"In the fine wine world," he explains, "there are excellent wines like this that cost a hundred, two hundred, three hundred dollars a bottle. Then there are the elite wines, mostly French, and they cost two or three times as much but only the greatest palates can taste the difference. I don't have a great palate and I don't want one. I top out in the three-hundred dollar range and I stick with American."

"Actually," he says, "I used to top out a lot lower than that, but your favorite president gave me a tax cut that makes it possible for me to buy a case of Cask 23 every week and still be many thousands ahead of where I was before."

He smiles good-naturedly, like he knows I hate Trump.

"What made you think Trump is my favorite president?" I ask, smiling back.

"I meant that ironically, of course," he says. "One need only sit in BeatNikki's for a few minutes to pick up the anti-Trump sentiment. And I understand it. But, please, forgive me for voting my own self-interest. The guy has been good for me."

"He's burning your planet to the core," I say, controlling my voice, but just barely. "Your tax cut is just an IOU—you're deferring trillions of dollars of debt that will come due in the next recession when the economy will shrink and the interest payment on the debt will become an overwhelming percentage of the annual budget and the country will have none of the usual tools for fighting recession—"

Alan holds up both hands in mock self-defense.

"Okay, okay," he says. "I was just kidding. I voted for the guy but I won't next time. I agree with you. But I have to say, you have a more sophisticated knowledge of economics than I expected."

We enter into a discussion of my life before Nikki, when I was a corporate animal and stood up to pee in urinals.

"Where did you go to school?" he asks.

"Community college, then a BS at Northern and an MBA at Northwestern."

"Northwestern. Good school. That must have set your family back, financially."

"Scholarships," I say. "They like to bring in some riff-raff so the one-percenters get a picture of the people they're going to screw the rest of their lives." I offer it as humor and he takes it that way.

"How about you?" I ask. "Harvard?"

"Stanford undergrad, because the weather sucks in the Ivy League," he says. "MBA at Chicago. Still didn't like the weather, but I love riding the L."

I smile at his humor. "Scholarships?"

"Trust fund," he grins. "I'm a born one-percenter. My parents came from poor families, but they did very well."

"Where'd you get your sense of humor?" I ask. I mean, really, he's the first rich toad I've met who has a sense of humor. The others only smile to celebrate someone else's pain, or to show off their new dentistry.

"Must have been rubbing elbows with the common folk on the L," he says. "The rest of my time was spent with bankers and lawyers and you're right, those people don't do humor."

"Poor you," I say. "Wife?"

"Divorced," he says. "A long time ago. I wasn't good at it."

"Gay?" For some reason, he seems open to such a personal question.

He grins. "I don't think so, but I keep an open mind."

"You better not share that information at the next Trump rally."

He waves a hand. "Please. Half those white supremacists are closet gays, don't you think?"

"That's what I mean," I say. "It wouldn't be safe for a good-looking guy like you to come out in that crowd."

Over dessert I get him to share a little more about himself. He grew up in an affluent suburb of New York, one of three kids in a wealthy family headed by a pair of surgeons. He was the only kid who didn't go into medicine. He went to Stanford to get away from a neatly plotted life, wasn't really comfortable with the California lifestyle, was drawn to the University of Chicago by its elite economics professors, fell in love with Chicago.

I openly question his sanity. "It's ninety-something outside with ninety percent humidity, and in six months the wind-chill index will be reading in the single digits and you jilted Palo Alto for Chicago?" I smile when I say it. The truth is, I'd make the same bargain. I was never a warm-climate kind of person, and I love Chicago for its combination of gilded culture and rough edges. I didn't think anyone else could possibly feel the same way.

"It grows on you," says Alan. "And I learned to ignore the weather."

He orders after-dinner drinks—a tawny port that's almost as old as I am. I don't object, though I probably should. Pouring more alcohol on my raging libido seems dangerous.

"Can I ask you a personal question?" he asks. I nod my assent.

"When did you know you were trans?" he asks. "I'm sorry, I shouldn't pry. But you intrigue me."

If my mind was a sex organ, I'd be in peak climax about now. No one has ever found me intriguing, at least not a handsome, cosmopolitan man like Alan. I get the occasional proposition from conquest-hungry males who are curious about what it would be like to have sex with a transgender woman, but that's a much different and utterly unsatisfying thing.

I find the power of speech. "Intrigue you? That's a first for me." I pause. "When did I know? That's a more complex question than you might think. I probably always knew, but I didn't admit it even to myself until I was in my twenties."

"Why would you do that?" he asks.

I try to dodge the question, but he's able to insist in a way that makes me feel interesting to him. It's powerfully seductive and I share with him things I've never shared with anyone.

"There's a stigma about being trans," I start. "It's better now than when I was growing up, but it's still tough. Lots of people shun you, sometimes even your own family, and most of the rest regard you like an alien. They don't want to get too close to you, like they might catch your disease. I saw this happen to other people all the way through school. Gay men. Lesbians. But especially effeminate men."

Alan is rapt, but I'm feeling horribly uncomfortable. "Are you sure you want to hear this?" I ask.

He nods; his eyes widen to add emphasis.

"It was very confusing until the internet came along and I discovered the word *transgender*. Before that, I had this desire to wear women's clothes and I dreamed of growing my hair long and having breasts, but I wasn't attracted to boys. I was attracted to girls, but it was complex because I could want to be with a girl sexually and at the same time want to be her. That was when the world was just straight and gay, and as queer as I was, I wasn't gay."

I sip the last of my port. "Are you bored yet?" I ask.

"Never," says Alan. "Please, go on."

"When I found out what transgender meant, I knew that was me, but I didn't want to admit it to anyone. I was good at being a male. I was handsome and smart. Girls liked me. I did well in school. I was a pretty good athlete and great at trash-talking. Never backed down from anyone. I had the world on a string as a man, but if I transitioned, I'd be one of those buffoons you used to see in movies, a huge, hairy guy in a dress, talking in a falsetto.

"So I buried it. I put the whole thought of being a woman in a box in my mind. It came out once in a while and I'd go out and buy a wig and some clothes. I even went to a gay bar in drag once. But I'd always purge and go back to my male life, ashamed and determined to put all the queer stuff behind me. I dated. I graduated. I got a great job. I married a great woman. We had a child. Then, when Morgan was three, the walls started caving in on me. I don't know why it happened then, but it did. I hated everything about being a man, everything except my wife and daughter. I couldn't stand seeing myself in the mirror. My clothes felt like a prison. It got so that I just couldn't face the world as Nick Finch any more. That's when I decided I had to transition, and that's when I lost my wife and daughter. I lost the rest of my family, too—I couldn't even get invited to Christmas dinner with my parents. And I lost my job, my whole career. I had to start all over again."

Alan regards me with open empathy. I'm relieved. He starts to ask another question, but I hold up one hand, asking him to stop.

"I've talked too much already," I say. "If I go on any more you'll fall asleep."

He laughs. "Never."

"There's got to be something more interesting than me."

Alan beams. "Want to see one of my places?"

15

When I was living as a man, I was a hetero man. I had male friends, but I was never attracted to men sexually, not that I thought about it much. That changed after I transitioned, though I was mostly just curious at first. I wanted to try out the new plumbing, as the saying goes, and maybe experience some of the fantasies I'd had about what it was like to be a woman. A few of my early assignations as a woman produced mutual orgasms, but none of the men were really interested in me and I began to think of male lovers more as a household convenience than a life-fulfilling adventure. Alan is proving to be the first exception to that in a long time and I have to remind myself to keep my crush to myself because he can't possibly feel the same.

He settles the bill and we walk a short distance to one of his buildings. It's breathtaking. It's an art deco monument to obscene wealth, a sleek, arty assemblage of steel and glass and concrete about twenty-five stories high and taking up half a city block. Retail businesses occupy the ground floor—boutiques, a Starbucks, service stores and a bookstore. I comment on the bookstore. There are hardly any left in Chicago, and none that can pay the rent in a new Gold Coast high rise a block or two from Lake Shore Drive.

"I love books," says Alan. "Always have. I solicited the owner. She has a store farther north. This is kind of an extension. I subsidize the rent. It adds class to the place, so everyone's happy."

He takes me in the condo entrance and we ride a gilded elevator with soft classical music to the tenth floor. He explains that his business plan focused on maximizing prices for the condos, so the first priority for the street level stores was to reinforce condo buyers' notions of luxury.

"We don't lose money on the commercial rents," he says, "but we aren't trying to wring every last dollar out of the tenants either."

I ask what the units sell for. He smiles. I brace myself for the old crack, "if you have to ask, you can't afford them," but he spares me. "Millions," he says.

We enter a unit. It is opulent and tasteful and beautiful, the kind of place that makes being filthy rich worthwhile. It has high ceilings, enormous expanses of window, breathtaking street views looking north and east, hardwood trims and wainscoting with wood that looks a lot like black walnut. The living room has facing sofas on a plush area rug and a walnut coffee table in between. A chandelier that could have hung in Windsor Castle floats just overhead. Overstuffed chairs and walnut tables form two other conversation areas in the huge room, one in front of a marble fireplace. The kitchen looks like something from the Food Network with glistening pots and pans hanging over a butcher block island, restaurant quality stainless steel appliances, and a dark-glass-fronted wine cellar next to the pull-out pantry. The master bedroom is done in soft colors and puffy textures that make just standing there seem like you're floating on a featherbed. The master bath has the same tasteful elegance as the rest of the place, done in porcelain white with walnut cabinets and accents.

"No gold toilets?" I ask.

Alan grins. "Trump owns the gold toilet market."

We continue the tour, Alan pointing things out, me trying not to gush. There are two more bedrooms, one set up as a library. Back in the living room, he seats me on one of the sofas and fetches two glasses of wine from the kitchen. I express my surprise that there are beverages in the place. "I thought this was a model apartment," I say.

"It is, sort of," he says. "I use it now and then, but we keep it showroom ready. I'll sell it eventually."

I shake my head in wonder. I've never personally known anyone who had a million-dollar condo as a spare place. We sip and chat. Before long, he steers the conversation back to me.

"Since I answered your questions about my marital status and sexual preferences, can I ask the same of you?"

He's really skilled at this. There were a dozen ways to ask that question that would have offended me, but he found one that's completely reasonable. And impossible not to answer honestly.

"All right," I say, cautiously.

"Men, right?" he asks.

"Either. It's been men for a long time, but if my ex had still loved me, it would have been her." I pause and sit straighter on the sofa, trying to decide how honest I should be. "But mostly I don't think about sex or romance."

"Why is that?"

"I had a run of disappointing affairs that made me realize there are some things that just aren't going to happen for me. So I focus on other things, the ones I'm good at."

Alan raises his eyebrows in surprise. "That works? You can shut off the urges?"

I blush. "For my weak moments I have a friend I can call."

Alan's surprise deepens. He's working hard to restrain his curiosity. "A friend?"

"An escort. He'd prefer "gigolo" I suppose because he's not

121

a full-time sex worker. He has a day job but he also has a side business pleasuring a woman who can't attract interesting men."

Alan blushes now, too, but his face is smiling and he's beaming at me. "You are amazing, Nikki," he says. After a pause, he starts again. "I don't buy that you can't attract interesting men. You're smart and funny and…" He pauses. I think he's blushing. "You're exotic."

I know it's false flattery but it still works on me. I feel pretty and sexy. For the briefest moment, I feel like a gorgeous cisgender woman, five-six, cute butt, tiny waist, turning men's heads when she walks into a room.

"Thanks," I say. "You don't have to humor me, but I love that you try."

He shakes his head.

"I'm completely sincere," he says. "I find you incredibly attractive. I did from the first time we met." He's blushing a deep red as he says this. I think he's telling the truth. In fact, I think he's trying to restrain himself. I think he'd like to jump my bones right now. A shiver of arousal passes through my body. I can't remember the last time I got laid and didn't have to pay for it.

He reads me. Not that it's hard. He stands up, reaches down and adjusts himself and offers me his hand. He leads me into the bedroom and lowers me on the sumptuous bed and lies on top of me and we embrace in a long, slow, lovely kiss. My heart flutters and my body hums. I haven't allowed myself to even fantasize about a romantic encounter in years. I can't believe it's actually happening.

Alan repositions himself beside me and combines his kisses with gentle strokes of my body. When he opens my top and massages a breast I almost pass out. My breasts are deeply symbolic to me, probably more than if I were a ciswoman, and having them touched by an amorous lover is so erotic I can hardly breathe. Somewhere in our clenching and stroking, he begins to whisper into my ear how sexy I am, and how I drive him crazy, and he's saying some of it in sex talk, which adds to my desire.

When his hand slides up my thigh and begins stroking my erogenous zone, I open my legs in surrender. But in the midst of my erotic ecstasy, an image explodes in my mind, the image of the last non-prostitute man I slept with. I remember him mounting me like we were dogs in an alley, and forcing himself inside me, no foreplay, him pounding up and down on me for a minute or two, grunting, then bellowing when he released, then getting up, getting dressed, and leaving without a word. It was consensual, but not what I thought I was consenting to.

"Can we stop?" I ask Alan. I'm not sure I want him to stop, but the memory of rejection is too strong.

"Of course," he says. He puts his arms around me and kisses me, lips, cheek, forehead. "Is everything okay?"

I try to explain. "It's wonderful," I sigh. "I haven't felt like this in years. You're like a dream I wouldn't dare have. But Alan, I'm not into quickies or one-nighters. They make me feel like I'm dying. So I'd rather go without, if that's how it is."

"That's not what I want," he says.

"Can we see?" I ask. "Let's see how you feel tomorrow and next week. Let's see if we enjoy each other's company on another date or two."

I can hardly believe what I'm saying. I try to avoid situations like this but once I've come this far, I'm usually in for the whole ride. I can't believe I'm turning this man down.

"Of course," he says. Which makes me want him even more. Some women are motivated by a man's appearance, some by his personality, some by his lovemaking prowess. For me, it's whether he respects me. We can figure out everything else.

Morgan gets home a few minutes before ten, the deadline we

had agreed on because we have work tomorrow. I've been home for maybe thirty minutes when she arrives, long enough to entertain fantasies of sex with Alan and get over them.

Morgan closes and locks the door and walks through the living room toward her bedroom. "Hi, Nikki," she says. Her tone is quiet and distant, but somewhat pleasant. "How was your date?" She asks the question over her shoulder as she walks to her room.

"It wasn't a date," I call after her. "But we had a pleasant dinner and he didn't pressure me to sell."

I wait for Morgan to return to the living room so I can ask about her date, but when her bedroom door opens, she's dressed for bed and goes directly to the bathroom. She comes out a few minutes later, her face washed, her hair pulled into a high ponytail for sleeping. She stands at the threshold of the living room. "Goodnight, Nikki," she says, with a little wave of her hand. She starts to leave.

"Wait," I say. "How was your date?"

"Fine," she says.

"What did you do?" I ask quickly because I can see she wants to go to bed.

"Dinner, talked. Nothing much." She shrugs.. "I'm really tired."

"Goodnight, sweetie," I say.

I've taken advantage of our truce to express my parental love for her in moments like this, by using words like *sweetie* and *honey* when I address her. She seems to accept it. Tonight she even shares a small smile before she goes to bed. It seems like a forced smile, but at least she's not snarling and calling me Dad.

I check the windows and door locks and turn off the lights before going to my room. I start to go to bed, but my thoughts are so full of Alan I know I'll never get to sleep. I pull out my laptop and log into the accounting program for BeatNikki's. Nothing puts me to sleep like numbers.

But it's not working tonight, at least, not as fast as usual. As I try to focus on a number, I hear a light tapping on the side of the building, like pebbles clicking against a window. The sound seems to be coming from Morgan's room. I immediately think it's lover-boy Ralph signaling her to let him in. I grit my teeth in anger. I can't keep her from having sex if she's intent on it, but I can sure as hell keep her from having sex in my home. I throw on a robe and slip quietly downstairs and out the front door. I stay in the shadows and slink barefooted to the side of the building where the noise came from.

The moment I turn the corner of the apartment building, I find myself standing behind two men about twenty feet away. There's just enough light from the building next door to make out their forms. They're roughly my height, short haircuts, wearing sweatshirts and jeans. And laughing. As I watch, they throw pebbles against Morgan's window and snicker. One of them calls out softly, in a sort of falsetto stage whisper, "Oh Morgan! Morgan honey. Did you lose your cherry tonight?"

The voice belongs to Ralph, the shit-eating snot who took her out tonight. My first impulse is to slam into him with all the velocity I can muster in this short distance, and jam my thumbs into his eyes so deep he'll never see again. Echoes of the testosterone-fueled reactions I once had as a male. I quell them.

"Hey, shit-for-brains," I call to them. Loud. They startle and turn around. Ralph staggers a little. They're both drunk. "The police are on their way."

"That's the she-male," Ralph says to his buddy, slurring his words a little.

"Get out, punk," I tell him. I'm picking my words carefully. I've watched too many courtroom dramas on television. If I end up killing or maiming one of them, I don't want to leave a trail of premeditation.

"Or what?" the friend challenges.

"Or wait and deal with the police."

They look at each other, still snickering, then stagger past me toward the sidewalk. As Ralph passes me, I block his way.

"If you raped my daughter, you will pay the price," I tell him.

He shoulders past me with a contemptuous sneer. They climb into a BMW and drive away. Back in my apartment, I knock on Morgan's door. No answer. I knock again. No answer. I open it and step in, keeping the door ajar so there's enough light to see her. She's lying on her back, covers pulled to her chin, crying. I sit on the edge of the bed and take her hands in mine.

"Did he force himself on you?"

"Leave me alone," she says.

"If he raped you, we have to get to a hospital right now," I tell her. "Don't let the bastard get away with it."

"Just drop it, Nikki," she says.

"I won't let him intimidate you," I tell her. "I'll protect you with my life."

"Don't be stupid," she says. "He didn't rape me, okay? Can you leave me alone now?"

"I think you need to talk about it."

"I don't care what you think," Morgan says. "What do you know about it? You buy yours, just like you bought your boobs and your nose."

I sweep aside her insults for now.

"It will help if you talk about it," I repeat.

"Not with you," she says, angrily. "Maybe I'll call Mom tomorrow."

"Do you really want to do that?"

"That's none of your business," she snaps. "What's your business is that I don't want to talk to you. About anything. Please go away. Now. God, please leave me alone."

Her voice is edging into hysteria. I stand up and adjust her covers a little.

"Okay, sweetie," I say. "But I'm here if you need me."

"I don't."

"If you do, I'll leave my door open. Come in any time."

She rolls over on her side, away from me. I stand next to her bed, a statue in the dark, completely unsure of what to do, hoping she'll change her mind. She doesn't. After a long wait, I leave her room and go back to mine. I won't sleep tonight. I'll agonize over my daughter's horrible introduction to intimacy and share her pain, albeit from a distance. I'll try to keep my mind off thinking of ways to torture and maim Ralph.

16

Dawn comes early in June, the first hint of light waking me around five. Morgan is already in the kitchen when I get there. She's fully dressed, sipping tea and studying her cell phone. Her face is puffy and her eyes look tired.

"Hi honey," I say, my voice soft and sympathetic.

"Don't start," she says. "It's not what you think. Just leave me alone."

I'm certain Blythe could talk through this with her, but I feel helpless and inept and I know there's no way in hell I can work through her anger.

"Okay," I say. "But I'm here if you need me."

She sighs and focuses on the phone.

When my tea is ready, I sit at the table with Morgan. She sighs and starts to leave. I put a hand on her arm.

"Stay," I command. "This will only take a minute and it's important."

She sighs again, trying to play the martyr, but it's easy to see the bereavement just below the surface.

"I need to know if you had unprotected sex last night."

"That's none of your business," she snaps.

"It's *our* business," I say. "Yours and mine both. If you had unprotected sex, we have to make sure you didn't contract a disease. And we'll need to know if you get pregnant."

"He's not the kind of person who gets STDs," Morgan says. "You should worry about your stud."

"If you think rich kids don't get STDs, you're horribly mistaken," I answer. "The risks are highest with people who take chances and engage in sex with a lot of partners. Ralph is a good candidate." I make her look at me again and raise my eyebrows to repeat the question.

"He used a rubber," she says, looking away. "Leave me alone now."

I let her get up and leave the table.

The day gets worse.

Little John is waiting for me when we get to the café. Since it's his morning off, his presence can only mean trouble. Plus, he's got a nasty shiner and an impressive bandage on his forehead. He greets us, and reassures Morgan that he's fine. She scoots off to help set up the kitchen and Little John asks if we can talk privately. We go to the office.

"Some thug followed me home last night," Little John begins. "I thought he was only trying to scare me, but when I got to my building, he closed in on me. He slugged me, knocked me down and then kicked me in the face."

I'm shocked. "Did you recognize him?"

"I think I've seen him before," says Little John. "He's a big, burly guy, but ever since you blinded that guy out back, I've been seeing fascist biker goons in my sleep. I'm not sure if I've seen this guy before, but I've seen another guy, all decked out in tattoos and Nazi symbols, following me. Marvin and Janet say they've been followed by a guy like that, too. I don't know if it's one guy or a nest of them, but we're being targeted and we're in danger."

My eyes sweep across the walls of the office and focus on a framed eight-by-ten photo of Little John and me, each with an arm around the other, posing for the camera with triumphant smiles. It's from our early days together, when BeatNikki's was turning the corner financially and we were gaining confidence in our combined genius.

"I think it's open season on us," I say. "I think these attacks are the work of the same kind of neo-Nazi goons that attacked us and put Billy in the hospital. That's why I passed out the pepper spray. Any other ideas?"

"Nikki, I'm risking my life coming to work every day." Little John's eyes focus on mine. "I can work somewhere else without risking my life."

My mouth goes dry. If Little John walks, it could set off a chain reaction. Our beverage offerings would become as static and routine as the chain shops, and some of the staff people would quit, too, because Little John is a big part of the culture of the place.

"Are you leaving?" I ask.

"I'm looking for a reason to stay," he says. We look each other in the eye.

"How about self-respect?" I suggest. "How about living the rest of your life knowing you stood up to the beasts rather than let them chase you from the best job you ever had? Your very words, Little John. The best job you ever had."

His eyes drop to the desk top, then back up to mine.

"You're very good at this, Nikki," he says, "but it's not your ass on the line."

"Are you kidding?" I say. "If you're a target, I am too. Maybe the main target. Me and Morgan, because they can get me through hurting her. But they will not run me out of my business. I won't be bullied, not anymore."

"And if they kill you?"

"They'll most likely get caught and get tried for a hate crime."

Little John shakes his head. "A lot of good that'll do you if you're dead."

"It beats living like a sniveling coward, running away every time some psychotic baboon decides to hassle a queer."

I'm getting red-faced and agitated as I speak. Little John thinks my wrath is directed at him and he's getting uncomfortable. I take a deep breath and raise a hand as if to say, hold on.

"I'm not mad at you, Little John," I say. "It's about me, and how I got here, to this point in my life." I repeat the story about getting severely beaten when I was transitioning. Little John knows the story, so I do the Cliffs Notes version.

"I had to decide right then and there whether I was going to let bigots dictate my life. Was I going to limit my life to my apartment and my workplace, to be safe? Or even stop transitioning altogether? Or I could keep doing what I was doing and hope the bad guys got interested in someone else or got arrested."

Little John smiles a little. "Or you could take self-defense classes and carry pepper spray. which is what you did. But this is a little different. Last time, your thug went away. I don't think this one—or this group—is going to go away."

I stare at Little John for a moment, trying to decide how much to share with him. He cocks his head as if to ask what I'm thinking.

"My assailant didn't just drift away," I say. "He came down with a severe case of shattered kneecaps and broken shin bones. He probably never knew which of his victims struck back, but even if he did, he no longer had the physical ability to commit violence, even on a queer like me."

"My God, Nikki," says Little John, looking at me with saucer eyes.

"I'm not proud of it," I assure him. "I had nightmares that I got the wrong guy, or that I killed him and went to jail for the rest of my life. I want to find a better way to solve this problem. But Little John, no matter what, I'm not going to let these gorillas dictate my life to me. I'm staying. I'd like you to stay too."

Little John shakes his head. "I wish you hadn't told me."

"I wish I didn't have to tell you," I say. "If you repeat it, it could ruin me."

"I don't want to kill anyone," Little John says.

"You don't have to. Just use common sense. We'll figure out schedules so that everyone comes and goes in pairs or groups, even on the L. We'll have our people alert the police in their home neighborhoods. Not all cops are like Brooks."

Little John nods his head in thought before he speaks. "It's still risky. Very risky."

"Every day is a risk for people like you and me. But we can handle it. That's how we win."

He nods again.

"I can do a short session for everyone on what moves to use after you blind an assailant with pepper spray."

Little John looks at me incredulously. "Surely you jest."

"I'm completely serious."

"Like with the guy out back last month?" says Little John. "What did that solve? These people threatening us now, they're probably his pals, trying to get even."

"They'll get the same treatment."

"Jesus, Nikki," he says, shaking his head in disbelief.

"I'm tired of people on our side sitting around with their thumbs up their asses while the crazy people take over everything. It makes me want to scream."

Little John grimaces. "What kind of example are you setting for Morgan?"

He has a point. But so do I. "The same one I'm setting for you," I say. "Stand up for yourself. They want to scare you away from a job you were born to do, a job where you get to own a piece of the action. Do you want to work at some Starbucks storefront factory, slopping crap in paper cups for people who see you as a minimum wage stiff too dumb to get a white-collar job?"

"Starbucks is a multi-million dollar company," says Little John.

"Yeah, and their baristas make a buck fifty an hour," I counter. "You have a salary, and benefits, and you get a piece of the action. Now all you have to do is man up to keep it."

"I can't believe a transgender woman is lecturing me about manhood," Little John cracks.

We smile as we always do when we exchange mock insults over our gender choices. Little John says he'll think about it. Meanwhile, I'm thinking about what he said: what kind of example am I setting for Morgan?

There's something about life—my life, anyway—that proves the old saying, "when it rains, it pours." My bad days are never about just one thing, and today is holding true to form. My deflowered daughter is moping through the day, my faithful business partner wants to leave, and now I have to sit down with a capitalist maggot and be polite while he tries to persuade me to do something I don't want to do.

Vernon I. Gibbs is seated at the very same table where Alan first pitched me on selling this building. Gibbs's card says he's a developer so he's here to make the same pitch. As I approach the table I know I wouldn't do business with him even if I was interested in selling. He's a wiry, gaunt-faced man with crazy eyes like the evangelist preacher who lived next door to me years ago.

Gibbs's eyes have the same kind of intensity as the

preacher's, but he's not crazy or stupid. He's a predator. He's wearing an expensive suit, white shirt, and narrow black tie. He looks enough like an undertaker to send a chill down my spine.

We exchange greetings and he launches into his sales foreplay, which is a riff on what a great place I've got here.

When he pauses to take a breath, I tell him outright I'm not interested in selling. He smiles patiently and asks me to hear him out. I shrug and let him speak his piece.

His pitch is different from Alan's. Whereas Alan talked about architecture and aesthetics as well as money, Gibbs is all about money, emphasizing how much money I'll make if I sell to him. He says the neighborhood is going to change anyway, so this is the time to cash in and find a new one. He adds that if I wanted to stay he'd cut me a great deal on space in the new building, though not as big as this space. When he's done, I thank him and again tell him I'm not interested.

"I know Campbell's talked to you," he says. He leans forward and locks eyes with me. "Be careful with him. He's a ladies' man. He'll wine you and dine you and bring you flowers, but when he gets what he wants, he's gone."

I'm tempted to point out that if you look up *man* in the dictionary, that's pretty much the definition, at least, in the dictionary written by women. I'm also tempted to point out that Gibbs's own proposition is the same thing, less the wining, dining, and flowers, and if I'm going to sell, why not get laid, too? But I don't want to extend this conversation any further so I thank Gibbs for his time and interest and send him on his way.

We stand and shake hands. He takes my hand like I'm a man, pushing past my fingertips to grasp my whole hand firmly. It irritates me, but I'm sure he has no idea what he's doing or what it means to me. He leans closer, still holding my hand and says, "Don't trust Campbell."

17

Morgan and I prepare dinner in silence. It feels like I'm beside a dark cloud. She's mute and the look on her face alternates between hopelessness and sadness. I finish washing vegetables for our salad as she stirs the soup.

"Five minutes," she says.

We have a system now. Whoever prepares the main course gives the other person a heads up five minutes before the dish will be ready. It's nice that at least this tiny touch of human communication has survived in her Dark Period. I mix the salad and heat rolls while Morgan sets the table.

After we sit for our meal, I push my luck. "Morgan, it will help if you talk about it."

She emits a martyr's sigh. "About what, Nikki?"

"About what happened with you and Ralph."

"Nothing happened." Her body language reeks with disdain.

"Something did happen," I insist. "You've been moody and miserable ever since you got home last night."

"I'm always moody around you," she says.

"But now you're gloomy at work, too," I point out. "You don't smile anymore. You don't chat with people."

"Maybe I didn't feel like it, okay?" Her tone is sharp and dismissive.

"He treated you badly," I say. "You'll get over it faster if you talk about it."

"With you?" She says it like it's the stupidest idea she's ever heard. "Why would I talk about anything with you?"

"Because I've been there," I say. "And I love you. And I'm a good listener."

"You've been there?" Morgan laughs. "You're not even a real woman, Nikki. Are you going to tell me about hiring men to fuck you? That's going to make me feel better?"

"It's not about me, Morgan." I try to control my anger and hurt. If I vent now, there will be a lot of broken glass, figuratively speaking. "It's about you. You'll feel better if you talk about it. That's how women cope."

"As if you'd know." It's another nasty dig, but her voice has returned to the conversational range and she looks down at her food as she says it. It's a retreat of sorts.

"I do know," I say. "I am a woman, no matter what you think. And you're a woman, a proud, strong woman, no matter what Ralph said or did."

"Oh good." Sarcasm, but it's more to save face than make me feel bad. She doesn't look at me, but I sense that she kind of likes what I said about her.

"I want you to talk about it," I say.

"Not with you," she says. She takes a bite, chews, swallows. "Maybe with Mom."

"Okay," I agree. "Tonight. Right after dinner. I'll do the dishes, you go call your mother."

"Sure," she says.

"I'll be calling her after you do." Morgan starts to object and I hold up my hands to stop her outburst before it starts. "I won't ask what you said. I have other things to discuss with her, but I will make sure you talked to her about whatever is troubling you."

We eat in silence. The house rules dictate that meals are taken without the accompaniment of electronic devices, so the silence is total—and as uncomfortable as an ear-blasting stereo. When we finish, I remind Morgan to call her mother right away, and start clearing the table.

She shrugs and retreats to her room.

An hour later, I deduce that Morgan isn't coming back. I was hoping she'd want to talk. I call Blythe's cell. Her wicked mother answers the phone with her usual warmth.

"What do you want?" Caller ID has made it possible for her to bypass even a single word of civility when taking one of my calls.

I'm tempted to say, "I want a handsome man with one of those four-hour erections they talk about in the boner-pill commercials," but it wouldn't be as funny if I couldn't see her face twist with rage.

Instead, I say, "Do you really have to ask? Let me make you a promise right now: I will never willingly talk to you unless the Earth is on fire and I want to curse you before I die."

She hangs up. Two minutes later, I call again. Blythe answers, though not with a cordial greeting.

"What did you say to my mother?" She's trying to be rude and her voice is almost strong enough to get there.

"You sound better," I reply. "I hope you're feeling better, too."

"I'm not, Nick," she snaps. "I'm going to die."

I collapse into a chair. "Seriously? That's the diagnosis?"

"Yes." She says it haughtily, then pauses and when she speaks again, her voice is tired. "For all practical purposes. They haven't given up, but it would take a miracle."

"Jesus."

"It might even be too late for him," she says. Graveyard humor, my favorite kind. I smile. If you can give the Grim Reaper the finger, you're still in the game. To hell with the doctors.

"I'm so very sorry, Blythe." I'm stumbling. I'm not good at

this. I have no command of the common platitudes that are safe to say at a time like this, and I also have no words to express the sorrow I feel. I'll always love her, no matter how much she resents me, and the world without her in it will be a hollower, lonelier place. And I don't even want to think about Morgan.

"Save your energy for raising Morgan," she says.

"Do you think she'd actually consent to live with me?"

"I think if it comes down to you or my mother, she'll choose you." I can hear Blythe's voice tremble as she fights off a sob. She takes a deep breath. "My advice to you is, don't alienate her so much she chooses her grandmother just to strike back at you."

"Yes," I say. "I understand what you're saying. I'll do my best." As I say it, I'm selfishly thinking it wouldn't be the end of the world if she chose her grandmother. I deal with enough hate and rejection in my world without my own daughter saying horrible things that I would never allow another other living soul to say to me. I quickly erase the thought. As much as Blythe's mother deserves the truckload of grief Morgan is driving right now, I don't think Morgan would ever recover from living with that awful woman as her primary parent. She'd get more nurturing being raised by wolves.

"What's this Ralph like?" Blythe asks.

"Rich, arrogant, entitled," I say. "In a perfect world, it would be legal for me to sever his head from his body and mount it on a pike."

"For once, I think you understate the case." Blythe tries to laugh, but it comes out a cough. She's getting weaker. "He used her, Nick. Nikki." I'm surprised she corrected herself. I was going to let it slide without comment. I'm going to let everything slide with Blythe. I can't even imagine how I would handle her situation. Spend what's left of your life in bed, in pain, and then you die.

"She's crushed," says Blythe. "She was expecting angels and violins and he treated her like dirt."

"What should I do?" I ask. "I can't get her to talk to me about it."

"Be patient," says Blythe. "She only talked to me about it because it was a way to poke you in the eye. Sooner or later, she'll come to you, too."

"Why would she do that?"

"Because you love her." Blythe takes a breath. "Really Nikki, stop being so sensitive. She says terrible things to you because that's how she vents and she knows she can say them to you because you love her." She takes another breath. "She loves you, too."

The way she says it I actually believe it. It's not like Blythe holds back when she talks to me. For a moment, I feel like a teenager whose secret crush has smiled warmly at her in the hallway at school. Then reality kicks me in the head. Blythe is dying. We've had our differences, but she's the woman I've loved for most of my adult life, and she's dying. She's not even forty yet. So much for a benevolent, interactive God. Good people like Blythe die young and evil drones like Trump slog into their eighties eating junk food and assaulting women.

Then the other reality hits me so hard I have to sit down: Morgan and I are about to become permanent roommates, at least until she goes off to college or the home for unwed mothers or a rehab clinic. My grim visions of her future have a little to do with her and a lot to do with how incompetent I am as a parent. I wish I'd had the toddler years and Blythe took over for the sex, drugs, and rock and roll chapters.

We talk a minute more and then I let her go.

Later, as I get ready for bed, I think about what Blythe said: Morgan abuses me because she knows I love her and she can trust me not to abandon her for acting out her anger. I try to picture myself accepting her next "Dad" insult with a warm smile, fueled by the inner knowledge that she's only misgendering me because she loves me. It doesn't work. Even in my fantasies, it pisses me off and it hurts. I can't imagine ever getting to a place in my life where I can absorb those kinds of insults with equanimity, so I start outlining some simpler objectives.

Don't swear at Morgan, no matter what.

Tell her I love her at least once a day, and mean it.

Keep the lectures short. She's going to make her own decisions no matter what I want her to do.

School! The thought explodes in my mind. What in the hell can I do about school? Would she even consent to going to the local high school? Would I want her to? I don't even know what high school kids in my neighborhood attend, much less whether it's safe. She has the grades to get into a magnet school, but it's probably too late to apply.

Maybe I'll have to move to Winnetka so she can stay in her current institution for the financially gifted. It's one of the two or three best high schools in the state, plus Winnetka has beautiful trees, and . . . And that's my complete list of benefits of being a transgender woman living in Winnetka.

As I lie in bed waiting for sleep or something like it to overtake me, I find myself wishing I was religious so I could pray for Blythe's miraculous recovery. My parenting abilities would be inadequate in the best of times and for Morgan, these are the worst of times. She needs her mother. Without Blythe, it's hard to see any way this doesn't end badly for Morgan.

"I'd like to have my own hours," says Morgan as we walk to the L station. Her comment shakes me out of my own roiled thoughts about how to talk to her about her mother.

"What?"

"I'd like to come and go on my own schedule instead of following you around everywhere."

I ponder her statement for a few beats before answering.

"I understand what you're saying," I start, choosing my words carefully. "I'm not quite ready to do that, yet, but it's something we can work toward."

She reacts with a modified martyred sigh, and a walking foot stomp thrown in for good measure.

"How did I know you were going to say that?" she fumes. "I'm not a baby. You've been giving me lessons on getting around the city on my own from Day One. I'd like to have my own life, okay? Nikki?" She adds my name in a sarcastic tone.

"We'll get there," I answer.

We walk in silence. Morgan dabs at tears forming in her eyes. I'd prefer to just keep going in silence and let her rage work itself out, but I know Blythe wouldn't do that. She'd face up to it, and now it's my turn. Of course, I have no idea what to do next.

"Last night, I told your mother about how deeply you resent me and how the things you say hurt me." I can't believe I'm saying this. "Know what she said?"

"How could I know that?" Morgan sneers. "But whatever it was, I'm sure she called you Nick."

"She told me to stop being such a wimp," I say, ignoring the insult. "She said you say those things to me because you're hurting inside and you have to let the venom out and I'm the one you can do that with because you know I love you and I'll take it."

Morgan does that gasping sound again. "Brilliant," she mutters. "Did she tell you I told her about your prostitute? When she comes home maybe you can fix her up with him. A little sex might be just what the doctor ordered."

Tears are streaking down her face now, coming too fast to be brushed aside with her fingers.

"She didn't mention that to me," I say. "But if she's interested, I'd certainly do it." I'm trying to sound matter of fact, but inside I'm outraged that Morgan would discuss my sex life with Blythe, who's on her death bed and has bigger problems. But also, it's embarrassing for my ex to know I'm such a pathetic woman I have to buy a stud service. I make myself shake it off.

"She's told us both that her prognosis is grim," I start.

"She's dying." Morgan says it like a bitch slap.

"Yes. And you and I are going to have to learn to live together."

Morgan tries to do another martyr sigh, but it comes out a sob. I put an arm around her. It's an instinctive move. If I'd thought about it, I would have anticipated her pushing me away and saying something terrible about me, and I wouldn't have done it. To my surprise, she doesn't resist.

"We're going to need to talk about things, Morgan," I say, pulling her to me, a sort of walking hug.

"What things?" Her voice is a blend of anger and broken-hearted despair.

"Where you're going to live. What school you'll attend." I pause. "And I think we need to talk about what happened with Ralph."

She pulls away, furious.

"I'm not going to talk about sex with you." She says "you" like I'm a disease.

"Then let's get you a therapist," I say. "Your mom's in no shape and talking to your grandmother about sex is . . . well, you'd be better off talking to a bowl of prunes."

Morgan actually smiles a little amid her sobs. "I don't need a therapist," she insists.

"It's me or a therapist," I say. "If you say no, I'll keep nagging until you really do need a therapist."

Her lips form a small, trembling smile. The tears have stopped.

"It's not a big deal," she says. "I wanted to see what it was like. It's over."

"It's not like that. It's not like Ralph. Men like him should have their balls cut off."

"Like you?" Morgan glances at me, embarrassed. "Sorry. That just slipped out."

"I shouldn't talk like that anyway," I admit. "But we need to talk through this. It's affected you and that worries me."

We've arrived at the L station. Our conversation dwindles as we join the rush hour crowd riding the escalator to the station platform. I push the issue when we get to the platform, albeit in a low voice.

"I'll think about it," Morgan says. "The therapist."

18

My phone rings just as the train is pulling in. It's Butch, the guy who opens the café three days a week. He tells me one of our display windows has been shattered. The tell-tale brick is sitting in the café, where it landed. The police have been called.

As Butch fills me in, the image of that laconic, Nazi-sympathizing detective looms in my mind. I will it to go away.

"Just one window?" I ask Butch.

He confirms it. I feel fortunate. The café has two huge display windows and replacing them both would kill me financially for the month. Actually, replacing just one is a big hit to my personal finances. Still, I wonder, why just the one? If you're there and committing a crime anyway, why not bring two bricks and get two windows?

I thank Butch and spend the train ride locating my insurance agent in my contact list. As soon as we get off the train, I find a quiet corner of the platform and call the agent. I get his voice mail and leave a message explaining the situation. Morgan hears me leave the message.

"What's that all about?" she asks when I hang up.

"I think our Nazi friends have paid us another visit," I reply.

"A brick through the window?" says Morgan. "Sounds more like teenage boys to me."

"Ever hear of *Kristallnacht*?" I ask.

Morgan shakes her head and makes a face, like it's a stupid question.

"The English translation is 'night of broken glass," I tell her. "It was one of the most infamous early chapters in the Nazi terrorizing of German Jews. Nazi stormtroopers ransacked Jewish homes and businesses and even demolished whole buildings. Nazis like to break things."

We descend to the street level and begin walking to the café.

"Maybe you shouldn't have beat up that guy in the alley," says Morgan.

"I'd be a target either way," I tell her. "They hate me because I'm trans. A freak. They're stalking Little John, too, and all he did was save that animal's life."

"You were going to kill him?" Morgan stares at me. I think I see shock on her face.

"I had to subdue him before he killed Little John and me. It wasn't so much that I wanted to kill him; it was that I had to disable him and I didn't care about his safety."

"So you're okay with killing Nazis." Morgan states it as fact. Little John's rejoinder echoes in my mind: what kind of example am I setting for her? But I'm too irritated to entertain a long philosophical discussion.

"I'm okay with killing a homicidal maniac in self-defense," I snap back at her. "And I suggest you get your mind into that groove in self-defense class."

Morgan snorts contemptuously.

"Believe me, Morgan," I say, "it's a lot easier to live with hurting a rapist or murderer than to live with the memory of them doing violence on you."

"Like, someone tried to rape you?" Morgan says it like no

145

one in the world would want to touch an ugly transwoman like me.

"Grow up, little girl," I snap again. "Rape isn't about sex. It's an act of violence and brutality. Yes, someone tried to rape me and I've had to fight off unwanted sexual advances, too, just like every other woman. You will too."

"Well, I'm not going to kill anyone." She says it with the moral certainty of the inexperienced.

"Give yourself the choice," I say. "If you empower yourself to incapacitate a rapist, you get to make a moral decision. He attacks you, you disable him, and you get to decide if he lives or dies. If you don't empower yourself, you volunteer to be his victim. There's no morality in that. That's cowardice."

Morgan starts to say something, then stops herself. Her jaw muscles flex and her eyes squint, like she's deep in thought, then she looks straight forward and keeps walking, silent and stone-faced, all the way to the café.

Detective Sergeant Brooks arrives a little before nine o'clock with a worker bee in tow. He doesn't bother with introductions and his greeting is as brusque as he can make it. The young man with him seems to be some kind of technician. He moves to the area where the broken glass and the brick lie and begins shooting photos. Brooks takes up a command post at the coffee bar.

The tech has the run of the place. We've all watched a million hours of *Law & Order*, so we knew to block off the whole room where the brick and the broken and glass landed. He takes some photos and examines the brick with gloved hands, but even I can see there isn't anything special about any of it. If Brooks had been paying attention, he would have said the same thing, but he was sipping a free latte and trying to make time with

146

Deborah, a barista who is as beautiful as she is gay. So much for the detecting powers of the brilliant Sergeant Brooks.

Brooks finally waves me over, like a tribal chieftain summoning his maid. I consider ignoring him, but I can hear Little John's voice in my head, telling me not to be petty.

"So, you've solved this, right?" I'm deliberately sarcastic even though I willed myself not to stoop so low. There's something about this man's blend of arrogance and ignorance that brings out the devil in me.

He ignores my quip.

"I don't suppose you have a security camera like most other businesses," he says, getting in his own little dig.

"No," I respond. "I didn't realize that law enforcement had become the responsibility of the victims. But now that I've seen how diligently you work, I see that we've reached a new paradigm and I'll invest in security cameras."

"That smart mouth of yours is going to cause you more trouble," says Brooks.

"Is that a threat, Detective?" I ask.

He laughs sarcastically. "I'm not your problem, missy. You've gotten yourself sideways with some people who play rough."

"Your Aryan pals?"

"Whoever it was, they're letting you know they haven't forgotten what you did to that poor bastard you blinded." Brooks looks me in the eye when he says it. He seems to think I was bullying the "poor bastard" who was assaulting Little John and me.

"Well," I say, "at least they've got you working for them."

Brooks flushes and shoots me a withering glare. "I'm going to pretend you didn't say that," he says.

"Okay," I say, "then I'll pretend like you're actually a detective. What's next?"

He glares at me again and slowly pulls a dollar bill from his pocket. He places the bill on the bar and nods to the tech, who's been waiting near the door. They leave together without another word. When they disappear, I become aware that Morgan has joined Deborah behind the coffee bar. They've been listening to my conversation with Brooks. Deborah flashes a smile that congratulates me on standing up to him. Morgan's face is more inscrutable. Deborah goes back to work.

"Is that how you talk to cops?" Morgan asks me.

"Just that one," I answer. "But you're right. I should have been more respectful."

"Why weren't you?" she asks.

"Because I despise authority figures who use their power to abuse and belittle the weak and vulnerable."

"You didn't sound very vulnerable," says Morgan.

"Good," I say.

Little John comes in at lunchtime and we take our meal together in a quiet corner of the café. I fill him in on the morning vandalism as workmen replace our window. His face, always expressive, goes through varying shades of concern, especially when I give him the short version of my encounter with Brooks. Little John is a lovely man and he looks like a man in a way I can only dream of looking like a woman. If you know his history, though, there are things about him that recall his former identity, especially when he's emotional. As he frets about the news, he wrinkles his nose a little, like a young girl. It's kind of cute, and for me it's quite distracting because he has a feminine nose that I can't achieve for all the money in China. He hides it with facial hair and tattoos on his arms that distract from his face, but it's there for me to appreciate and sometimes envy.

The other feature I fix on is his eyes. He's flashing alarm right now, but not the kind of anger that so many men show when they feel threatened. His eyes are a soft brown color, and they are set in the wide, open orbits of a woman—a feature I paid a small fortune to acquire.

"We're sitting ducks," he exclaims. "Those Nazis know it."

I shrug.

"This is crazy, Nikki," he says. "Do you really want to die for this business?"

I concede that I don't, but I repeat my whole sermon on not letting bullies dictate my life to me.

"Sometimes, discretion is the better part of valor," he says, invoking the ancient aphorism.

"And sometimes what we call discretion is merely capitulation."

He does his bunny-nose thing again and says, "Who cares? I just don't want to get beat up again, or killed."

We lapse into silence for a minute; then I mention that I had another developer come calling this morning. This isn't exactly hot news—they've been all over the neighborhood for weeks—but it hits Little John like a thunderbolt. His eyes light up. "Well, that's the easy solution!" he exclaims. "You sell and we set up somewhere else."

"Why would that satisfy the Nazis?" I ask. "They're not trying to run us out of this neighborhood, they're trying to run us out of this life."

We spar, Little John arguing that it would take them months or years to find us again, and by then maybe the crisis would pass, me arguing that we'd be easy to find, and besides, the Nazis would have already won if they made us move. Like all hypotheticals, it's an argument with no resolution.

"Are you still thinking of leaving?" I ask.

"I don't know," says Little John. "I'm going to talk to some people, take some interviews, see what's what."

He doesn't ask my permission, and he doesn't need to. We practice a purer form of free enterprise than most capitalists: everyone here serves at their own pleasure, including Little John and me. If he'd be happier somewhere else, it's his call. Same with me. I have license to sell and move on. It would break a lot of hearts on this staff, but no one would begrudge me my freedom of choice. Except me.

Those of us who have survived nightmarish experiences carry them around with us for the rest of our lives. Mine are locked away in compartments of my mind, but they still hang over me, just waiting for some random stimulus to burst them out of confinement—an incident, a dream, a cross word from a stranger. And when they descend on me, they overwhelm my view of everything I see or feel or understand about my life. I'm so conscious of these clouds it's hard to remember that good things happen to people like me, too. That's why nights like this are so special.

Morgan is out for the evening with a group from the café, led by Little John, so I know she's in good hands. No sooner had I consented than Alan stopped by for a coffee and a chat, something he seems to do with regularity now. When I mentioned that Morgan was going out tonight, he asked me out on a date.

Really!

I'm recalling all this and trying not to look like a love-struck teenager as I gaze across the table into Alan's eyes. They are blue, but more than the color, they always flash with a kind of electricity that arouses me if I let it. And just now, there's also a softness in his visage, like a warm and welcoming lover. My mind quivers. I can feel his strong body on mine, his rigid manhood linking us together, his lips caressing mine, his face soft with love. I imagine locking my legs around him, holding us as one person, the heat from our bodies melding us together.

"I hope you're thinking good thoughts when you look at me

like that," he says, with a twinkle in his eyes.

I feel like I'm blushing. Goodness knows, I should be.

"I am," I say, though it's not easy to make my mouth work properly. I'm so aroused, I think if he just touched me or told a dirty joke involving a woman's climax I'd have one myself.

"What are you thinking?" he asks.

I return his smile and try to think of something safe to say that isn't a lie.

"I'm sure I'm no different from your other women in that regard," I say. "What are you thinking?"

"No fair," he says. "I asked you first. Come on."

"You're the first man to pick me up for a date in years," I say.

"That's what you're thinking?" he asks. He's a little disappointed but hides it well.

"No," I say. "That's why I'm afraid to tell you what I'm thinking. You'd laugh and lose all respect for me."

"Never!" He says it with a blend of humor and sincerity. "You tell me and I'll tell you. I would never laugh at anything you confide to me, Nikki."

It's perfect, the way he says it. I wish we were in a private place right now, so I could sit on his lap and get him hard and we could tumble onto the floor and make mad, passionate love like a couple of kids.

I take a deep breath. "I'm thinking how wonderful it would be to make love with you."

He smiles and takes one of my hands in his. "That's what I was thinking, too." He kisses my hand. "Your place or mine?"

19

Alan and I lie panting and sweating in my bed. If this wasn't quite the fulfillment of all my fantasies, it fulfilled at least one. Alan actually seduced me. No one has ever done that. Most of my sex partners engage in foreplay for all of about sixty seconds, mostly to get themselves aroused. William takes more time, but he's almost clinical in where he touches and rubs and for how long. None of them ever unclothed me. I suppose they would have if I had asked, but that wasn't their mission. They just wanted to get laid, and frankly, I wasn't complaining because that's all I wanted, too, so I could get on with the rest of my life.

Alan stopped me in the living room and embraced me. His kiss was soft and warm and it had a sincerity I've only ever known as Blythe's husband, never as a woman. His caresses were even more seductive. The warmth of his hands on my body, the tender, leisurely movements up and down my back, the gentle fondling of my butt. In the bedroom, he undressed me, kissing each patch of newly revealed skin as he went. Even when he lowered me onto the bed it was a slow, sensuous journey to penetration, filled with sensations I've never known before and so much pent-up desire I nearly passed out when he entered me.

Now, with my body and mind turned to postcoital mush, he lies on his side, one arm around me, his lips nuzzling against my neck, my breasts, my lips. It's different than when William does it. It's part of William's service, and it's fun and even erotic. But Alan's attentions feel different. He's expressing something for me, a kind of passion that goes beyond male trophy hunting or a job well done.

He massages my breasts and gently squeezes my nipples. I smile dreamily. He kisses me on the lips.

"You're a wild woman," he says.

"Can you still hear out of your left ear?" I laugh self-consciously. I'm often loud and uninhibited in sex, but I think tonight I set new records for volume and sex talk.

Alan smiles. "I'm fine," he says, "but my right ear wants in on the action now."

I sigh. My mind fills with the possibilities of a second tryst. My body is in full tingle when my phone rings and vibrates. In that instant, all my amorous thoughts disappear with the suddenness of a balloon popping. Maybe it's because Morgan is out on the town, or maybe because of being targeted by the Nazi thugs; whatever, the ringing phone pierces my thoughts like a fire alarm and I know this can't be good news.

The caller-ID is a downtown hospital. My heart sinks.

"Hello?" My greeting is a question.

The voice on the other end is female. I miss her name and title. She tells me that my daughter and one of her friends are being treated for injuries in the emergency room. She has no details about the injuries or what caused them. Morgan is being seen now. The voice on the phone is matter-of-fact about it all. This is something she does every day, I suppose. Which is the last rational thought I have. My mind goes into full panic mode. Mental images of my daughter with a battered face and body flash into my imagination, one after another, each driving my guilt engine further into overdrive. How could I have been so stupid as to turn my daughter loose in the city when these Nazi thugs are out there, looking for trouble? I knew Little John was a target. I knew Morgan might be targeted, too.

My self-recriminations are in full swing when I hang up. Alan's face is filled with concern. "Is everything okay?" he asks.

I fill him in as I get dressed, my hands shaking, my teeth clenched. He dresses, too, and when we're presentable, he takes my hand and leads me out to his car. We arrive at the hospital maybe fifteen minutes later, though it seems like hours to me. I've been crying and shaking all the way here. I keep seeing pictures of Morgan as a toddler in my mind; then I see Blythe's face, horror-stricken, lying on her deathbed and receiving this news. I'm so overcome with guilt and regret I have trouble making my body move to get out of the car. Alan comes around to my door and extends a hand. I take it and when I get out of the car, he loops his arm through mine for support. As we enter the building, I realize I'm leaning on him. In one instant, I'm so gratified to have someone to lean on for once, but in the next I command my body to stand and walk on its own. I know better than to depend on anyone for anything. It's nice when I can get help like this, but I know better than to count on it.

As dire as my imaginings have been, the sight of Morgan hits me like a cannon blast. She's lying on her back, mouth slightly open, eyes closed, a pitiful expression on her face. Her forehead is swathed in white gauze and even though her left eye is covered with a thick bandage, I can see it's swollen and grossly black-and-blue. She may be sleeping, or she may be in shock. I'm certain she's had a concussion, maybe even a fractured skull. I step to the bed and examine her exposed skin, looking for cuts and abrasions. There aren't any. I struggle to contain my sobs, but little squeaks eke out. Morgan's unbandaged eye flutters open. Her mouth makes a brief attempt to smile. I take her hand and kiss it.

"I'm here, angel," I say, bending low to her so I can speak quietly. "You're going to be fine."

She tries to smile again but it's too hard. She strains to move her other hand to mine. For a moment, we touch, and stack our hands, like pancakes, a game we played when she was just learning to walk and laugh. I bend over her again and kiss her softly on the cheek.

"I love you, Morgan," I whisper. "Whoever did this is going to pay, and you will never be harmed again. Not ever. I swear it."

She smiles a little and pats my hand.

"Are you in pain?" I whisper in her ear.

She starts to shake her head, but winces in pain and stops. Her lips form the word *yes,* no sound coming out. I hover over her and kiss her cheek again as tenderly as I can. She moves one hand laboriously and strokes my cheek. It is a tender touch, and a complete surprise. I'm overwhelmed. My eyes tear up.

Her lips say a silent, *Thank you.*

"I love you so much," I whisper back, my voice feverish and desperate. I feel her hand on my shoulder, then on my face, then she hugs me. There's no strength in her hug, but I can feel the love.

I'm in mid-sob when a nurse whisks into the bay, sweeping the curtain open and closed like a gust of wind, and pushing a mobile computer in front of her. She emits a chain of questions, each a variation on "how are you feeling?" but doesn't wait for answers. Instead, she checks the machines that monitor Morgan's condition, checks her IV pouch, enters data into the computer, then comes to the bedside and addresses me.

"Are you family?" She asks the question professionally, but there's a dubious note in her voice. I stand a good nine inches taller than her and I don't look like a mom or a sister. She's not being snide, it's just a reaction I get sometimes.

I nod. "I'm a parent," I say.

The nurse starts to ask another question, but Morgan interrupts, her voice just above a whisper, somehow loud enough to be heard, even by a nurse in a hurry.

"She's my mom," Morgan rasps. "I have two moms."

While I reel with emotion at this unexpected acknowledgment from my daughter, the nurse focuses on the pragmatic.

"You're talking," she says to Morgan. "That's great." She rattles off a string of cautions about not trying to do too much too soon and flies off as suddenly as she arrived, her final words—"the doctor will be by in a little while"—hanging in the air.

"How is Little John?" Morgan whispers.

"I don't know," I answer. "I'll look in on him next."

Morgan tells me to go ahead and see him, she'll be fine. "Not yet," I tell her. She starts to argue, but a doctor bursts in. He nods to me and examines Morgan, moving quickly and surely, oblivious to everything but whatever his eyes are focused on. He pulls the covers back and opens her gown, revealing bandages across her chest and bruises on her ribs.

"How's the pain?" he asks Morgan.

"I'm not sure," she whispers. "My head hurts when I move it, but mostly I feel like I'm floating."

The doctor smiles a little and I do, too. She's clearly on pain-killing narcotics, not the kind of trip she was threatening me with a few weeks ago, and certainly not the circumstances she envisioned, but a drug trip nonetheless. He checks her face and head injuries and pounds notes into the portable computer station at Morgan's bedside. I wait for him to address us. He keeps typing. Minutes pass. I can't take it anymore.

"What is my daughter's condition?" I ask. My voice is a little sharp, reflecting my impatience. The doctor looks at me quizzically, as if surprised I can express words that make sense.

I get that sometimes from people who make me as transgender and associate it with a lack of intellectual depth.

"Well," he clears his throat, "she's suffered a lot of trauma. She's had a concussion and a number of hematomas on her face and torso." He stops typing and peers closer at Morgan's face. "No facial fractures," he murmurs. "That's a minor miracle. Someone really worked her over, someone very big and very strong." He casts a second glance at me, as if measuring me to see if I was the attacker.

I see tears form in Morgan's eyes and I take her hand in mine.

"Her ribs are bruised but not broken," the doctor continues, "not that it makes much difference. The bruises are just as painful as a break and take about as long to heal." He continues his monologue as he returns to the computer and reviews the notes and data. "We'll need to keep her overnight at the very least," he says, glancing at me again. This time, he stops what he's doing.

"Are you related to the patient?" His question is pointed and even less diplomatic than the nurse's.

"I'm Morgan's parent," I say. I see Morgan's unbandaged eye open wider and her lips start to form an objection. "I'm her mother," I add. "She has two mothers."

The doctor nods. He's figuring it out. Ten years ago, I would have had to explain it to him. Today, the medical community is more aware of transgender people. He starts talking again, addressing both Morgan and me, going on about concussion protocols and avoiding long-term brain damage. His cautions echo the information that has accompanied newspaper stories about fallen football heroes. It shakes me up, thinking about the consequences if Morgan is attacked again by hoodlums. The doctor finishes his talk and asks if we have questions. Morgan gestures for him to come closer.

"How is Little John?" she whispers.

"He's one of the other victims," I explain.

"I can't really talk about another patient," says the doctor, "but I think he'll be available for card games and chess when you're recovering." We all smile. The doctor pauses at Morgan's bedside before leaving. "The police may come back again. Your companions answered their questions earlier, but you weren't coherent." His exit line is an invitation to call him or the nursing staff if Morgan's condition changes.

I sit at Morgan's bedside until she falls asleep, then move two bays down to Little John's bed. The sight of him is just as shocking as my first glimpse of Morgan. His face is swollen and misshapen, like he's just gone a few rounds with Muhammad Ali or run into a meat grinder. One eye is nearly closed from the lump on that side of his face. There are bandages all over his skull and upper body. One ear is wrapped in white gauze.

For all that, he's awake and alert. He's sitting up, his bed tilted to put his upper body at a forty-five-degree angle. His eyes are bright and attentive, following my every movement. He smiles when I enter his curtained bay.

"Jesus, Little John!" I exclaim. I don't mean to be so demonstrative; it's just an emotional reflex, especially after seeing Morgan.

"You should see the other guy," he quips.

"I just came from Morgan's room," I say, not laughing.

His face clouds. "Yes. Sorry. I did my best."

"I know," I say.

"It could have been worse," he says.

"How?"

"They could have had tanks." Little John started playing World War II games on the internet when he was transitioning. He swears it made him think more like a man. Personally, I doubt it, but there's no doubting the fact he became a student of battle tactics, and especially of Rommel's tank tactics in Africa.

This time I smile with him.

"What happened?" I ask.

"Morgan didn't tell you?"

"She's not in conversational shape," I reply.

Little John trains his eyes on me and nods sadly.

"We had dinner and caught a set at the House of Blues and we were walking to the L station and everything was fine. We're talking about the band, and you, and your date"—he smiles impishly—"and there's this guy coming the other way, just another pedestrian, we'd passed lots of them. He was big, but most guys seem big to me. He looked normal. Jeans, T-shirt, Cubs hat. He starts to pass us and then, all of a sudden he jumps between Morgan and me and grabs us. He throws me down and stomps his heel into my solar plexus. I don't remember anything after that.

"Janet was with us and she managed to run," he continues. "She called the police. When I came to, Morgan was lying beside me, bloody and moaning and out of it. I was in agony, too, and the guy was gone. The police got there a couple minutes later and here we are."

I try to absorb what he said.

"Did you recognize the guy?" I ask.

Little John gives me a painful shrug. "I think it was one of the guys who's been stalking me."

"Which one?" I'm trying to jog Little John's memory a little.

"I don't think this one had any tattoos or swastikas. He might have been the same guy who assaulted me before, but I didn't get a good look at that one," says Little John. "This one looked kind of normal, at least, from a distance."

"A normal Nazi," I say.

"'A white nationalist,'" Little John smirks. "That's what the cops said when I called him a Nazi."

"But you can't identify him?"

"I didn't get a real good look at him," says Little John.

"What did the cops say?"

Little John shrugs again. "Not much."

"They're just going to drop it?"

"I didn't give them much to go on," says Little John. "I'd hate to get the wrong guy locked up."

I throw my hands up in the air. "Are you crazy? If we locked all those bastards up the world would be a better place. And not one of them is innocent."

Little John gives me his disapproving look. "Come on, Nikki, we can't lock up people just because we don't like them. That's persecution. That's what they do."

"No," I say. "This is what they do." I gesture toward Little John, then toward Morgan's bed. "They hurt people. They kill people. It's about time we struck back."

We argue the point back and forth for several minutes before I let Little John think I'm wavering. I'm not, but this thing has a smell to it that's triggering my paranoid instincts. I think this crap with the Nazis is going to go on until people get killed. I don't think the police see them as an enemy. Plus, these apes are smart in their own brutal way. We don't have a description for the police to use because they strike fast and hard and people like Little John and Janet and Morgan aren't equipped to deal with such outrageous, spontaneous violence.

I'm probably not either, not at the moment of attack, but I've been the victim before and if they set upon me or mine, they will face consequences. If the police don't deal with them, I will.

Little John reads me loud and clear.

"Don't even think it, Nikki," he says.

"Think what?" I flash him my innocent face.

"Let the cops deal with him," says Little John.

"I will," I say. "If they will. But I'll say this, Little John, it's a bad sign when the cops want us to call those thugs 'white nationalists' instead of what they are."

"It's probably part of their sensitivity training, like calling us 'trans,'" says Little John.

"Or maybe they all belong to the same Nazi cell." I try to say it humorously, but even I can hear the edge in my voice.

"Promise me you won't take matters into your own hands," says Little John. "Surely you remember what happened the last time you confronted one of those people."

"Yes, I saved you from a beating."

"And what happened, Nikki?" says Little John. "You took one out and another one shows up. Maybe two. These people are like cockroaches. You can't stop them by stepping on them one at a time."

I'm fighting to control my temper now. Little John is maybe the finest person I know, but this passive morality crap makes me crazy.

Little John and I banter back and forth a little. Not much. We've walked this ground together many times and nothing ever changes. Still, I tone down my rhetoric. This is a time for him and Morgan to heal. It's also a time for me to start planning. The time for talk is over.

It's after two o'clock in the morning when I finally leave Morgan and Little John to their slumbers. I remember Alan when I start to leave and feel a pang of guilt for not bidding him farewell when he dropped me at the hospital. I check my phone to see if he sent a text or phone message. He's waiting for me in the emergency room waiting area, sitting in the back row of chairs, typing away on a laptop computer. He looks up as I enter the room. A sympathetic smile forms on his face.

"I can't believe you waited all this time," I gush.

He stands up and kisses me. "I dashed home and got my computer," he says.

He offers me his arm and we begin walking to the parking garage. On the drive to my place, I fill him in on what happened, and how Morgan and Little John are doing. When he pulls up to the curb, he turns off the engine and comes around the car to get my door.

As I unlock the front door, he asks, "Would you like some privacy now?"

It takes me a second to understand what he's asking. I turn to face him, our faces so close I can feel his breath on my skin. My memory fills with him kissing me in the waiting room, a public place, not O'Hare Airport, of course, but still, a public place where a dozen people could see a good-looking man kissing a broad-shouldered transgender woman like she was someone special. The recollection lights up all my circuits.

"If you're offering me a choice," I say, "I'd like to get laid again, and I'd like to go to sleep with your body next to mine."

20

Janet, the barista who got away from last night's assault, is part of the crew that opened the café this morning, so by the time I roll in, everyone knows about the incident. The four people on duty cluster around me for an update on Little John and Morgan. I end my briefing saying that I'll need people to work an extra hour each day so I can look in on our wounded comrades. I thought there would be a lot of sympathy in the group, and a general willingness to do whatever it takes to keep things rolling, but I was wrong. All I got was blank stares and silence.

Not even twenty minutes later, Janet and Marvin corner me in the kitchen. Janet launches into a long soliloquy about how terrified she is. I listen for a while, then cut her off. "Janet," I say, "are you giving notice?"

Janet blushes, looks at her feet, looks up again, and nods her head.

"Yes, sorry Nikki. It's just not worth the danger. I love it here, but this is getting scary. I think someone followed me again this morning."

Janet is probably seeing boogeymen behind every tree and

under her bed, but there's not much I can do to talk her out of it. I turn to Marvin. They've started dating in the past couple months. They're probably living together. They're white and straight, so they can quit and melt back into the untargeted population.

"Are you giving notice, too, Marvin?"

He nods his head. "Nikki," he says, "she really was followed this morning."

"Are you sure?" I feel a tingle of fear run through my body.

"I'm sure," he says. "We both saw him. He wasn't trying to hide."

I ask what he looked like.

"He's big, like the guy who jumped us last night, but more Nazi-fied," Janet says. She describes a burly, heavily tattooed guy wearing a MAGA hat, a leather vest adorned with an Iron Cross and swastika, and a sneering face.

While she's talking, fires of rage begin building inside me, burning away my fears. I keep seeing Morgan's battered face, and Little John's cuts and bruises, and my staff abandoning the café, me unable to look in on my daughter because I have to run the shop, or me losing the business because I have to close to look in on my daughter.

"He was still out there ten minutes ago," says Marvin, gesturing to the sidewalk outside.

I grab Marvin's arm and pull him toward the back door. "Show me," I say.

We dash out the alley to the street and look south. Nothing. We walk to the corner and look east. Marvin jumps back and pulls me with him.

"He's on the other side of the street, Nikki. He's sitting in the bus enclosure."

I peek around the corner. Sure enough, there's a man sitting in the plexiglas shelter at the bus stop. I can't see him very well from this distance, but he's obviously large, tattooed, and he's wearing a red baseball hat backwards on his head. I should be afraid, and I am a little bit, but mostly as I stare at him, I envision driving a spear through his chest.

"Do you have a phone with you?" I ask Marvin. He nods that he does. "Good. Stay here and watch me. If World War III breaks out, call in the cavalry."

Before he can say anything, I walk boldly to the intersection, wait for the light to change, and cross to the other side of the street. My heart is hammering inside my chest and I'm feeling a little short of breath because of my nerves. I know this is crazy, but it feels right. I walk casually toward the bus shelter, pulling my pepper spray from the pocket of my jeans as I go. When I get to the bus shelter, I uncap the can and palm it in my left hand.

The homicidal urge that propelled me this far seems to evaporate when I enter the bus shelter, but I'm committed. I sit beside the goon. A brief, sidelong glance confirms Marvin's accusation: the man is a neo-Nazi gorilla from central casting. He's large and thick with upper arms the size of my thighs, some of it pasty fat but plenty of it muscle—more than enough to deal with me. Shiny Nazi symbols dot his black vest, and he has Iron Crosses and swastikas prominently tattooed on his arms. He has a shaved head, a scowl, and a day's growth of beard on his face. Stalking coffee shop workers is a tough business, what with the early hours and all.

He glances at me, just for a fraction of a second. As his eyes revert back to the café across the street, his lips curl into a sneer.

"Jesus Christ," he says, "I thought this was a bus stop, not a drag bar." His voice is clear and his diction is surprisingly precise.

"Disillusionment is everywhere today," I reply. "Do you know what *disillusionment* means?" My mouth is so dry I have trouble forming the words, but my rage hasn't abated.

He looks at me, his sneer deepening. "It's what happens when you find out a white man with all the advantages turns out to be a fucking queer."

"Or when you find out a white man with all the advantages turns out to be a brain-dead thug," I say, returning his stare.

A woman from the neighborhood approaches the bus stop. She glances into the shelter, sees us jawing at each other, and positions herself outside, at the curb.

The Nazi stares at me, his mouth forming a cruel smile, his eyes blazing into mine.

"What you got in your hand, queenie?" he taunts. He nods toward my left hand which is tucked against my thigh, just out of his field of vision.

"I have the end of your life in that hand," I tell him.

He laughs. The woman on the curb turns nervously to look at us. "I'll give you this," he says. "You have more nerve than any pervert I've ever met."

"And you're the first Nazi I've met who has an intellect superior to a toad," I reply. "But that doesn't mean you're smart."

His face turns deadly serious. "I'm trying to decide whether to crush your pansy-ass body here or wait until I can take my time with you."

"A coward like you will wait until you can sneak up on a victim," I say. "If you tried something now, you'd have the disillusioning experience of getting the shit beat out of you by a drag queen."

His face breaks into a sarcastic smile. His lips tighten into taut rubber bands, his teeth clench and he seems to be holding his breath. I'm tense, too, my peripheral vision locked in on his body, ready at the slightest movement of either hand to swing my pepper spray into his face and let go a blinding blast.

He exhales loudly. The cruel smile returns. "You're right," he smirks. "Why take you out here when I can wait and really enjoy it later?" He stands and starts to leave.

"Hey, Adolf," I call, stopping him. "Leave my people alone or I'm going to inflict more pain on your body than you ever thought possible."

He leaves, laughing loudly. I watch him go, unsettled by the encounter. The way he talked and acted, he seemed educated and intelligent, a terrifying combination. I'd been counting on him being as stupid and arrogant as the alley guy had been.

I return to the café, my legs so watery I can barely walk, but I fake it lest the whole staff get the willies and quit.

"What did you say to him?" Marvin asks, his eyes wide. Janet and the rest of the staff cluster around me, waiting to hear.

"I told him to leave my people alone."

"What did he say to that?" Janet poses the question like she doesn't quite believe I challenged him.

"He thought I had a lot of balls," I say. "Which I took as an insult. But he left."

"Do you really think he's done with us?" asks Janet.

"We'll see," I reply. I know he's not, but maybe now he'll at least focus on me and leave everyone else alone.

At two o'clock, before the morning crew goes home, I conduct a brief staff meeting. I update everyone on the assault and on the condition of Little John and Morgan. I tell them I've made our local police department aware of this morning's stalker and they promised to send patrols by more frequently. I share the tips I've picked up over the years about how to check for stalkers, how to ready yourself with pepper spray, and to stay with the crowd if you're being followed.

The mood is somber when I end the meeting. No one speaks. Their faces are thoughtful and concerned, but no one gives notice and Janet and Marvin tell me they're going to give it another day.

I get away for a brief visit with Morgan and Little John in the midafternoon. It's a desultory visit. They're both bored stiff and physically uncomfortable and more than ready to go home.

When I get back to the café, Vernon I. Gibbs is hunched over a laptop at a corner table. He manages to fill a table for four, his brief case on one chair, his suit coat draped over another, his person filling a third. His papers and files are scattered over the table top, along with his computer and phone. When I enter the room, he looks up and tries to flash a friendly, ingratiating smile, but it's an act. Even from twenty feet away, he's all crazy eyes and manipulation. I approach him, wanting to get this over with fast.

"I hope you're enjoying our hospitality," I say as he stands to greet me.

He adds raised eyebrows to his phony smile. "Absolutely," he says.

He gestures for me to sit opposite him on the one chair he hasn't yet claimed. I comply. As I do, one of the staff brings me a glass of cold water with a squeeze of lemon and a squeeze of lime. We actually named this drink the Afternoon Refresher and put it on the menu for two dollars a shot. We sell a lot of them on summer afternoons, especially to people who come in to camp out for an hour or two between appointments.

After a minute of excruciating small talk—he does it poorly and I receive it even more poorly—Gibbs gets down to business.

"I heard about your employees' misfortune yesterday," he says. "I want to express my sympathies. There has been way too much of that sort of thing lately. It's a threat to all businesses, but especially minority-owned establishments like yours."

He stops for a moment so I can express my eternal gratitude, or perhaps vent my pent-up emotions. I don't do either. I sit silently waiting for him to make his point.

"Well," he continues, "the thing is, you're a sitting duck in this location. Middle class, upper middle-class neighborhood, not much crime, not much police patrolling. The local station isn't all that friendly to LGBTQ folks."

"So I should sell to you and move to Key West?" I interrupt him rudely. I don't have time for this crap.

"No, no," he says, flashing his phony smile again. "Look, things are coming together here. Your property value is peaking. Bad people are targeting you and you're not getting much protection. You could sell for big bucks and relocate your business to Boystown or Andersonville, where you'd have more neighborhood support and a more sympathetic police force."

"Why would you want to invest in such a poorly policed area?" I ask. I'm being deliberately sarcastic, but the truth is, he has a point.

"Let's face it, Nikki," he says. "Money talks. Here, there, and everywhere. If I don't get what I need from the police, I go to the mayor. If it still doesn't happen, I hire my own security. It kicks a dent in the profits, but just a dent."

"Or I could hire security myself," I say.

"You could, but it's going to cost more than you clear," says Gibbs. "I can spread that cost around a much bigger operation. I'll build up, and I'll have dozens of condos and several commercial units generating revenue." He lets that sink in for a minute, and it does. "These are signs, Nikki. It's time to take the money and relocate. I'll make you the deal of a lifetime."

I eye him silently for a moment, thinking about Alan. "Why would I sell to you?" I ask. "I've had other suitors."

"First of all," he says, "I've got the resources to buy you out in cash. When you get down to the fine print, most of the others are going to offer you a buyout deal—some cash up front, the rest in installments over a period of years. Don't trust them. We're all speculators, and we all protect ourselves. If the business projections don't materialize, or there are problems with the construction—permit problems, environmental issues, you uncover an ancient burial ground, whatever—the speculator has the option of going belly up and cutting his losses."

"Good to know," I say, noncommittally.

"I know you've been seeing Alan Campbell," says Gibbs. His face, which had seemed almost sincere for moment, gets tense and his eyes get that crazy look again. "He's one of the people I'm talking about. Watch out for him. He's very good with the ladies, not so generous with the contracts."

I blink. Something about the way that he says this makes me think he knows I've slept with Alan. Does he have people looking in my bedroom window? He's doing everything he can to imply that this is how Alan works—romance the buyer, get them distracted, then get them to sign an unfavorable deal. I try to envision Alan like that: insincere, opportunistic, investing time in seducing me just to get my property. Then I look at Gibbs and his crazy eyes and taut body language. He looks like someone who'd say anything to get the deal he's after, and Alan doesn't.

"I have to get back to work," I say. "My building isn't for sale, but I appreciate the advice."

I stand as Gibbs starts to speak. He wants to recycle the discussion, go back to the part of his pitch that I didn't accept and rebuild his argument. Some salesmen do it intuitively, some after being instructed or mentored. I'll never know which branch of the sales tree Gibbs comes from because I'm a coldhearted bitch who knows how to say no, and I'm too impatient to reargue done deals.

To his credit, Gibbs realizes today's game is over as soon as I stand up. He rises too, pastes his phony smile on his face, and extends his arm for a handshake.

"Thank you for hearing me out," he says. "If you don't mind, I'll stop in from time to time to enjoy your wonderful café and see if you've changed your mind."

I smile, shake hands, and get back to work. On my way to my office, the afternoon floor manager intercepts me and reports that one of the waitstaff has quit, and others are thinking about it. As I sit at my desk, he asks, "Are you selling? Is that what your meeting was about?"

I shake my head *no*. I don't trust myself to speak. I'm too angry about people quitting and threatening to quit. I pay a competitive wage. We have health benefits and a positive workplace where people can't be harassed for anything, not by other staff and not by customers and certainly not by the bosses. We're liberal about giving people personal time off. We have a generous vacation policy. People get a half day off on election days. The list goes on and on. Really, if you don't have the sand to stand up for a place like this, and you run and take some shit job just because someone might mess with you here, well, don't come whining to me about your minimum wage or your nonexistent health benefits. Sometimes, you just have to stand up and be counted if you want to live a good life. If you choose to live in a hole like a reptile, I have no sympathy for you.

21

Ophelia Francis Langston came out as a trans woman in a very public way years before the American public was prepared for such a thing. She was a much-heralded tax attorney whose client list read like a who's who in Chicago's crop of Fortune 500 companies and millionaires and billionaires. When she stepped out as a woman—a six-foot-two woman who favored heels and hose and an endless variety of big-hair wigs worthy of a Houston belle in the sixties—all of her conservative clients were shocked. Many abandoned her, but many stayed because she was so much better at what she did than most of the straight people in the tax attorney corral. By the time I met her, she was drifting into retirement, providing consulting services to favored clients and companies part time, and spending the rest of her time leading transgender lambs like me through the valley of terror.

We still talk frequently, and she drags me to charitable events several times a year, so my call doesn't come as a shock to her. As always, when she answers the phone, she skips all the normal small talk and gets right to her sardonic humor.

"Let me guess," she says, "you want me to write a personal

services contract for your concubine."

My paid assignations with William are a source of humor between us. She has paid for sex, too, so it's not a morality play; it's more her way of mentoring. Among the many things Ophelia has taught me is not to apologize for my interest in sex or my taste in men.

"No," I say. I tell her about the assault on Morgan and Little John, and the pattern of violence that preceded it.

"It's happening all over," Ophelia remarks, "but usually it's just a single, spontaneous assault. This sounds more personal."

"It is personal," I say. "They want to drive me out of business. Meanwhile, I've got real estate developers offering me the deal of a lifetime to sell."

"Do you think they're connected?" Ophelia asks.

"The Nazis and the capitalists?"

"The developers hiring a couple of thugs to scare you off," says Ophelia. "It's not like our white nationalist friends are blessed with qualifications the employment market is crying for. I'm sure you can hire them cheap."

"That never crossed my mind," I say, trying to imagine Gibbs or Alan hiring a neo-Nazi goon to terrorize me. I can't quite get there.

"It fits, though, doesn't it?" Ophelia says. "The thuggery started around the time the real estate boys began calling on you, right?"

The thought hits me like a punch in the gut. My perfect lover, Alan, cloaking his consuming desire for my property in a two-pronged attack: violent hate crimes on one front, and fake passion on the other. I relive his seduction in my imagination, this time imagining him grinning slyly to himself as I surrender my body, my pride, my secret self. Or perhaps he was secretly gritting his teeth, imagining he was with an attractive woman, just going through the motions with me so he could gain my trust and buy my building.

"You're very quiet, Nikki." Ophelia breaks my reverie. "Did we hit a nerve?"

"I slept with one of the developers," I confess.

"Good for you!" says Ophelia. "If they're going to play you, at least get an orgasm out of it." She seldom talks about sex with others, especially the puritanical matriarchs who lead our community, but she's quite ribald with me, no doubt because we share similar urges and employ similar tactics for satisfying them. She wants a blow-by-blow, but I have to get back to work. I put her off until we can grab a meal or coffee together and get to the point of my call.

"Morgan's coming home tomorrow and she'll be in a concussion protocol for a while," I say. "Especially for the next few days, she needs to go slow, take it easy, pamper herself, and most of all, avoid any more traumas to the head."

I pause, choked with emotion. It takes a moment to get my voice back. Ophelia waits. I explain about challenging the Nazi by my café.

"They're still coming after me, Ophelia," I say. "And Morgan's the easiest way to get to me."

"How can I help, sweetie?" Ophelia asks.

"Can she stay with you?" My voice breaks. Asking for this makes me feel like a terrible parent who can't even protect her daughter.

"Of course," says Ophelia.

Morgan is restless and cranky and sick of hospital food when I visit. She's in a private room with her own television set and her laptop computer so she has plenty of diversions, but the walls are closing in. I tell myself it's a good sign as she continues an unending monologue about how miserable she feels being cooped up like this. The only reason she can go on living, she tells me, is that her doctor has promised to release her tomorrow if there are no complications overnight.

"We need to talk about what happens when you are released," I say.

She looks at me dubiously. "Why do I think you're about to tell me something I don't want to hear?"

"It's not that bad," I say. "It's just, since you need to take it easy, I've arranged for you to stay with my friend Ophelia for a while."

Morgan's face turns into a mask of righteous indignation. "You're trying to hide me from the Nazi. That really pisses me off!"

I let her vent for another minute or two, then admit the obvious. "Yes, I'm hiding you from the goon squad. You can't afford to take any more blows to the head and I can't watch over you every minute of the day."

"I don't need a babysitter," she fumes. "If I ever see that ape again, I'm going to nail him with pepper spray and kick his nuts into his lower intestines."

I'm shocked at her aggressiveness, even though she sounds like me, but I recover. "Well, your knowledge of male anatomy is impressive," I say, "but your recollection of facts is a tad hazy. You didn't see his face, remember?"

"I'll know him if I see him."

I don't argue the point. She knows I'm right. I talk her through my reasoning for her R&R with Ophelia: She has to rest and must avoid any possible head trauma. It makes sense to lie low for a few days or a week, and hope the police can get everything sorted out.

Morgan flashes the kind of lemon face I would make if I were in her place. "You don't run from these pigs, so why should

I?" she asks.

"I'm not the one with the concussion," I say. We debate the issue for several minutes. She's determined and a mentally agile debater and I don't have enough energy to draw it out. I tell her I'll talk to her mother about it tonight.

For once, Blythe's mother puts me through to her without insult or delay, but that pleasant surprise is short-lived. Blythe's voice is thin and weak. She sounds like she's floating on drugs.

"Nikki," she says. It's like she's too weak to say "hello," but she uses my female name. I tell her about Morgan, pacing through my empty flat as we talk. Each time I pass through the living room I pause to look at the photo of Blythe and Morgan on the fireplace mantel. They look happy and loving and, most of all, healthy, as if they could live forever. When I get to the part about Morgan being in the hospital, she groans, "Oh God." She doesn't have enough strength to say more, and I feel terrible for adding to her burdens, but she has a right to know.

I fill her in on my plan for stashing Morgan with Ophelia after the hospital. When I say it, I add the part about, "until the police sort things out," but I don't tell her I don't have any faith in the police sorting things out. "What would you do?" I ask her.

"You're going to have to make these decisions yourself," she says. Her voice rises a little, like she's irritated that I keep calling her about these problems.

"Morgan's saying no," I tell her. "Actually, she's saying hell no which means she won't comply anyway."

"I'm not any better with belligerent teenagers than you are, Nikki," Blythe says. "Why do you keep asking?"

It's a good question.

"Because you know things I don't. Because you might share something that saves her life. Because I want you to have a say in what I'm doing." I pause. "Mostly, I'd like your approval."

I'm tearing up and getting sloppy emotional as I picture Blythe, drugged and dying, her emaciated body in a sterile room shared only by her mother whose image is enough to scare the shit out of the Grim Reaper.

"Nikki," she sighs. "Do your best. That's all anyone can do. You love her. She loves you. You're smart. You'll be okay. Just don't give up."

The line abruptly goes silent. I wait, thinking she's summoning energy to say something more. There's a rustling sound, then her mother comes on the line. Her voice is surprisingly human. "She can't talk any more, Nick. It's not personal. That's all the energy she has for now."

"Should I bring Morgan to see her, Virginia?" I'm so unsettled by Blythe's condition and her mother's sudden moment of humanity I actually use her mother's name. This sounds like a death watch.

"Not yet. This is from all the meds and chemo. If the doctors give up, I'll take her home if I can. Either way, I'll let you know."

It takes a full half hour for me to get control of myself after that conversation. I can't stop pacing through the flat and I can't stop feeling how empty it is without my angst-ridden daughter here, even though she'd be locked in her room if she were here. When I finally feel like I can carry on an adult conversation, I call the police and ask if they've made any progress in finding the man who beat Morgan and Little John. It's a fruitless waste of my controlled emotions. A detective tells me they've canvassed the area, but no one saw the assault and unless Little John or Morgan can provide a description, there's not much more they can do.

I tell him about the goon who followed two employees to the shop yesterday. "Three of us can identify him."

"I'm sorry," he says, "but what did he do, Ms. Finch?" he asks. "What law did he break?"

"Maybe he's the same guy who attacked my daughter and Little John. Can't you at least question him?"

"Can one of you categorically state he's the same guy?"

I give him the obvious answer, then explain the situation with Morgan coming home and me worried about her safety. I ask if they can check out the goon we saw.

"I'm sorry," he says. "I understand your concern, but we have no reason to check out someone who hasn't broken any laws. I'll ask for increased patrols in the neighborhood. That's the best I can do."

I can't control myself. "That's what happened last time and somehow these Nazi fucks keep slipping through your protective shield and terrorizing my people."

He tries to sound conciliatory again, urging us to give him hard information about actual law breakers. I control my temper long enough to say a civil goodbye, then continue to pace through the flat like a crazy woman. I want to scream loud enough to rattle the windowpanes and raise the dead, but I manage to control myself.

Alan calls and asks how I'm doing. I vent. He wants to stop by and give me a hug. I warn him I'm somewhere between possessed and homicidal. He says he's coming anyway. Thirty minutes later, he knocks softly and when I open the door, he opens his arms. I fall into a warm hug and sigh. Part of me is ashamed of being so needy, but another part of me is basking in his body warmth like it was the summer sun. I hear myself purring. Really. I've lost all pride.

When we break the clinch and I usher him inside, I issue the standard offer of a beverage or snack.

He puts his hands on my upper arms and we look into each other's eyes, me wondering if these could possibly be the eyes of a man who's only interested in my real estate. "You've had a terrible day," he says. "Let me give you a massage."

In that moment I realize several things in a split-second

sequence. His eyes are an exotic shade of blue, right at the border of pale gray. He has a masculine, Roman nose that adds intensity to the way he looks at me when we're so close. His skin tone is a tawny tan, created by the summer sun and lake-effect winds and now that I notice it, it's so sexy it sends a charge through my body. I'm wondering why I didn't notice these things when he was pitching me on selling my building, or when we chatted at dinner, or for sure when he was seducing me. While I wonder, his lips come to mine in a tender embrace. I'm ready for some torrid sex, but when we go in the bedroom and I peel off my clothes, Alan has me lie on my front and he begins kneading my tense muscles: neck, shoulders, upper back, lower back, butt, thighs. If he's playing me, he's extraordinarily good at it. Who needs sincerity when you can have a great massage and hopefully an orgasm by being taken advantage of?

When he reaches my thighs I can't take it anymore. I roll onto my back and put his hands on my breasts. He smiles and gives me a *wait a minute* gesture and gets himself naked. As I wait for him to join me, Vernon Gibbs's warning about how Alan uses his power of seduction passes through my mind. I watch Alan as he takes off his clothes, searching for some sign of insincerity. All I see is his lovely body, his handsome face, and his aroused manhood. I'll worry about reality after we make love. For now, it's enough that the prospect of getting laid has blocked out my mountains of anxieties, at least for the moment.

22

Morgan is still peevish when I arrive to take her home from the hospital. She paces and frets as we wait for the hospitalist to sign off on her release. I don't blame her. Little John, under a different doctor's care, has already departed. No one knows where Morgan's hospitalist is or what he's doing. He could be in China or in a bathroom or tending to a hundred new patients. It takes thirty minutes for the nursing staff to contact him and get an electronic release, and another ten minutes to get a hospital volunteer with a wheelchair to Morgan's room. The wheelchair protocol pisses me off as much as it does Morgan. The hospital says you're fit enough to go home, but not fit enough to walk to the door, even though when you get to your home you might have to walk up several flights of stairs. Plus, the hospital says I can't be trusted to push the wheelchair, even though it will trust me to care for my child after we leave the facility.

Our next stop is the accounts department. Morgan stews as I settle the bill. It only takes fifteen minutes, but Morgan twitches and fidgets and complains nonstop while I sign away my financial life.

"You could at least show a little appreciation," I admonish her. "I've just invested a small fortune in your health and well-being."

"Serves you right for antagonizing Nazis."

Her outburst stops me in my tracks. "Do I understand you correctly, Morgan?" I say. "I'm responsible for you being attacked because I didn't let some Neanderthal beat Little John to death? Do you really believe letting bullies have their way makes the world safer for any of us? If you believe any of that hooey, your fancy school has failed you badly. Your brain is not fully functional. Your sensory systems may be first-rate but you don't process reality worth a damn."

I'm fully prepared to go on, but Morgan looks broken-hearted and tears are streaming down her face. A tsunami of shame shuts me up. I bend down, and hug her. She tries to pull away, but she's trapped in the chair and I hold tight. I whisper apologies in her ear and feel her hot tears on my neck. I feel like a bully anyway, but when we break the hug and I see the accounts clerk staring at me, open-mouthed, I really feel like a bully.

I put my hands on Morgan's and say, "I love you.

Morgan nods, her face still sad.

"Ophelia's looking forward to having you over," I say as we head for the exit.

"I want to go home," Morgan says.

I start to answer then stop, wondering what she means by "home." She reads my thoughts.

"I want to go to your place," she says. "Actually, I want to go to the café and be among people for a change."

"My place is our place," I say. "But thanks for clarifying. Your doctor advised rest, so no work today. Sorry."

Morgan insists on staying at our home. I relent and settle for a compromise. Morgan will stay at the apartment, for now, but she'll move in with Ophelia at the first sign of trouble. Our plan explodes before we even get home. Butch calls to report that Janet and Marvin have quit. They were followed to work again this morning and they quit on the spot.

The news knocks all the energy out of me. My pep talk to Janet and Marvin was good for twenty-four hours of loyalty. Now, I have a critical staff shortage—those two, and Little John is on bed rest for another day or two. I have to go in. I can't stay with Morgan as I had planned and I can't leave Morgan home alone. I break the bad news to her that she'll have to stay with Ophelia after all.

"No," she says. "I can come with you and do light work. You need the help. The shift will be over in a couple of hours anyway."

She has a point. I direct the cabbie to the café.

The staff of BeatNikki's gathers in the entertainment room. They have questions about their safety so I called this meeting.

Little John has come in for the meeting. He's surrounded by our anxious staffers. They're concerned for his health, and they look to him for leadership. He has assured me that he'll hold off on any resignation until this crisis is over, which is good news because if he quits there's a good chance I'll lose everyone or close to it.

I call the meeting to order and Little John joins me. Our first announcement is that he's back and glad to be here. The applause and cheers are heartfelt and make me wonder if I would rate as much love.

Then I announce we're going to start closing after the lunch service, at three o'clock in the afternoon. It's just temporary, until the Nazi crisis passes. This way, we don't have to hire replacement staff right away, and our people will be able to come and go more safely in daytime hours when there are more people on the streets than at night. I make sure everyone has their pepper spray and thank one and all for their loyalty. I see no enthusiasm on anyone's face, though. When I stop, they're quiet. It takes a few seconds before they break into small groups, talking among themselves. Morgan has joined Little John and two others. No one talks to me.

Alan stops in when I'm taking my afternoon break. I serve him one of Little John's experimental concoctions, a whimsical blend of fruit, tea, chocolate and goodness knows what else, with an umbrella on top. I send Alan to a table and ask Little John to join us.

As we walk to the table, Little John asks, "So it's true? This is the new beau?"

I flash a playful frown and quip, "That implies there was an old beau."

I introduce Little John and Alan and we sit down.

"Alan," I start, "I wanted Little John to hear this from you. What do you think BeatNikki's Café is worth, lock, stock, and barrel?"

Alan's eyes round in surprise. "Well," he says, recovering, "I don't know about the business, but the property is worth a lot."

"What would you pay for the business and the building if they had to be purchased together?"

"I don't know why you'd sell the business, too, Nikki," he says. "For me, personally, I'm a developer. I'd probably offer something upwards of a million for the property, but I'd write off the business."

Alan makes a little speech about how he'd love to buy the property and suggests Little John and I could relocate the business and cash in on the customer equity we have in the café. When he's done, I tell Little John we can talk about all this later. He smiles, shakes hands with Alan, and gets back to work.

I watch him leave, then shift my gaze to Alan's handsome face and sip my tea. It has been quite a twenty-four hours. I've given my body to a capitalist, a piece of my mind to my daughter, and a bald-faced bribe to my business partner.

Morgan and I are packed into a rush hour L-train. It's six o'clock and hordes of commuters are heading for home or their favorite bar. The car is hot and humid and there's a vague aroma of human bodies and perspiration hanging in the air. We're both standing and grasping a pole in the aisle near one of the exit doors. As I look about, a fellow passenger exhales through his mouth and showers me in sour breath. I turn away. At least I don't have to worry about Morgan falling and hitting her head. We're packed so tight you couldn't fall to the floor even if you died.

Morgan and I share a glance. It's too crowded and noisy to talk, but she flashes a partial smile, as if to say she's being brave. A month ago she'd have been crying at the dehumanization of sharing an uncomfortable space with so many ninety-nine percenters.

The train stops at a station, and passengers shuffle off and on, briefly opening up space for us to see people who were previously hidden in the crowd. As the train jostles out of the station, bodies weave and stagger and I catch a glimpse of the Nazi bastard I confronted at the bus stop, the one who followed Janet and Marvin. I lean close to Morgan's ear and ask her if he's the one who attacked Little John and her.

"I don't know," she says. "I don't remember him having those tattoos, but I could be wrong about that."

She takes a second look. "But I think I've seen this guy before. I think I've seen him on the L before." My blood starts to boil but I try to focus on making a plan.

We ease our way toward the other end of the car, away from

the thug. I keep it slow, so it just looks like we're moving to less crowded spaces. We stop a few feet from the door. "That's the man who's been following Janet and Marvin," I tell Morgan. I move my lips close to her ear so I don't have to yell to be heard.

"At the next stop, we're going to let everyone get off and everyone get on, then we bolt off the train," I tell Morgan. "Smile, like I just told you you're getting a pony for Christmas, okay?"

She smiles. She understands the game.

"The trick is to time our exit so we don't make the doors reset because that would give him enough time to get off, too."

Morgan nods and flashes her happy smile again.

"When I say go, go like a bat out of hell," I continue. "If someone's in your way, push them aside."

Morgan grins cheerily. "No more Miss Personality awards for me."

In spite of myself, I smile back. When the kid's not having a snit fit, she's really funny and bright.

The plan works. Morgan bolts when I give the word and it turns out she's a natural born tunnel rat in a crowd. She sifts between bodies leaving a gap just wide enough for me to wedge through, and I follow her off the car onto the platform. The doors slide shut behind us. We pivot to watch the train leave the station. The goon glares at us through the window of the rear door. He didn't quite make the cut. I control the urge to smirk, but Morgan raises a middle finger and yells, "Fuck you, Adolf."

I can't decide whether to admonish her for her language or for antagonizing a knuckle-dragging ape who's already violent. "I think we could have done without you baiting him," I say.

"Well, duh," she says, "if that's the guy who's been following Janet and Marvin, yesterday you told him he was stupid and you were going to do terrible things to him if he didn't stop. What's one more middle finger and a 'fuck you' more or less?"

I shrug. "Okay, but you can cross Miss Congeniality off your honors list, too."

When we get to the street, I get directions to a hardware store and purchase a hammer. I treat us to a cab ride home. In between text exchanges with her friends, Morgan asks me what the hammer's for.

"Home improvement," I tell her.

Blythe is having a good day when we call after dinner. She's alert and her voice is stronger. Morgan talks to her first. I wander into the kitchen and take care of dishes to give her some privacy. Ten minutes later, Morgan brings me the phone and takes over kitchen cleanup.

"This is an impressive first," Blythe greets me. "You two calling me together? Have you bonded?"

"I hope so," I say. "But I don't feel confident about anything. A Nazi goon who's been following some of my staff people followed us on the L tonight. We don't know if he's the same one who attacked Morgan and Little John, but I'm not taking any chances."

"What are you going to do?" asks Blythe. I can hear the concern in her voice.

"I'm going to take care of it," I say. "Morgan can stay with Ophelia for a while. She'll be safe there."

"I don't like the sound of this, Nick," she says.

"It's Nikki," I say.

"I'm sorry. Nikki. Please tell me you aren't going to shoot that man."

"Absolutely not," I say. "I hate guns. I wouldn't have one in the house."

"Or commit any other act of violence," she adds.

"I'm not going to let anyone hurt our daughter ever again," I say.

"Talk to the police, Nikki," Blythe says.

186

"I did that. They told me the guy wasn't breaking any laws following people."

Blythe frets and stews. "You could get yourself killed. Or thrown in jail. Who would take care of Morgan then?"

I chuckle. "It's tempting to imagine Morgan and Granny— excuse me, Grand-mere—trying to coexist."

I can hear Blythe's breathy laugh. "Seriously, Nikki," she says.

"Seriously, Blythe, it's going to be okay. Whether or not something happens to me, you're going to beat this cancer and you're going to be there for her."

Blythe sighs. "I pray for that every day and night, but let's not kid ourselves. It would take a miracle."

"You're due for a miracle," I say. Not that I believe in miracles. But I know medicine is an inexact science and sometimes people who shouldn't recover do. I think Blythe has the mental strength and the motivation to be one of those people.

23

Ophelia picks up Morgan at five o'clock in the morning, an hour that Morgan has gotten used to, but not one that fits Ophelia's lifestyle. She looks ten years older than her usual self, partly because she skipped the makeup and the carefully selected outfit, and partly because she's operating on half a night's sleep which has left her with deep creases in her face and bags under her eyes.

"I feel like I'm dead," she complains when I walk Morgan to the car. "You owe me, Nikki. You both owe me. Morgan, you can give me a cup or two of your youth. Nikki, it's going to be an arm or a leg. I'll let you know."

She motors off before I can summon a comeback or thank her.

Back inside, I set my mind to dressing. Like Ophelia, I always put a lot of thought into my daily outfits. Usually, I'm focused on shapes that flatter my figure, and color combinations that project my spirit and mood. Today is different. Today, I need to fly under the radar. I need to be one of those unremarkable people no one notices and no one remembers. I choose nondescript blue jeans, a baggy gray Cubs sweatshirt over a summer tank top and a pair of older black Nike walkers. I pull my hair back in a bun. I'm not wearing makeup and the sweatshirt makes my breasts less obvious. From straight-on in front, it's hard to tell if I'm a boy or a girl. From the side, I look somewhat more feminine—more butt than a boy and more chest, but neither feature is as obviously feminine as I'd like under normal circumstances. Today isn't normal, of course, so I swallow my vanity and proceed with the plan.

I sip coffee as I transfer the essentials from my purse into a bag that can be worn like a backpack or carried like a shopping bag. The last item I put in the bag is the hammer I bought yesterday. It's a wooden-handled model with a sixteen-ounce head—the cheapest one in the store. I sling the bag over one shoulder and check myself in the mirror. Not bad. I could pass for an older student, or maybe a teacher, carrying books to school, androgynous enough for one casual bystander to describe me as a male, and another as a female.

My heartbeat picks up when I walk to the L station. I don't feel fully committed to following through with this plan, but every step I take brings me closer to the moment I have to either do it or run—and spend the rest of my days looking over my shoulder.

The morning is dewy with soft rays of sun bringing warmth to my skin and lighting up the neighborhoods in the pastel colors of dawn. The humidity is still at a comfortable level and the morning breezes are just waking to the whisper stage. At this hour of the morning, I won't see another pedestrian until I get closer to the L station. It's like walking in an urban wilderness that belongs only to me. Getting up this early has disadvantages, but these dappled moments are a huge reward. I take deep breaths and try to soak in the perfect setting. It's not easy. My mind constantly shifts to the plan, and all the things that can go wrong with it.

My plan falls apart when I get to the L station. There are a dozen or so early commuters on the platform, but my terrorist isn't among them. I'm surprised and disappointed. His method is to follow his victims to work and follow them home. That's what he did with Janet and Marvin and I expected him to do the same with me today. I was up until midnight studying Google Earth for places to lead him, somewhere far from my home and far from my café, a place that probably wouldn't have CCTV cameras recording things that happened on the street. But he's not here. What a waste of time and energy and angst.

I get on the southbound train and take one of the many open seats in the car. I stare idly out the window opposite me and try to come up with an idea for dealing with the Nazi. It takes just a few minutes before I realize the Nazi might be terrorizing someone else on the staff. Maybe one of the ladies. Maybe Little John. He returned to work yesterday. He'd be a great target. My blood runs cold. I text him with a warning. I'll follow up with a call when I get off the train.

At the stop before mine, the car begins to fill up. I stand so someone else can sit, and cling to one of the poles near the door. My eyes are fixed on the door because it's a safe place to stare and my mind is still trying to invent a way to get rid of the Nazi. I don't think of myself as a violent person, but sometimes there's just no other way. Like with the man who assaulted me when I was transitioning. My mind begins to fill with images of that showdown, a brutal and violent confrontation that felt good at the moment of inception but plays poorly in my recollection. His was a hate crime. My crime was revenge, but it was fueled by hate, and when my memory replays the gore and the groans and whimpers of agony I want to vomit and bathe and think about sun-drenched prairies covered with wildflowers and tall grasses. It doesn't work.

I blink and change my line of sight to rid myself of that terrible vision. I scan the passengers on the car again. Almost immediately, my eyes focus on the leering countenance of my Nazi nemesis. His shaved head glistens in the morning sun. His tattoos seem somehow more plentiful in the morning light, maybe because he's standing just eight or ten feet away on a subway car still lightly populated with early morning commuters. I hadn't noticed the tats on his neck before. I will myself not to look him in the eye, but I do anyway. As soon as I catch his eyes, he sneers, his face as repulsive as a bucket of snakes. Fear shoots through my body. My breathing gets shallower, my chest tightens. I have goosebumps on my arms and my hair feels like it's standing on end. I try to decide where to get off the train. Maybe head for one of the Loop stops and lose myself in the crowd?

But when the doors open for my regular stop, I get off, my phone in one hand and my bag over my shoulder. Better to stay in familiar territory, I think. The phone is set up to speed dial 9-1-1, not that I can expect much help from the police while I'm still among the living. I take the escalator down to the street level and glance back. My Nazi follows about twenty feet back. When I glance at him, he smiles like a giant cockroach eying a crumb of moldy cheese. He scares me stiff, but his disrespect pisses me off, too. He thinks I'm weak, easy prey, a sniveling queer whom he can abuse at will because polite society doesn't care much about my particular kind of minority.

As I make my way toward the café, the anger overtakes me. I glance back a few times. He's trailing me by thirty feet now. Very few people are motoring by at this early hour, and even fewer are walking. He waves when I look back, that same sneering expression on his face. He thinks I'm going to curl up and die when he attacks, whenever he decides to get down to the serious business of beating or killing me. I'm so furious I could attack him now, but I make myself form a plan.

I take a roundabout route to the café that passes a construction site. It's a massive, dusty bit of landscape where they're getting ready to build some sort of mid-rise building. If I'm lucky, they won't have installed security cameras yet, but even if they have, I'll be a vague—vaguely—male blur. I'll take my chances. I glance back at Mr. Nazi. He's thirty feet back now, strolling like a tourist, not a care in the world. He knows I'm going to BeatNikki's and he can catch up to me any time he wants.

I hug the wall of an apartment building that borders the construction site and pray the pedestrian gate in the security fence still has a gap wide enough for a person to walk through. It does. I hang a fast right turn and dart through the gate. Mr. Nazi sees me turn, but the apartment building obscures his view of the construction site—and me. An office trailer occupies that corner of the site, and I scurry to the shelter of its far side. I can picture the Nazi trotting now, surprised and maybe alarmed by my disappearance. I tuck myself behind the back of the trailer, throw my phone in my bag, and pull out the hammer. Then I crouch and wait.

I hear his footfalls. He's coming fast, not the slightest caution, no inkling that his prey might be setting a trap for him. When he reaches the edge of the trailer, I pivot out to greet him, still in my crouch.

I almost screw it up. I expected him to hug the long wall of the trailer, but he's farther away from the trailer than I thought he'd be and I'm already starting my swing. To hit him at this distance, I have to use one hand instead of two on the hammer, and even after I extend my arm as far as it goes, I could miss him. His face registers surprise, shock, and amazement when he sees me. His eyes widen and his mouth opens. His momentum carries him forward even as he watches my weapon arc toward his leg.

The long reach and the weight of the hammer throw me off balance. I drop to one knee to avoid falling over. The hammer almost misses him entirely, but the head manages to clip his kneecap. My head explodes with fear because the contact is so slight, but to my amazement, he drops to the ground screaming and holding his knee. I stand over him and slam the hammer down on his ribs, once, twice, three times, working feverishly, knowing I have to disable him because if he recovers he can overwhelm and kill me in seconds.

The blows to his torso feel like they're breaking ribs which is the objective, but the thud of my hammer on his body also makes me want to vomit. He curls into a fetal position, then rolls onto his back, groaning and screaming, holding up his hands in a defensive posture.

"No! Stop! Please! Please no! I'm an actor!" He waves his hands frantically, even though the motion makes him wince in pain. "Honest. I was hired to scare you. I've never hurt anyone!"

I drop the hammer to my side. I don't believe him, but his explanation is so weird it makes me pause.

"Honest," he says through the gritted teeth of pain. "These tattoos, they're fake. They wash off. The shaved head, fake. It's from a costume shop. Go ahead, feel it."

Keeping the hammer poised, I touch his head with my other hand. I can feel softness underneath. Looking closer, I can see where the seam of the scalp piece meets his forehead.

"What the hell?" I say.

"A guy hired me. Just to follow people who work at that coffee shop," the Nazi says. "It was just to scare you."

"Who hired you?"

"Some guy who works for a guy," he grunts.

I don't try to hide my doubts about his veracity.

"I think they want you to sell the business."

That takes all the wind out of my sails. I stand up, almost dizzy with realization, the hammer dangling at my side. I believe him because it makes so much sense. And my next thought is, could it be Alan doing this to me? It hits me like a cannonball. Of course. He plays the good cop, seducing me, playing on the emotions of an oversized, sex-starved transwoman, getting my head focused on true love at last and the miracle of multiple-orgasm trysts, while a paid employee picks up where the real Nazi left off, keeping the fear and pressure on me and my staff until I have to close the business and sell the building. And who would I sell to? Mr. Climax Producer, of course.

Anger and hurt flood my mind.

"Can I get up?" the actor asks.

I glance at him. He's still in pain.

"Can you?" I ask. "Physically, I mean. Can you get up?"

He struggles. "I may need help. You're not going to hit me again, are you?"

"Not unless you attack me," I say.

I offer a hand. He shakes his head. "Give me a minute," he says. He groans as he tries to push himself up onto his hands and knees. Pain overtakes him and he lies down again, on the side I didn't attack with the hammer. "I think I have broken ribs."

"Probably," I say. I'm feeling guilty. He looks pitiable, lying there. "Want me to call a cab?" I pull out my phone and put the hammer back in the bag.

"You want to pay for it?" he grunts. "I don't have insurance. I'm a fucking actor." He struggles to his hands and knees again. His pain is so acute I can feel it, too.

"Jesus," he swears, "you really fucked me up. Let me guess, you used to be a Navy SEAL?"

"No," I say. "I'm just a garden variety queer who got beat up once too often."

He struggles onto his knees. The pain of moving flashes across his face. He grunts and yips. I can't figure out how to help him without making the pain worse. I offer him a hand to hold when he tries to stand. He eyes it, starts to reach for it, then collapses to his hands and knees again, coughing, grunting, moaning in pain.

"I don't think I can lift my hand that high," he says. "Even if I could, the pain of pulling on one side of my body would kill me. You really fucked me up."

"Sorry," I say. I mean it. I feel like such a bully, even though he's bigger and younger and much stronger than me.

"Are you sorry enough to call me an ambulance?" he asks.

"Can you pay for an ambulance?" I ask back.

"No." He shakes his head in despair. "I'm fucked."

"I'll call an Uber," I say. "I'll put up the first twenty dollars and you can go to a hospital or go home or whatever you want to do."

While we wait for the driver, he gives me his name—Rudolph, as in Valentino—and the name of the man who hired him. "Bob" could have been a phony name. He was in his twenties and wore an expensive suit and conducted himself like a hotshot who knew the secrets of the universe. Rudolph's description has me picturing a junior genius on the staff of a real estate developer, making more money than he ever thought possible and equating the money with brilliance, and doing his master's bidding without a second thought about ethics or morality. For some reason, I can't picture "Bob" working for Vernon I. Gibbs. Gibbs is an asshole of the first order, but I can't see him orchestrating this. And for some reason, I *can* picture Alan doing it.

Morgan and Little John confront me as soon as I enter the café. Little John's face is furrowed with worry. What surprises me is that Morgan's face is just as worried. She's shown glimpses of affection now and then, but this concern for my well-being comes out of the blue and sends a charge of warmth through my body.

"Where were you?" Morgan starts. "We were really worried."

"We were ready to call the police," says Little John.

"Glad you didn't," I say.

Something in my tone changes their expressions from worry to disapproval.

"What did you do?" Morgan asks.

"I made a few home improvements," I say. "Actually, I think I improved things here, too."

"Please tell me you didn't do violence on that man," says Little John. His face changes into a macho scowl.

"I took care of the situation," I say. I don't want to say anything else in case the heroic detective Brooks or some competent member of the police force should come calling. If Little John and Morgan don't know anything, they won't have to say something that could incriminate me. But neither of them looks like they're going to accept my stonewalling.

"You killed him, didn't you?" says Morgan. "With that hammer, right?"

"Nikki?" Little John's reproval cuts off my denial before I can utter it.

"Let's get to work," I say. "We have a business to save."

Morgan stares daggers at me, as if the fake Nazi was her best friend.

24

When I close the door to my office, Alan tries to kiss me. He's a gentleman about it, his hands soft on my arms, turning me slowly to him, bringing his lips toward mine, his eyes closed. I put my fingers between our lips before they can meet.

"We need to talk," I say. I gesture for him to sit down, and take my place on the other side of the desk. "Have you heard from Rudolph yet?" I ask.

Alan looks confused. "Rudolph?"

"I guess not," I say. "He's the guy your guy hired to stalk me and my people and scare me into selling."

"What?" Alan's good at this. Either that, or he's innocent. What a kick in the head that would be. I'd love to sit back in my chair and put my feet up on the desk, like when I was a hotshot junior exec. Instead, I remain ladylike, keeping my back straight and my tummy pulled in, leaning forward to put my elbows on the desk, all the while staring at him, looking for a tell of some kind. A facial tic. Moving his eyes from mine. A nervous smile. Alan just looks back, holding my gaze, his face open and friendly.

"Nikki?" he says. "What's going on?"

He's the only loving lover I've ever had and he looks as innocent as a choirboy, with his blue eyes wide and his soft lips forming words that I barely hear because I want so badly to have those lovely lips caressing mine. I want to say it's all a mistake and I want to have him come over tonight and run his beautiful hands all over my body and insert himself into me, locking us together as one organism, sighing and petting. I can see him making love to me and I can feel his body on mine even as I stare at his face here in my office, even as he blinks and averts his eyes.

"Will you at least tell me what this is about?" he asks. His eyes come back to mine, but it's too late. It's not that he broke the stare, it's how he did it. It's his body language, the awkwardness he shows in looking me in the eye again. He's guilty. I have a choice. I can let him off the hook and maybe have another night of hot sex, or I can confront him. I sigh and call up Alan's corporate website on the office computer. I click on "Meet the Staff" and scroll down to the profile of Robert Bart. He's a twenty-something with a cocky smile and loud tie, listed just below the company's top officers and just above the office staff. He's someone on his way up. I pivot the screen around so Alan can see it.

"He said his name was Bob when he hired an actor named Rudolph to stalk my staff, and Morgan and me, dressed up like a neo-Nazi to terrorize us."

I say my lines sadly. I'm grieving. I've been grieving since I pulled this page up and saw Robert Bart's image, all decked out in a Brooks Brothers suit and a shirt and tie that cost enough to rebuild a hurricane-ravaged house in Puerto Rico. And the smile that was almost a sneer, the perfect stereotype of the meat-eating young capitalist who's tasted success and glory and buckets of money and just knows he's destined to rule the world and if everyone was like him there'd be no poverty. I know, because that's about what I would have looked like at the same age, before my secret eked out, before my need to release my inner woman became a compulsion I couldn't deny.

Alan looks at the screen, shakes his head slightly, looks back at me.

"Robert's a good kid," he says. "He works like a dog to put together deals and he's been very successful. I can't believe he'd want to harm you or anyone here. Really, he's a good kid."

Yes, Alan is really good at this. It would be so easy to go along with him. Why not? It's over. He's not going to do that again anyway. I could have my lover, at least until he gave up on buying my building. But one thing about coming to grips with your gender identity, you learn that the truth's the truth. You can try to run from it or ignore it, but you can't get away from it. It stalks you like an unrelenting cop, especially unpleasant truths, like having the body of a linebacker and the mind of a cheerleader. Like having a lover who is perfect in every way except he's just fucking you to acquire your possessions.

"The actor's name is Rudolph," I say. "He's a big, burly guy. When he puts on one of those things that makes you look bald and a bunch of fake tattoos and biker clothes, he looks like the Fuhrer of all neo-Nazidom." I pause for a moment and turn the screen back to face me. "Your boy Bob is probably getting a phone call from him just about now, wanting some help with medical expenses."

"What?" Alan almost keeps his innocent face intact, but there's a tiny break in his voice and his eyes widen just a hair as he processes the fact that his queer girlfriend has probably administered a serious beating to his hired goon. You can't blame him for flinching. In the newspaper business they'd call that a man-bites-dog story.

"You don't have to keep bluffing, Alan," I say, my voice calm and level. "I'm not going to bring charges. I just wish you'd be honest with me. It's bad enough to realize how awful it must have been for you making love with me, treating me like a lady, taking me to nice places. At least now you could just be honest. You wanted the building. You didn't think anyone would get hurt."

I stop for a moment, to see if he has anything to say. He stares at me. "I don't know where this is coming from," he says.

"Rudolph is probably telling Bob I almost killed him," I say. "He's not exaggerating. I was all set to plant a sixteen-ounce hammer head in that man's skull, because I thought he was the Nazi who beat my daughter and Little John damn near to death. Do you understand that you almost got a man killed and me maybe serving time? Just for another building? Jesus Christ, Alan, you already own half the real estate in Chicago! Are you so desperate for another project you'd sacrifice lives?"

Alan stands up. "I don't know what you're talking about, Nikki. I'm crazy about you. I love being with you. Socially. Sexually. I don't know anything about any violence. I'll talk to Robert, but I'm sure he doesn't know anything about any of this either. I'd like to put our relationship back together, but you'll have to let me know about that."

He opens the door and leaves. I watch him weave through the tables, the cuffs of his suit pants falling precisely just above the heels of his priceless shoes, his footfalls strong and steady and as quiet as a big cat's. He exits the café with the nonchalance of a man who just dropped off his laundry. I should be furious but instead I feel a cloud of sadness descend on me with the weight of an anvil.

"What is it with you?" Morgan's words burst out of the watery air like so much heat lightning. We've been walking in silence for several blocks. The hot day has turned into a sweltering night; the temperature is still well above ninety and if the humidity gets any higher the whole city will be a lake. I glance at Morgan. Tiny beads of perspiration collect along her hairline. Her sleeveless blouse is splotched with wet spots. Her face is furious.

"What?"

"You look like a hooker, Nikki."

"Is that a compliment?" I ask. I'm not in the mood for her histrionics. It's been an awful day and it's not going to get any better for a long time to come.

"Do you like having every creepy old man we pass stare at your big fat fake boobs?"

I know she's upset about her mother dying and the violence she's suffered and she's taking it out on me, but she's hitting me in my most vulnerable place. Am I real? In deference to the heat, I took off the blouse I wore over this tank top before we left the café. The tank top was pretty revealing when it was dry. Now, moistened by perspiration, it leaves little to the imagination. On the other hand, quite a few other women are similarly clad. You'd be insane to wear anything more than you have to in this weather.

"How much did they cost?" Morgan's still talking about my breasts.

"Shut up, Morgan," I snap. "Just shut up!" We descend into a surly silence for several minutes, while I get control of myself. "What's really bothering you, Morgan?" I ask. We're a block from the apartment and I'm coming to grips with the fact that I have some parenting to do.

"Oh, gosh, Nikki, let me think." If sarcasm was money, she could buy the city. "My mother's dying. I've been beaten unconscious. My father's a flaming queer who just tried to kill someone with a fucking hammer. Shall I go on?"

I hold my temper for several steps, willing myself to silence rather than an equally sarcastic retort. I take a deep breath. Another.

"I'm sorry your life is so difficult. Really. I am." I put a hand on her arm and stop us. We face each other. "I'm heartbroken

201

about your mom," I say. "Dealing with that Nazi the way I did probably wasn't the smartest option." I take her hand in mine and we begin walking again, slowly. "But understand, as long as I'm alive, no one will get away with trying to do you harm. Whether I'm a flaming queer or an emancipated woman, I'm your parent and I love you and I won't let anyone or anything threaten you ever again."

"Did you kill him?" Her voice is low.

"No," I say. "But I could have."

"You need to work on that," says Morgan.

"Oh?" I'm confused. "Be more efficient at killing?"

Morgan forces a smile. "No, Nikki. You need more self-control. What am I going to do if Mom dies and you're in prison?" I turn to look at her in time to see the tears running down her face, and I finally realize what she realizes: whatever else she thinks of me, I'm all she's got. I think about that for a moment. She'd have her lemon-sucking grandmother, of course, the meanest bitch in all right-wing Christendom, but Morgan's saying she'd rather tough it out with me. Not everyone in the world would consider that a compliment, but in my little world, it's a good enough reason to strike up the band and fire the cannons.

"I don't want to wake her." Morgan's grandmother sounds almost human when she says it, like she did the last time we spoke, no insults or tantrums. That makes me worry.

"Is she okay?" I ask.

"She's sleeping," the old lady says. She's hedging, trying to keep the bad news from Morgan. As if Morgan didn't know her mother was dying.

"You might as well tell me how she really is," says Morgan. It dawns on me that she probably appreciates my candor with her after her Granny's guarded secrecy.

"Is it okay with you, Nick?" she asks. She's trying to be courteous, and even when she tries, she can't keep from being a bigot.

"Her name is Nikki," says Morgan. "And you don't need her permission."

I'm starting to comprehend the world as Morgan sees it, and that crabby old lady and I will soon be the last family connections Morgan has in the world. And considering that I'm a middle-aged, gender variant woman with a penchant for beating the crap out of large, angry men, perhaps I should be a bit less judgmental and a tad more generous in my assessment of Blythe's mother, starting with an end to my insulting nicknames for her. I resolve to use her proper name from now on. Virginia Bascomb. Or Grandmother. I can't do Grand-mere, I'll choke.

"She's very weak," says Virginia. "We're trying to get her strong enough to go home."

Morgan sobs on the other line.

"She wants to die at home," the old woman says, her own voice breaking.

I'm pacing in the living room and I can see Morgan in her bedroom, sitting on her bed, doubled over in sorrow, her body racking with sobs. Her phone lies unattended on the bed beside her. My heart breaks.

"Would there be a good time for us to call back?" I ask as I walk into Morgan's room.

"It's unpredictable," Morgan's grandmother says. "I'll call you, if you want."

If I wasn't so worried about Morgan I'd faint at the utter compassion of her offer.

"Better make the call to Morgan," I say. "She'll link us up."

We sign off and I sit next to Morgan and throw my arms around her. She fits her face in the niche between my cheek and shoulder and cries. It's a good cry with lots of wet tears and she doesn't try to muffle the sobs and the little wailing sounds that accompany the tears of the truly heartbroken. After a while, she lets go of me, and sits up straight. She rubs her eyes and wipes away her tears.

"I can't believe it's happened so fast. A month ago I had a mom. I had a house. I had friends. Now, all I've got is you and Granny."

She doesn't mean this as an insult, and I don't take it as one.

"I was thinking that, too," I say. "Your grandmother and I represent two distant branches of the definition of the word 'bitch.'" Morgan forces a smile. "If you're going to call me Nikki, maybe, to be fair, you should start calling her Grand-mere or at least Grandmother, even behind her back."

Morgan makes a face. She's still mourning, but she's playing along with the humor.

"Okay," I say. "I'm trying to think of her as Virginia Bascomb. You could try that. Grandmother Virginia. Grandmother Bascomb. Lots of syllables in those names. It might help keep your bee-stung lips soft and supple as you get older."

Morgan laughs, short and quiet, but genuine. A good sign.

Neither of us feels like cooking, so we set out on foot for a local diner that Morgan favors.

"Maybe for dessert we should go to Chaya's Tea House," I suggest. We haven't been back since the night of the attack there.

"That would be nice," Morgan says.

"You know," Morgan says, "the man who hit that customer at Chaya's, that wasn't the man you beat up."

"No," I agree.

"And the man who beat up Billy at the beauty salon, that wasn't the man you beat up, either. Or the man who attacked me and Little John."

"No," I say. "He was an actor, only trying to scare us."

"So the real bad guy is still out there. Or bad guys."

"It's a sobering thought," I say. In truth, I hadn't really

thought about it. There's something about almost killing a man that really closes down my latent macho aggression. "Be sure to carry your pepper spray at all times." I'm not sure what else to say.

Morgan reaches into the pocket of her shorts and shows me the can. "Maybe we should get me a hammer, too," she says. She forces a smile so I'll know it's a joke. She's starting to pick up my graveyard humor. I start singing the words to the song *If I Had a Hammer*. Against all odds, Morgan knows the words too. We sing together, Morgan's voice clear and on key, mine awful, but artfully broadcast to be overwhelmed by hers.

25

The mood in the café is morose. Morgan navigates the world in a body that almost sags with sadness and a face befitting a widow on the morning after her loved one's death. She plods along like her feet are clad in concrete blocks. She tries to smile and converse, but the effort saps her energy. I understand this is a necessary process. I feel it, too, though my many years of banishment from Blythe's world reduce the sting. I give her space.

Little John reacts differently to stress, darting around the shop edgy and angry. Everything pisses him off. The pushy customers. The slow-moving staff. Me. There's so much tension in here it feels like the whole place would blow up if someone lit a match. When I can't take it anymore, I sidle up to him and throw an arm around his shoulders. "Let's talk," I say. He frowns but follows me to the office.

"What?" he says when we sit down.

"No fair, I wanted to ask you first," I say. My attempt at levity falls flat. I've never seen him so glum and stone-faced. "What's bugging you, Little John?"

"Everything." Little John throws his hands up in the air. "Janet and Marvin aren't coming back. They've had enough. Which means we'll lose more staff. Friends. And we'll have to recruit newbies and train them and some of them will be jerks and we'll have to fire them and start the cycle again. And Morgan's living a private hell right now and no one can help her. I'm so jumpy I look over my shoulder every five seconds expecting to see a skinhead crackpot as big as a mountain coming down on me with a baseball bat. I can't sleep. Coming in here is like returning to a nightmare. I'm scared to death, Nikki."

"But Little John," I object, "I took care of that situation."

"You took care of one Nazi," says Little John. "There are lots of other ones still out there, including the monster who attacked Morgan and me."

"Hopefully, they've all moved on to other targets," I say. "They don't like brown or Black people, or Jews, either. And for the mob that worships Trump, there's something like eighty million liberals."

"Good theory," says Little John, "but I don't think it's working."

"What?" I look at him intently. There's something in his voice that tells me he knows something I don't.

"Remember the guy who attacked you and me?" Little John locks eyes with me. "The one you beat up? The thing that started all this?"

I nod. "And?"

"And someone who looks a lot like him was standing in the doorway of a store across the street last night when I closed up." Little John arches his eyebrows to add emphasis to what he said.

"I don't get it," I say. "He was probably waiting for a bus. People wait for buses all the time."

"This guy was almost a clone of the first one. Big, stupid looking. Younger than the first one. Maybe his little brother."

"Come on, Little John," I say. "Big and dumb describes half

207

the male population of Chicago."

"Well, at least three buses stopped there after I noticed him, and he didn't get on any of them." Little John's face creases with worry. "I don't think we can afford to take chances. I took a Lyft home last night. Had it pick me up in the alley. But I can't afford to do that every night. Or every morning."

"Is he there now?" I ask.

Little John shrugs. "I don't know. I haven't had the nerve to look."

After a moment, I say, "Okay, I'll take care of the bad guys; you take care of the shop."

Little John leans forward over the desk so our faces are just a couple feet apart. "I don't want any part of your vigilante act," he hisses. "And you aren't getting it. I'm afraid for my life. You're acting like we have a delivery problem with the coffee supplier and I'm telling you there are people who want to kill us. What makes you think a ten percent stake in this business is worth risking my life?"

"You talk about ten percent like it's peanuts." I can hear the anger in my voice and so can he. Good. "It's not ten percent, it's equity. You got a piece of a successful business without having to risk a dime of your own money, without having to face off with bankers and accountants. You didn't have to establish credit lines or open accounts, sign leases, deal with vendors. You didn't have to sweat the first day or the first month or wonder where in the hell the money was going to come from to pay the mortgage or the staff. Ten percent? You're an hourly worker anywhere else and you pay for your own Obamacare. Here you're on salary and your health insurance is subsidized by the company. And you make enough money to be a fucking Republican."

My slip into obscenities is a sign that I'm losing control. I shut up, take a deep breath, look away, take another deep breath until I can continue in a normal voice.

"We're the Israelis in 1967," I say. "We just want to live our

208

lives and enemies are massing at our borders to kill us because they don't want Jews as neighbors. We can give up and leave or fight for what's ours. I'm going to fight." I pause a moment, trying to decide whether to give voice to my next thought.

"Of course, I've always wanted to be Golda Meir." I manage to get the sentence said before laughing. Little John laughs, too.

"We're both Jews, Little John," I say. "I need you to take care of the shop so I can take care of the Nazis."

"I won't be a party to any violence," says Little John. "I'd rather run than go to prison."

"You won't be a party to anything I do," I tell him. "And relax, my first move will be to visit the local gendarmerie."

"Detective Brooks?" Little John's voice drips with disbelief.

"I'm desperate, not stupid," I say. "No, I'll find someone else. There must be some form of intelligent life there."

Sergeant Moore is attentive and sympathetic as I explain our situation. He's part of a hate crimes unit. He takes notes, and interrupts a few times to get specific times and places regarding recent incidents, and he probes for particulars about our encounters with Detective Brooks. I'm impressed he would give me the time.

"But you can't give me a description of this latest guy?" he asks, as the interview winds down.

"My partner can," I say. "And we'll try to get some photos of him if he keeps hanging out in the neighborhood."

Sergeant Moore nods thoughtfully. He's a middle-aged guy with a handsome face and a fringe of graying hair at his temples, a big man still in relatively good shape. He wears a uniform and he looks good in it.

"Okay," he says. "That's good. But Ms. Finch, please understand there's not much we can do. He hasn't committed a crime that we know of. I'll get that photo to our patrols so they can look out for the guy, and you can keep us on speed dial, but until he breaks the law, we can't do much else."

I thank him and issue an invitation to anyone in the department to stop in for a cup of coffee on the house.

"It's not a bribe," I tell him before he can object. "We'd all feel more secure to have some uniforms stop in from time to time. It might discourage our friendly white nationalist, too."

When I stand up to leave, he rises, too. He's being polite, but he appraises me physically while he's at it. My height sets him off. He's startled to realize I'm just as tall as he is. From there, his eyes move down my body: eyes, nose, mouth, chin, chest, waist, legs. I don't blame him. My outfit is tasteful, but it shows off my feminine attributes to good advantage. When I was a man, I checked out women the same way. I still do, but I'm more subtle about it and motivated more by curiosity than sexual assessment. He wishes me well and urges me to stay safe. As I walk to the exit, I wonder if he's watching my butt. It's one of my proudest possessions.

Morgan, Little John and I work the last evening shift with Butch. Tomorrow we start closing after the lunch run, but we had to stay open tonight because we have a live show booked. It makes for an endless day because we're so short-staffed.

The entertainment is a flamenco guitarist who has a strong following, so the place fills up by seven. We're running like wild horses to keep up with the orders—a good night for receipts and tips, but a hard night on our bodies and minds. I take a short break near the end of his first set and go outside for a few minutes, mostly to get some fresh air, but also to see if there are any hulking goons loitering in the area. There aren't.

I go back to work. Since Little John and Morgan are both

more efficient than I am at creating drinks, they're holding down the food and drink preparation and I'm part of the waitstaff. It's not a bad night to be a waitress. The guitarist's crowd is well-mannered and upscale. The tips are generous, most of the orders come with a "please" and are delivered to a "thank you," and several people have taken the time to tell me how much they like the café.

At the guitarist's next break, Butch intercepts me at the coffee bar to say one of his customers wants to say hello to me. I start to say no, but Butch stops me. "Please, Nikki," he says. "The guy is really insistent."

I follow him to a table occupied by a single male. He's a large man, young, with thick shoulders and a muscular chest shown off to good advantage by a T-shirt that fits him like a glove. A body builder, I think as I approach. Up close, he has a large head with buzz-cut hair and a lantern-jawed face. His default expression is a kind of sleepy arrogance, like he's the biggest, toughest guy in town and he can ignore everyone around him. Of course, that's just a genetic accident. Appearance, not reality. He's enjoying a flamenco guitarist. He's a man of culture who was given an unlikely body at birth, just as I was. On the other hand, I don't recognize him at all.

I greet him with a friendly smile and thank him for being here tonight. He smiles back but doesn't say anything and remains sitting.

"Butch says you wanted to say hello," I say, stopping the awkward silence. "Do we know each other?"

He shrugs and his smile shifts into more of an insolent smirk. "Got me," he says. "Do we?"

I can't tell if he's being deliberately rude or if he's one of those men who think they want to make it with a transwoman, then clutch when they get close to one. Either way, this is not an audience I want to extend.

"I don't think so," I say. "But thanks again for your patronage."

I turn to leave but he stops me. "Excuse me," he calls. When I turn back to him, he says, "Come on, don't you recognize me?"

I shake my head apologetically. "Sorry," I say.

"Think of someone a little bigger than me, a little older, lots of tats."

I shake my head again, but I'm starting to get the picture.

"Out back, by the alley?" the guy says. "All he wanted was a feel and maybe a blow job?"

My face flushes red and my hair feels like it's standing on end. My heart races. I scan the area with my peripheral vision in search of a weapon. There's a fork and a plastic plate on the next table. Throw the plate, stab with the fork, I think.

"Oho," he says. "You've made the connection. Congratulations. You're not as stupid as you look."

"It's time for you to leave," I say. I want him out of here without a scene. We've lost enough staff already, and we don't need to horrify our customers, either.

"Sure," he says. "I just wanted to say hello. That was my big brother. You blinded him in one eye and you got him sent up for another stretch. Parole violation. We'll be seeing more of each other."

He stands and walks casually to the exit. Butch calls to him about an unpaid check, but I put a hand on Butch's arm and tell him to forget it.

I work on autopilot for the rest of the show, my mind flaring and grinding about the eerie visitor and what to do about his implied threat. My body is on full alarm, my skin tingling with fear, my hearing alert to every sharp sound, my eyes darting around the room looking for thugs and hooligans. Amidst the flashes of outright fear and visions of horror at the kind of thuggery that man might perform, I wrestle with cold, logical assessments of my new nemesis. The most striking thing about him is how normal he looks. No swastikas or tattoos. No biker-gang jewelry. Even the arrogance of his face is something that could be as easily worn by a banker as a hoodlum. The other thing is, and I realize it with a start, he comes across as being intelligent, not like the moronic ape he claims as his brother. He speaks in complete sentences and he has the crisp, clear diction of an educated person. He doesn't stand out in a crowd. That makes him even more dangerous.

I fight back panic attacks and concentrate on my problem. I skim quickly past talking to the police. I've done that, and they can't help until he kills one of us. For me, the only rational action is offensive. I need to get him before he gets me. It won't be easy. In fact, it's probably impossible. He is way too powerful for me to confront directly, and probably too smart to be easily surprised. I think about acquiring a gun, a pistol maybe, a black market purchase that can't be traced to me. Or a knife, something that can be hidden until the last split second then delivered to the gut, maybe on a crowded sidewalk. My mind runs through hits I've seen on television and in movies. This isn't really helpful on a practical level. I'm not a gun or a knife person. I don't have access to poisons or know how to use them. These aren't much more than fantasies, but they get me through the rest of my work night without shaking uncontrollably or crying in public.

It's nearly ten o'clock by the time we close. I order a Lyft to take Morgan and me home. I don't bother with an alley pickup. Our new goon undoubtedly knows where we live, where we work, and most likely, what trains we take on which days. He probably knows everything about us and we know nothing about him except that he claims to be related to the evil moron I beat bloody back in May.

As we roll along the Chicago nightscape, I call Little John. "You're going to have to run the show for awhile," I tell him.

He's startled, and more than a little dismayed at having to run the café by himself while we're shorthanded. He wants to know why. "We've got trouble," I tell him tersely.

"Butch said you kicked someone out tonight."

213

"That's right," I say. "The baby brother of the guy who assaulted us out back. Probably the guy who attacked you and Morgan. He's not going to go away."

"Please don't say you're taking care of it, Nikki," he objects.

"You just keep our business going," I snap. "I'll keep us safe."

"Or die trying," he mutters.

"Yes."

Morgan turns her gaze from the stores and shops lining the street to peer at me, her face questioning.

"We're back to Plan B," I tell her. "Tomorrow, you'll go stay with Ophelia for a few days."

"It's that guy you were talking to, right?" Her face is animated. "Is he the guy Little John saw yesterday?"

I'm impressed at how much this kid picks up. They were churning out drinks and food so fast I can't imagine how she could find even a few seconds to look up and scan the room and find me talking to a customer.

"Yes," I say. I lower my voice. "And we're in danger. I'll explain when we get home."

We spend the rest of the ride with Morgan arguing to stay with me. Her protestations touch me deeply. She's still outwardly cool to me much of the time and she still resents me becoming a woman, but she wants to be with me now, even when it's dangerous.

26

Marcus Leonard is in his early thirties with dark African skin, braided hair, a handsome face with piercing eyes. He's a good six-two, with narrow hips and wide shoulders and he's clad in shorts and a T-shirt that reveal lean, ropy muscles in his arms and legs. He looks like a boxer, a cruiserweight, maybe, ready to go ten hard rounds with the best. Marcus teaches martial arts in a dojo in a South Loop neighborhood but he also provides a very private consulting business on the side—private as in, you have to be referred by a source he trusts, you pay with cash up front, and if you get in trouble he'll deny ever knowing you. My self-defense instructor sent me here. I'm Marcus's first transgender client and my peculiar blend of female and male characteristics has momentarily upset his poise, but he quickly recovers. He asks me what I want to achieve. I tell him I have a stalker problem, a neo-Nazi type who has threatened to hurt me and people I love.

"I'm here because I don't want to wait for him," I say. "I want to make the first move."

Marcus's eyes widen in surprise, and he smiles. "Okay," he says. "You understand, that's a different program than my classes."

"I know."

"It's cash up front, nothing written, nothing said after you leave the dojo."

"Yes."

"Okay," he says. "I'm going to ask you some questions about who you are and who he is. I'm going to get an idea of your capabilities. Then we'll work on some things. But first, before you give me the money, are you sure you can go through with it?"

I nod.

"You don't just beat up someone like this," he says. "They just come back at you, maybe with a bigger weapon, maybe with a mob. You have to stop him. Permanently."

I nod.

"Most people can't go that far," he says. "They think they can, but somewhere in the process, they nerve out."

I tell him about my self-defense class and taking down the Nazi behind my café.

Marcus studies me for a moment. "Killing's different than disabling. Most people can't do it. The worst outcome for you would be to go all the way through with this, right up to the kill shot, and not be able to finish the job. Think about that, because when you get that far and don't go through with it, you're going to die badly."

"I'm in," I say.

Ophelia calls as I step out of the shower. She picked up Morgan early this morning for a day of shopping and cavorting around Chicago. I wasn't expecting a call.

"Houston, we have a problem," she says. "Your white power pal has been following us this morning." Ophelia describes coming out of the ladies room at Water Tower Place and seeing our Nazi of the week staring at them. "There was no reason for him to be there," says Ophelia. "I asked Morgan if she knew him. She looked at him and pulled out her pepper spray. The kid has a way with words."

"Are you in danger?"

"No, honey," Ophelia says. "He's too smart to try something in a crowd and he's keeping his distance so we don't have grounds to call the police. But Nikki, this means he knew Morgan was with me today. That's trouble."

I take a deep breath and sit down. "Can you keep her safe for a day or two?"

"Of course," says Ophelia. "My condo has better security than the Pentagon. But Nikki, please don't do anything rash."

"Not rash, no," I say. "Just give me a couple days."

Ophelia objects. She asks what I'm planning but I dodge her questions. Where I'm heading, I have to go alone, and if I make it back, it's best if I'm the only one who knows what happened.

When we finish, I throw on a robe and go down in the basement to my storage area. I find the plastic-wrapped bag on a top shelf, back in a corner, dust-covered, as if it had been resting in this dark place for years and years. It has. I clean the outer surface and take it upstairs.

Inside the bag is a complete Halloween costume for a woman who wants to go to a costume party as a male Parisian painter, everything from black clothing to a beret to paint brushes and a palette. Those are but props to explain the rest of the package, should someone in law enforcement ever find it and begin asking questions.

The image staring back at me in the mirror makes me want to gag. My face is gone, the one I bought with money and endless hours of pain and worry, the one that finally came close to looking like the woman within me that no one could see. In its

217

place is a male face, camouflaged in facial hair, a Van Dyke goatee and moustache and side burns. My pretty blonde highlights and sculpted bangs are hidden beneath a mousy brown male wig that blends with the facial hair. My breasts are flattened by a compression garment that feels like a medieval torture device. It has taken just fifteen minutes to apply these features and just that fast I am transformed back to manhood. I look more like a man than I ever have looked like a woman. The sight makes me feel physically ill.

I look away from the mirror and block the male image of myself from my mind. I put on baggy jeans and a plain, baggy T-shirt, no logos. I complete the look with generic sneakers and dark-framed glasses that give me a nerdy, scholarly look.

I slip out the door and make my way to the L station and begin looking for my pet Nazi, but he's not here. I take the train to the stop nearest the café and check both sides of the platform for him. Nothing. I go down to the street level and scan the area but again, he's nowhere to be seen. I sigh. It would have been too easy picking him up this fast. I call Little John to see how things are going. He's still angry about being dumped on and risking his life. The staff is edgy and snappish, too. He vents for several minutes, then abruptly signs off.

"I have to get back to work," he says. "We're short-staffed. But everything's fine."

Instead of going home, I go to a couple of costume shops. I still get home well before rush hour and before any neighbors are there to see me and start asking questions.

I turn up the sidewalk to my building and let myself into my apartment. I barely have time to take a deep breath before I hear a sharp rap on the door. I look through the spy hole. It's Alan. Alan Campbell. Seeing him reminds me of what easy prey I've been.

My impulse is to open the door and share some unladylike epithets with him, but I catch myself and stand back. No need to answer. This is not a man who deserves that kind of consideration. Let him walk away thinking I'm not home.

Another knock.

I will myself to walk away, but I can't. I can still feel his arms around me. The memory of being seduced is burned in my mind. I try to focus on my fury at being used, but somehow what comes through is the sensation of his warm, hard torso on mine, his body covering mine like a second skin, feeling his heart beating, his breath in my ear, my mind fluttering, then flashing with lights of an arousal I've never felt before. I shake my head. I'm pathetic.

Another knock. "Nikki," he calls, "I know you're home. I saw you come in." He pauses for a moment. "Please, let's talk. I have something to say to you."

I'm frozen. His voice has drifted to my ears like a melody.

"Please, Nikki."

I remind myself he paid someone to terrorize me. I imagine him saying, *She's a fool. Scare the crap out of her. and go home and laugh. She's not really a woman. She's a man who wanted to sit down to pee.*

It helps. I'm focused on how he used me now, and how useless it made me feel.

"You'll never set foot in this house again," I yell through the door.

I want to say more but words don't occur to me.

"Let me apologize," he says. "Let me come in and give you a proper apology. I just want to apologize the way a man should apologize to a woman."

Calling me a woman is more powerful than hitting my erogenous zone in sex. And as he says it, I'm looking at his gorgeous face and seeing nothing but sincerity. I know better than to melt, but I do. I open the door.

Alan beholds me and freezes. I realize I'm still in my Nick presentation.

"Can I speak with Nikki?" he asks. He's staring at me as if he's wondering if I'm Nikki's new lover or a long-lost sibling.

It's too late for anything but honesty. "Come in," I say.

"Nikki?" He recognizes the voice. I nod and gesture for him to enter. "What's going on?" he asks as he brushes past me. "Are you—?"

"Nothing's going on," I tell him. "I like to cross-dress sometimes. It's not your business."

"Right," he says. He looks away for a moment, trying to regain his composure.

"What did you want to say?" I'm being cruel, pushing him like this. I understand what's going on with him. He came to apologize to a woman and now he's got to tell a six-foot dude wearing a beard and moustache that he loves him. I strike a male pose, arms crossed over a flat chest, the toilet-paper-crafted penis-bulge in my jeans more obvious.

"I want you to know—" he stops. "Do you do this very often?"

"None of your business," I say. "State your piece and go." There's something about thinking of myself as he sees me that brings out the latent male in me. As a man, I wouldn't have been attracted to Alan, so I can speak even more forcefully.

Alan stutters and stumbles. Pouring his heart out to a man has him off balance.

"It's my fault, Nikki," he says. "I told Robert to get you to sell. I didn't tell him to terrorize you or hire an actor or any of that. But I didn't clarify and I didn't follow up with him so I didn't know what he was doing. It's my fault. He's just a kid, finding his way. I let us all down. I'm so sorry."

He goes on for a while. I'd be touched if I were still in full Nikki mode, but I'm not.

"I can never make it up to you, but please let me try," he says. "Give me a second chance."

"Second chances are for people who make mistakes," I tell

him. "You didn't make a mistake. You set one of your dogs on me so you could buy my building. Fuck you, Alan. Now, get out of here."

His face goes all puppy dog. His voice is soft. "I know I have no right to ask forgiveness," he says. I interrupt him with a groan, though in my lady voice.

"I just wanted Robert to keep calling you."

I try to make a face that tells him I think he's full of crap. "My building's not for sale."

"This isn't about that," he says. "I love you."

"Is that it?"

He nods. "I'm going to call you every day. If the impulse moves you, you can answer and we can talk."

"Is that it?" I ask again.

"I guess so. Thanks."

"Go," I say.

27

Mr. Nazi boards a southbound train a little after ten o'clock, much to my relief. I've been loitering around the station for two hours, waiting for the man of my nightmares to give up on finding his target, a six-foot-tall transgender woman going to work. I'm not her, not this morning. I'm back in guy mode, hating it, already hot and damp from wearing the compression garment under my butch T-shirt on a muggy day. I take solace in the fact that I'm invisible to him and pretty much to everyone else, just another tall-ish male on his way to work with the rest of the masses.

He was already at the station when I arrived at eight, Nikki's usual Wednesday morning commuting time. He was sitting on a bench facing the southbound train tracks, his head buried in a newspaper, like in a spy movie. I hovered out of his line of sight, keeping an information board between me and him. Every few minutes, I peeked around the board to see what he was up to. He was pretty good at surveillance. He had a way of glancing to the side of his opened newspaper every time another person entered the platform from the escalator. It was a subtle movement. You wouldn't notice it if you weren't watching him.

After two southbound trains came and went, he strolled down to street level. I followed him with a crowd of passengers getting off a train, carefully staying in the mix. It's not that he'll recognize me—even a neighbor who knows me pretty well walked past me this morning without a hint of recognition—it's that I'm going to be following him a lot today and it's important he not be aware of me. He spent another fifteen minutes in the area, pretending to be a commuter, but staying in positions that let him see everyone who got on the escalator to the platform. After another southbound train came and went, he strode off down the street, following the route I take to and from the station. I didn't follow him because I knew he was coming back and he did. I figured he'd check out the trains until nine thirty, which was the latest train I ever take to work. I was right, and shortly after nine thirty, we both boarded the same southbound train.

Mr. Nazi stands near the front exit doors. I'm near the back doors, sitting in a front-facing seat, holding a newspaper in front of my face, peeking over the top of it at every stop to see if he's getting off. The magic moment comes at a north Loop stop. I follow him, keeping a cluster of people and twenty or thirty feet of distance between us. My anxiety level rises when he transfers to a Green Line train heading west. I have no trouble making the train, but I'm a north sider and I don't know much about the west side other than a lot of it is dangerous.

To take advantage of the thinning commuter crowds in mid-morning, I get on the car behind the one he boards, and I sit near the front window so I can watch him. A young teenage couple burst into my car and position themselves against the front window, laughing and whispering to each other, but I still have a good view of Mr. Nazi, who's standing at a pole near the exit door. The kids make a nice shield should he glance back this way.

223

Adolf seems to live a life of leisure. He gets off the train in a scabby neighborhood lined with rusty industrial buildings and weather-beaten houses, many of the former looking vacant, many of the latter converted to apartment buildings. In Chicago, this kind of neighborhood is referred to as blue collar or middle class, mainly because most of the residents are white or white enough. If they were people of color, it would be called a slum. Even presenting as a white male in good shape, I feel vulnerable wandering these streets. I constantly monitor my walk and whisper words to myself to practice masculine enunciations. This would be a dangerous place for Nikki and maybe even more dangerous for an effete Nick.

Adolf stops at a storefront gym on a dying commercial strip. Many of the surrounding stores have boarded-up windows. The ones that still operate offer bare essentials—a laundromat, a currency exchange with a sign about payday loans, a mom-and-pop convenience store. Against all odds, the street also includes a café. It looks dirty and old from the outside, like a place where the special of the day is zesty ptomaine poisoning. I enter it anyway, promising myself to launder my garments as soon as I get home. It provides a view of the gym door and it's out of the sun. To my surprise, the place is fairly clean, though the tables are rickety and the aged chairs are plastic and about as comfortable as a cast-iron saddle.

A middle-aged woman with an Eastern European accent waits on me. She has tired eyes and scraggly hair that has been bleached into a cotton candy consistency. Tufts of it pop out of her ponytail here and there, like imitations of a fireworks show. I order coffee. She leaves and returns quickly without uttering a word, setting a pale brown beverage in front of me and gesturing to a dish on the table that holds packages of cream and sugar. She leaves a check on the table and goes back behind the lunch bar to wash dishes. I pull out my phone and start reading emails and news bulletins. From the looks of Mr. Nazi, his workouts must last at least an hour, maybe more. Eventually, curiosity overcomes my coffee snobbery and I deign to taste the discolored water in front of me. No surprise. It's disgustingly weak, barely recognizable as coffee. I have to fight off the sensation that I'm poisoning myself.

The Nazi's workout lasts well over an hour, and he emerges from the gym with shower-wet hair and a new T-shirt. I've used the time to change some of my clothing, donning a loose-fitting blue cotton work shirt over my tee, front unbuttoned, sleeves rolled up, and trading my blue Cubs hat for a green baseball hat with a John Deere logo on it. I settle my bill when I see him come out of the gym, then watch as he walks toward the café. For one horrifying moment, he looks like he's going to stop in and see me, which would make tailing him impossible for the rest of the day, but he passes the entrance. I wait a couple of minutes, then leave the shop and trail him from a safe distance.

His next stop is a grocery store, several blocks from his gym. It's a small establishment in an old building with worn linoleum floors, not much bigger than a suburban convenience store. I pop in long enough to buy a bottle of water, then wait outside, a few doors down in a storefront. He comes out with plastic grocery bags dangling from each hand and walks briskly west, then south. The late-morning sun is hot and the air is getting wet again and he's cruising along like an Olympic race walker. My T-shirt has dark wet spots from my perspiration, and I can feel beads of sweat running down my face and my back.

I trail far behind him, trying to stay out of his line of sight. I want to see where he lives. I can take a couple shots at it if I lose him today, but tailing him is hard work, requiring a lot of concentration. I'm a block behind him when he hangs a left. I turn into an alley that parallels his street, then I jog and try to catch sight of him between houses. In minutes, I'm soaked in sweat and feeling a little lightheaded, but still trotting and craning to look between houses. All of a sudden I see Mr. Nazi walking toward me, between houses. I freeze in place, partially screened from his view by bushes and a wire fence. He doesn't see me because his vision is fixed on something else.

A little girl, maybe two or three, is sitting in an inflatable wading pool in the backyard of a rambling old house that used to be white, her mother a few feet away in a beach chair, a hat brim and sunglasses protecting her eyes, her hair pouring over the straps of the hat. The little girl, a tow-headed blonde with long, loose, angelic curls, is in a swimming suit and chats unintelligibly with Mom. Mom chats back happily. Mom's in a tank top and shorts, thirtyish, matronly. Her smile is quiet and pretty. The Nazi greets them as he enters the backyard. The little girl claps her hands and runs to him. Mom stands and gives them space. He drops the grocery bags and picks up the little girl and hugs and kisses her. The little girl worships him.

After the love-in, Mr. Nazi nods to Mom who nods back with a friendly smile. She picks up the grocery bags while he plays with the girl in the pool. I piece the scene together. He's the dad. They could be divorced or maybe they never married; maybe Mom thought being a single parent was a better gig than being married to a Nazi. The groceries could be a form of child support, or just one of Mr. Nazi's chores. Whatever the adult relationships are, the little girl adores him, and he adores her. She splashes him and orders him around, and he obeys like a domesticated T. rex, getting on all fours so she can ride him, then lying on his back so she can sit on him and flexing his abs so she can walk on his stomach. It's like a scene in an old *Saturday Evening Post* cover, or maybe one of those idyllic Terry Redlin paintings.

Jesus Christ. I can't help myself from swearing. Of all the things I expected to see in an alley in a west side shithole neighborhood, this wasn't even on the list. Junkies or winos getting high, maybe. Bums sleeping off last night's bender, maybe. Doddering retirees sitting in the backyard, staring blankly into space, yes. A neo-Nazi jamboree of some kind, for sure. But family hour? Knock me over with a feather. Mr. Nazi as a human being? Impossible. And yet, there it is.

I move behind a neighbor's garage for better cover and watch awhile longer. At length, they all go inside. Twenty minutes later, Mom comes out in a nurse's uniform, Mr. Nazi carrying the little girl on his back. They head toward the Green Line station. Mom probably pulls a late shift at one of the hospitals in the medical complex a few stops down. They stop at another shabby apartment building before they get to the Green Line station. Mom takes the toddler to the door and surrenders her to a matron who welcomes the child with open arms and a warm smile. The tot goes willingly. Mom and Mr. Nazi continue on to the Green Line station. They get on the same car, but he gets off before she does. I stay with him.

His home is a sagging, four-story tenement, a sort of rabbit warren for derelicts and Nazis, or so I conclude. I stroll past his building slowly, looking for movement in the upstairs windows, trying to locate his apartment. Nothing. I go down the street another fifty yards and come back on the other side, closer to his building. Again, I see nothing moving in the windows.

I hang a right at the end of the block and find the alley that runs behind his building. A scraggly hedge at the back of Adolf's building offers a little cover, so I park myself there, half sitting on a garbage can. I scan the back of the building. Fifteen minutes pass. A door opens and closes further down the block. My hair stands on end. If someone walks past me in the alley they'll remember me. Minutes later, the door opens and closes again. Same door, same place.

Then the back door to the Nazi's place opens. It's him, carrying a plastic garbage bag, his face buried in a cell phone.

I dash up the alley and duck into a fenceless backyard with a dilapidated shed that gives me cover. My heart is pounding. I can hear him lift the lid of a garbage can and drop his bag inside it. I can hear the lid being replaced. I catch sight of him as he returns to his back door, his attention still focused on his cell phone. I dash back to the hedges behind his place and watch him enter.

As soon as the door starts to close behind him, I sprint to it and catch it before it closes. I open it a silent, cautious crack. A narrow staircase rises steeply to the second floor then doubles back to rise to the third floor. I peek in just in time to see Adolf enter a door on the second-floor landing. I wait, counting to ten, in case he comes back out again, looking for an escape route if I need it. There's no movement from above. I crack open the door again and peek in. The stairway is narrow and dim and silent. The ground floor apartment is silent. I slide in and ascend the stairs slowly. The second step squeaks. I freeze and listen for movement. Nothing. I take another stair, placing my feet at the far edge of the stair to reduce any further squeaking. It works. I make my way almost noiselessly to the second floor.

The Nazi's door is solid wood. No peephole. No names posted to identify the occupants. The back stairs are strictly utilitarian, for taking out garbage or getting access to the backyard. The stairs continue up to the third floor where they double back and ascend to the fourth floor.

I go back to the ground floor and let myself out. I walk around to the front of the building and step into the vestibule. There are eight mailboxes fixed on one wall, just above a small table. The mailboxes are numbered, 1-A, 1-B, 2-A, and 2-B and so on. There are also names taped onto most of the mailboxes, but not the unit I care about, not number 2-B.

I slip out of the vestibule and walk casually away, as if I belong there, another anonymous stranger in a neighborhood of anonymous strangers. I walk back to the Green Line station, checking behind me now and then to see if anyone is following me. I don't see anyone. Meanwhile, my mind is churning. Part of the time, I'm trying to create a plan for disposing of the Nazi, once and for all. And part of the time, I'm trying to conceive of a way the police can intercede and get him off my back. The truth is, I don't think I can handle this guy. He's not stupid like his big brother and he's stronger than two of me. If I attack him in his home, he'd have every right to kill me, which he can do without a weapon in a few seconds.

Even if I can somehow incapacitate him, I'm not sure I can take the final step. For all my bluster, for all my fear and anger, I don't think I can kill a helpless human being. In the heat of battle, maybe. In self-defense, yes. But a defenseless man trussed up in bonds, pleading for his life, maybe not. The vision of the Nazi playing with his loving toddler rises in my mind. I try to replace it with his evil, threatening countenance, the part of himself he shares with me. I can't make it happen. I'll work on it. I have to. This is no time for doubt or sympathy.

Morgan's grandmother, the subject of a great deal of my anger and resentment over the years, calls while I'm looking through the wares of a costume shop in Andersonville. Her tone is so civil I wouldn't have recognized her greeting if she hadn't identified herself.

"Hello, Nikki," she says. "This is Virginia Bascomb, Blythe's mother."

My mind fills with dread. There can be only one explanation for her call and her civility. "Is Blythe okay?" I ask reflexively, no return of greeting.

It was a stupid question to ask and I immediately wish I could retract it, but Virginia continues, unoffended.

"Blythe is dying, dear," she says. "I'm bringing her home

tomorrow. She won't last long after that. She'll just be given medications to keep her comfortable. She wants to say goodbye to you."

Her news rocks me, though I've been expecting it for days. I stagger to the wall of the store and lean against it. It takes a minute to collect my thoughts.

"Morgan?" I can only get out the one word, but Virginia knows what I'm asking.

"I'll call her next," says Virginia.

I realize she's calling me first as some sort of recognition that I'm Morgan's parent and I should be prepared to help my daughter through this trauma. Her consideration is almost as profound as my grief.

Virginia and I struggle through a few more minutes of conversation, my mind constantly flashing back to memories of Blythe, events, moments, and portraits of her that are painted in my mind, her beauty, her kindness, her courage. I stay focused long enough to find out we can visit Blythe in two days, giving Virginia time to get her comfortable and set up a schedule with the hospice service. There won't be any meals to share; Blythe is being fed by intravenous tubes. When we hang up, I beg access to the store's bathroom and go inside and cry. They look at me like I'm an alien when I come out and I realize why. I'm still dressed like a man, but in my sorrow, my voice went back to my female range, and my tears started falling well before I got to the bathroom. Sobbing sopranos are not a common hallmark of American manhood, even in a place as enlightened as Andersonville. I leave without buying anything. I'll buy from a store where I'm less memorable.

Morgan and Ophelia are waiting for me in the living room when I get home. Ophelia tipped me off by phone that they'd be there, thank goodness. I sneak in the back door and slide surreptitiously into my bedroom. I glimpse Ophelia walking to the kitchen just as I duck into my room. She may not have seen me, but I wouldn't bet on it. She doesn't miss much.

I peel out of my costume, wash my face, fluff my hair, and put on a comfortable cotton dress I wear around the house. When I enter the living room, Ophelia hugs me and Morgan starts to cry. I go to her, offer her my hands and help her stand. We embrace. She sobs, her cheek on my chest, wet with tears, her eyes closed tight. She wants to stay here tonight, she says. She has to stay here. She can't bear losing all her family.

I try to stay rational and calculating. I tell her she can stay here tonight, but I'll have Ophelia pick her up in the morning. It will be the last day of my life without her. I have one day to remove the threat to us all.

28

As I prepare myself for another day as a man, the face I see in the bathroom mirror again makes me queasy. This morning, it's even worse. Today, I have to kill another human being, and get away with it and be home in time to receive my heartbroken daughter who is coming home to grieve with me and prepare for our visit with Blythe tomorrow. I think about the pressure implicit in all that and I feel lightheaded and nauseated—not figuratively nauseated, the real thing. I drop to my knees and throw up in the toilet. My retching produces little vomitus. I haven't eaten anything since a slice of toast last night. I lie on the floor, letting the cold tiles chill my body and clear my mind. When the dizziness and nausea pass, I stand up again and resume my labors.

I'm incorporating the materials I bought yesterday into a new disguise. I have a new beard, longer and fuller than the Van Dyke. It comes with sideburns that connect to my hairline. The color match isn't perfect, so I have glasses and sunglasses to help camouflage the transition area, and I'll try to avoid scrutiny as I move about the city today.

In the mirror, I look like a typical dumpy, middle-aged man. My hair is pulled back in a short ponytail which I slip through the back of a White Sox hat. I'm wearing black-rim glasses, khaki slacks, and a billowing pin-striped shirt. I look like a nerdy guy trying to pass as a metrosexual. It's a legit look, and I don't look anything like me.

The rest of the disguise was more challenging than my face. I'm wearing a compression T-shirt again to flatten my breasts. It's not enough to give me a male chest, which started to become an issue yesterday. The more I perspired, the wetter and clingier my T-shirt became. By the time I got home I looked like a man with small female breasts. Today, I'm solving the problem by giving myself a different body shape. I'm wearing a padded belly that came with a Santa suit I found in a resale shop. It makes me look like one of those egg-shaped men whose torso sort of rounds from chest to hips. My pin-striped shirt flows from my shoulders to my belly, and even if it starts to collapse on my flattened boobs, fat guys have boobs about that size so no one's going to make me. The rotund look also makes my butt conform to the profile of an overweight male.

I check the contents of my backpack for the hundredth time. I'm tempted to rehearse my movements for the moment of assault again, but resist it. I've been through it at least a dozen times in pantomime, and dozens more in my imagination. I throw the backpack over one shoulder and slip out the back door.

I take the train down to the Loop and spend a few hours walking around, stopping for coffee, sitting in public places, killing time. I don't have to follow the Nazi today. I know where he lives. I have a pretty good idea of when he'll get home. All I have to do is wait, and not get recognized.

If nothing else, my roaming provides proof my disguise is working. No one notices me, not even on the L. No one cares enough about a fat, middle-aged white guy trudging off to work with a backpack slung over one shoulder. Just another IT nerd or

CPA, trying to look interesting and failing. My internal struggle is a lot less placid. My mind feels like a fireworks store going up in flames, with closed doors and windows trying to contain the shrieking mayhem that makes the earth shake and people scream. If I let myself think about what I have to do, I'm soon overwhelmed with panic.

Discipline. Marcus drilled me on mental discipline, blocking out everything but the objective, focusing on what needs to be done. I call on myself to assert the discipline. I have no other choice. The best I can do today is to kill a man and get away with it.

The derelict shed in the yard next door to the Nazi's place gives me a good vantage point for watching the back of his building. I'm trying to see if he's home and if there are other people in the building. I sit for thirty minutes, my heart pounding, my nerves on edge. It's torture. I'm tempted to go up to his back door and get on with it, taking my chances with interference from other people. I fight back that urge but I'm beginning to realize that my plan is impossible. I won't know who's in his apartment until I go in. There's no chance I can subdue the Nazi without raising the kind of racket that will alert everyone else in the building. I'm too weak and timid to have any chance against the man. I should leave now and hope the police find a reason to get him before he gets me. Or Morgan.

But I can't gamble with Morgan's life. Somehow, I hang on.

At ten o'clock, I ease out of the shed and stroll around the block, searching the windows of his building for signs of life, especially on the second floor. My pass reveals nothing. I don't see anyone stirring in any of the windows. I don't even know for sure if the Nazi is in his apartment, let alone a second goon or a lover, but it's late enough in the morning that anyone with a day job would be gone by now. I circle back to the alley. When I get to the Nazi's building, I see him in back, not far from the rear door. He's talking on a cell phone and smoking a joint. When the joint is smoked down to a nub, he drops it to the ground and grinds it into bits with his shoe.

He slides his phone into his back pocket and heads for the door. My heart pounds and my mouth gets dry. I will my mind to stop thinking. I'm going to do this. I'm going to do it now. I'll kill this thug and walk away without so much as a drop of conscience about it.

He goes back inside the building. I reach into my backpack and make my final preparations, my mind focused on each task. Put on the vinyl gloves. Slide the pepper spray into one front pocket, and a plastic gift card into the other. Slip the weighted pipe inside my belt and under my shirt at the small of my back. Close the backpack. Sling it over one shoulder.

I enter the property and walk to the back door, my pace businesslike, as if I live there. I use the plastic card to beat the lock on the back door, just like Marcus taught me. I open the back door a crack to make sure the Nazi has gone into his apartment. The staircase is silent and empty. I step inside and close the door. I pause to let my eyes adjust to the dim light, then ascend the stairs, slowly, placing my feet at the margins of each stair to reduce the squeaks.

When I reach his door, I pull out the pepper spray, remove the cover, and ready it in my right hand. I check the stairs for movement, up and down: nothing. I count to ten, listening for sound or movement. Nothing. I will myself to knock on the door, sweat trickling down my back, my hands shaking.

My mind races with what-ifs. What if there are two goons in there instead of one? What if there are more Nazis in the other apartments? What if they all come for me at once?

What if there's a woman inside? A biker babe, maybe. Do I kill her too? I'm on the verge of walking away, but the thought that stops me is Morgan. She'll never be safe as long as this maniac is prowling the earth. It's now or never.

I knock softly, three, four raps. Silence, then the sound of heavy footfalls coming for the door, just one person as best I can tell.

A gruff voice. "Who's there?"

"Lois from next door." I say it softly, in my most feminine voice. I turn off my mind. My roller coaster has crested the big hill. There's no turning back now.

"Well, Jesus H. Christ," he curses while he unlocks the door. "Why didn't you—"

He's in mid-sentence when the door opens and I douse his face in pepper spray. He recoils and steps back, hands to eyes, grunting and cursing, in shock, not sure what hit him. I deliver a massive kick to his groin and catch it perfectly. He topples to the floor writhing in pain, and I clobber him with the pipe. The blow stuns him into silence. I step inside, close the door, look about and listen for signs of another person. None. I pull a length of 300-pound-test nylon line from my backpack. It has a noose on one end which I loop around one of his wrists. I try to pull it behind his back. Even in his semi-stupor he resists and he's as strong as a bull. He tries to kick, but the groin shot and the blow to the head have dimmed his strength. I stand away from him and he tires in a few seconds. I deliver a kick from behind, to his liver. He cries out and reaches to the afflicted area with one hand. I hop to the other side of his prone body and deliver a kick to his solar plexus. It freezes him. He can't breathe. He can't make a noise. He can't move.

I tie his wrists behind his back and use another length of line to secure his ankles. My bonds are just temporary. When he's secured, I yank plastic ties out of the backpack and fasten his wrists and ankles with them. He'll need a knife to get out of them.

The gag is much harder. I try to push it into his mouth but

he closes down. I tap his lips with the weighted pipe. "Open or start losing teeth," I whisper in his ear. It's a loud whisper in my most masculine voice with a lot of vehemence. To my surprise, he opens his mouth. I shove the gag into his mouth and tie it behind his head.

I sit back, panting, sweat pouring off my body as if I had been running in place in a sauna. I look around. We're in his kitchen, which is surprisingly spacious and clean, despite roly-poly linoleum tile on the floor and an ancient metal-and-Formica table and aluminum-frame chairs with cracked vinyl seats.

As soon as I can breathe, I run through the apartment to make sure no one else is present. No one is. The rest of the place is as neat and clean as the kitchen: two bedrooms in use as bedrooms, a third set up as an office with a desktop computer and printer. Above the desk is a black and white poster of Hitler addressing a massive crowd. I resist the urge to tear it into small pieces, and go back to the kitchen. I search through the drawers until I find a knife with a blade that's long enough and strong enough for what I need to do. I can deliver a lethal blow with my pipe weapon, but Marcus says the knife is a surer kill tool.

I go back to the Nazi, aware that I'm just seconds away from completing my mission and getting out of here. He's groaning and moving a little, still dazed from the trauma I inflicted on him. I'm astonished at how calm and cold-blooded I am, and how easy it is to kill someone. I snarl at him to lay still and I pull up his shirt, looking for the correct entry point for my knife thrust. I'm on automatic pilot, blocking out everything but my mission, focused on where the knife goes in, and what angle it has to take to sever the heart. Marcus's counsel plays in my mind: "Thrust the blade toward the heart, then slice down to maximize the damage."

When he said it the first time, I just nodded and took in the information. Now, as my mind tells my hand to do it, bile rises in my throat; nausea overwhelms me. The world gets wavy. I stagger to a chair. Adolf writhes and makes some feeble attempts to yell as the effects of the pepper spray and blows start to wear off. I wait for him to stop. His eyes flutter open and shut, red and swollen. He's angry enough to tear my limbs from my body.

"Keep your eyes shut and you might get out of this alive," I tell him, my voice low and butch and threatening.

But I'm stalling. Reality has overwhelmed me. All that's left to do is shove the knife into his heart, and I realize this is the one part of the plan I can't do. Even if I could make myself kill a man in cold blood, what kind of example am I setting for my daughter?

My mind fills with the image of this man coddling the toddler girl and treating her mother like a human being. I seize on the idea that he's actually a decent person, capable of love and compassion, and maybe now he'll leave us alone because I've scared him. It's a stupid fantasy. I can hear Marcus's warning that it ends badly if you back out at the last minute. But that's exactly where I'm at.

I try to run a bluff. "I'm a messenger," I say in my most masculine voice. "You're stalking protected people. Stop or you will suffer unimaginable pain."

I wait a beat. "Do you understand me?"

He nods his head and grunts. It's what he has to say.

"You don't seem sincere," I say. "I have to kill you if you don't seem sincere."

He's still. I can't read him. I need to get a reaction from him.

"Maybe I should cut off a couple fingers."

He shakes his head and grunts earnestly, as if to say, *you don't need to do that.*

"Okay," I say. "How do I know you'll honor your promise?"

He grunts and tries to make words. He's asking me to remove the gag. I do.

"You have my word as a Christian soldier," he rasps.

I almost laugh out loud. On my personal list of people most

likely to lie, there's no daylight between right-wing bigots and religious crazies. "You'll have to do better than that," I say. I'm so distracted by my inner thoughts, my voice travels back up to my feminine range.

He notices it. A smug smile crosses his face. "You're the queer, aren't you."

I don't say anything.

"You're the tranny. What's this about? You're trying to scare me?"

He blinks his eyes open and looks at me. I look back, really look this time. When I've seen him before, my mind translated his features and his body language into images of fear. That's still there, the caricature of evil, but I fight through that to see his flesh the way a camera would. A meaty face, clean shaven, a receding hairline with fine, fair hair, blue eyes. A twenty-first-century version of the Hitler youth.

"I'm giving you a chance to save your own life by leaving mine alone," I say. I try to sound tough but I'm not disguising my voice. I realize my eyelids are fluttering as I try to stop the tears from forming. My words don't fool either of us. For all my bombast and bravado, I'm not able to do what needs to be done.

He laughs. "You're not going to kill me. You don't have it in you. You're a fucking swamp creature. Cut me loose and get out of here!" I'm expecting the hatred I see on his face, but there's something else, too. Intelligence. I've always thought of neo-Nazis as morons, but this one's eyes are clear and comprehending and his diction is precise and calibrated. He's an educated man. His IQ might be higher than mine. He hates me like his brother hated me, but he's also capable of rational thought, reasoning, planning. He's far more dangerous than an ordinary thug. I feel the handle of the knife in my hand. I have to kill him, here and now. I try to envision the blade plunging into his body, just beneath the ribs, angling toward the heart. I try to convince myself I can do that, I must do that. Just do it and leave and don't look back. He stares at me in silent fascination. He's reading my mind.

"Come on, queenie," he sneers. "You better do it or start running. My roommate will be home pretty soon and I don't want him to kill you. I want that pleasure for myself."

I can't do it. Not even to save my own life. Not even for Morgan. He knows it. He smiles. It's not even a blood-chilling smile. It's contempt.

"That's what I thought," he says. "You might as well cut me loose. Maybe I'll let you live if you do."

I put the knife back in the drawer where I found it, and conduct a quick search of the apartment to collect my belongings. As I do, the Nazi serenades me with taunts.

"You're as stupid as you are ugly," he says. "Why clean up the crime scene? I'm not going to the cops. I know where you live. I know where you work. I know where your daughter is. I own you, bitch."

He's got a point, but I keep the gloves on when I let myself out the door, taking them off only after I descend the stairs and close the outer door. The Nazi screams insults at me as I leave, but the noise doesn't seem to bring neighbors to their doors. His voice fades as I step into the backyard. I tuck the gloves in a pocket and head for the L station. I'll drop them in a garbage can there and use the remaining few hours of my life trying to think of a way to inflict pain and injury on the Nazi when he comes for me. Maybe I can kill him if he's attacking me. For the first time in my life, I wish I owned a gun.

29

"Did you do it?" Ophelia's face is filled with horror. She and Morgan arrived twenty minutes after I got home—just enough time for me to shed the male disguise and begin reassembling myself as Nikki. Ophelia and I have a private moment together while Morgan is changing clothes and I'm doing my makeup.

I glance at Ophelia in the mirror of my makeup table. She's sitting on the bed, staring at me. "I have good news and bad news," I say. "I won't have to worry about any murder warrants."

"What's the bad news?" she asks.

"That is the bad news." As I say it my mind fills with the vision of the Nazi bashing all three of us in the head as soon as we leave the apartment. My horrid imagination gives me a particularly graphic view of Morgan's skull being crushed. I drop my face into my hands. I'm too filled with dread to cry, and I can't shake the horrific images from my mind.

Ophelia comes to me and begins kneading my shoulders and upper back. It's a gesture that chases the ghoulish visions from my brain just because it's so unexpected. Ophelia is the most decent of human beings, and as kind as a religious saint, but she's not a touchy-feely type and she's never been one to coddle a heartbroken sister. When I raise my head and look at her in the mirror, she smirks a little and asks, "Okay, Nikki, what's the good news?"

"He hasn't killed any of us yet."

"Proof of a benign and interactive God," Ophelia mutters.

I finish my makeup. "Are you going to tell Morgan?" Ophelia asks.

"I have to," I say. "But not until after we see Blythe."

"What a daily double," says Ophelia. I can only nod.

I slide into a pair of sandals and check myself in the full-length mirror. I'm wearing flared jeans and a light blue button-front blouse that understates my bosom. I look casual-nice and maybe I can keep Blythe's mind away from comparing my breast size to hers.

Morgan emerges from her room at the same time I come out of mine. "You look adorable," I tell her. She does. She's in a pink and white top, a pink skirt that falls to mid-thigh—long enough to be appropriate, short enough to show off her perfect young legs—and white sandals. Her outfit is much cheerier than she is. She looks at me with red-rimmed eyes and a funeral face. I wrap my arms around her. She lets me hug her and slowly, tentatively puts her arms around me. She buries her face in my chest and sobs. Her arms tighten around me. I try not to dwell on how wonderful it feels. A truly selfish thought when I should be conjuring the right thing to say at a time like this. But there is no right thing. There are lies you can tell, but that just denies reality: Blythe is dying. She shouldn't be. It's not right. If there was an interactive God who was kind and just, this wouldn't be happening. Morgan's mother is dying. Morgan has every right to mourn. I'm mourning, too.

When we break the embrace, Ophelia hugs us both and we head for her car and the long drive to Winnetka.

As we approach the front door of her grandmother's mansion, Morgan seems to shrivel into herself, her arms folded, her shoulders hunched, her head looking downward. The sight of her fills me with heartbreak. I feel helpless and inept. I ask myself, what would Blythe do? But I know the answer and it scares me to death. Blythe would do what I want to do. She'd put an arm around Morgan and press her close, maybe even stop and do a proper hug. I start to do that and stop myself, anticipating Morgan pushing me away and saying something nasty, and her grandmother seeing it and greeting me with a sneer. I fight through the vision, knowing Blythe would overcome any fears she might have in order to comfort our daughter, and I have to at least try.

I put an arm around Morgan and pull her toward me. She seems to sag into me. The door opens before we can ring the bell. Grandmother Virginia stands in the threshold and opens her arms for Morgan. Morgan falls into the hug. It's a long, soulful bonding. Virginia's eyes are closed tight. I can see traces of tear residue below her eyes. She's been suffering, too. Morgan takes deep breaths every now and then, Virginia rubbing her back each time. "Oh, my beautiful babies," Virginia keeps murmuring. It's like a funeral dirge and I understand what she's feeling. No mother wants to outlive her child, and no grandmother can bear the pain of seeing her grandchild suffer such a grievous loss.

This may be the first time I've ever seen Virginia Bascomb as a human being. Even when I was a young man with prospects, she treated me like the illegitimate child of a scullery maid and conducted herself like a royal in the court of Louis XIV. Sorrow is a great equalizer. I wonder as I watch my daughter cling to her grandmother if Virginia will revert to who she was after Blythe dies. I hope not, but if she doesn't, it may be that Morgan will decide to live with her instead of me. The thought is painful and humiliating, but I try not to wallow in it. It would make sense for Morgan to stay here. She'd finish high school at one of the best schools in the state. And she'd be safe.

They end the hug, Virginia brushing a tiny tear from Morgan's cheek, and Morgan returning the gesture. They smile at one another. Morgan enters and begins ascending the staircase to Blythe's room. Virginia gestures to Ophelia and me to enter. She smiles, a sad smile, but not judgmental.

"Please come in, Nikki," she says. She raises one hand to squeeze my arm as I pass by. She does the same with Ophelia, saying, "It's Ophelia, right?"

Ophelia is as flabbergasted as I am. It has been a good ten years since they met, the last time Morgan was allowed to invite her "father" to her birthday party. They exchange pleasantries as the three of us climb the stairs.

Entering Blythe's room is like visiting a gilded leper colony. Sunlight streams in from the windows on the south wall, warming the hardwood floors and teak furniture, and bringing radiant color to Blythe's sumptuous area rugs and her pastel-colored walls. A teak bookcase holds hardbound volumes of great literature and a compact sound system plays classical music at an elevator volume providing a sort of aristocratic white noise. In the midst of all the splendor, Blythe lies on the four-poster bed, a skeletal facsimile of her former self. My first thought is that she's dead, but Morgan runs to her and Blythe's bony arms strain to surround her daughter in an embrace.

We wait politely while mother and daughter share their moment. Virginia dabs at her eyes with a tissue and sits in a chair on the perimeter of the room. When Morgan breaks the hug, Blythe weakly gestures for Ophelia and me to come forward. I let Ophelia greet her first—she's masterful at it, expressing grief for Blythe and admiration for the daughter she raised in a few quick words before tactfully standing back. When I get to

Blythe's side my rational mind shuts down. I sit next to her and bend to kiss her cheek, then hold my face next to hers. Tears come as if a spigot had been turned on. When I get control of myself, I sit up. Blythe smiles at me.

"You cry like a woman, Nikki," she says.

I try to dab my tears from my face without causing my makeup to run.

"I may not be much of one, but I am a woman," I say.

She takes one of my hands in hers. "Don't be so modest. It doesn't become you."

I nod. Her eyes flutter. She's in a dreamy state. Virginia warned us of this. The hospice service has pain-killing narcotics constantly available to her. She's living the last hours of her life floating on the edge of consciousness, like passing over a throng of loved ones on a soft cloud, just close enough to hear them and be heard.

"Let's talk," she says. "I don't have long. You, Mom, Morgan, me. No offense, Ophelia."

Ophelia nods and leaves the room. Morgan and Virginia come to Blythe's bedside. I move so Morgan can sit next to Blythe.

"Have you decided who you're going to live with?" Blythe asks Morgan.

Morgan's lips quiver, but she gets control of herself. "Nikki," she says.

Virginia starts to say something, then stops herself. I interject, "We'll have a chat about that, the three of us. Morgan may want to change her mind. Either way, we'll all remain close."

"You and Mom?" Blythe's face breaks into a broad smile. "I wish I could live to see that."

"We've been working at it," I say. Virginia nods, her face still registering some surprise at what I said about a family conference.

Blythe focuses on Morgan. "Are you doing sex and drugs?"

Morgan's face clouds. "Not so much, Mom."

"Good," says Blythe. "Your poor father needs a break."

"She's not my father." Morgan says it softly, almost apologetically.

"You're right," sighs Blythe. "I'm so sorry, Nikki. I didn't mean it that way."

"I didn't take it that way," I tell her.

After a few minutes, Blythe asks for time alone with Morgan. Virginia and I leave the room and sit on two chairs on the landing. There's a small table between us, polished walnut, crafted in some kind of classic French style with ornate feet and legs. Above it is an oil painting of an eighteenth-century aristocrat. As Virginia and I sit in anxious silence, my memory takes me back to the first time I saw that painting. Blythe and I were young, upwardly mobile professionals. We were involved, maybe not in love yet, but engaged in a ribald affair that included lots of sexual experimentation and adventure. One of the adventures started with a trip to her parents' house to water plants and look after things while they were on a cruise. When we went up to the second floor, I asked if the man in the painting was a relative. Blythe threw herself against me and smiled. I could feel her breath on my face and her hand on my penis as she said the painting was just a painting and the important thing was, she needed to get laid on her bed. That might have been the sexiest coupling of my life as a male. In fact, it was the wild satisfaction of sexual experiences like that one that helped me keep my gender secret locked away in a dark place for so many years.

"Morgan wants to stay with you," says Virginia, pulling me out of my trance. "What is there to talk about?"

I shift uncomfortably in my chair, trying to decide how candid to be. I've lived long enough to know that it's even money Virginia reverts back to her sour, disapproving self after Blythe dies.

"School, for one thing," I say. "I don't know that I can get her into a school anywhere near as good as she's in here."

We talk about schools until Morgan comes to get me. Her face is red and moist and she seems to be in a state of numb grief.

"Mom wants to talk to you, Nikki," she says.

When I sit next to her bed, Blythe puts both of her hands around one of mine. Her hands are warm and her touch is still soft, even though her fingers have been reduced to skin and bone. She smiles.

"Do you have a boyfriend?" she asks. "Or a girlfriend?"

"My social life is a good definition of pathetic," I say.

Blythe smiles again. "You've gotten good at avoiding the question," she says. "Morgan told me you have a lover."

I blush. "It's complicated," I say. "I didn't mean for her to know about that. I promise, I'll be more circumspect. I'm working on being a good example."

"You worry too much, Nikki." She grimaces as she shifts her body to a more comfortable position; then her smile returns. "Paying for sex is, uh, unorthodox, but not lying about it is a good thing. You're a good example. She knows it. I do too."

"Thank you." I can't think of anything else to say.

"What is there for you and Morgan and Mom to discuss?" Blythe asks.

"I still have a Nazi problem."

"You, specifically?"

I nod. "Yes. I'm worried about Morgan's safety. And I'm not sure we can get her into a school anywhere near as good as yours."

"The police?"

"They haven't been able to help yet," I say.

"Nikki," she sighs, "please tell me you aren't going to take things into your own hands."

My failure to kill the Nazi burns in my mind. I can see his

fleshy face snarling insults at me as I left him in his flat, bound but alive. I squeeze my eyes shut and shake my head, trying to rid myself of the memory. Blythe misreads my reaction.

"Oh my God, you killed someone!"

I shake my head wearily. "No, love. I didn't have it in me."

She pets my hands with hers, softly. "That's a good thing, too, Nikki. You're a woman now. You're setting an example for our daughter."

"I failed to make her safe."

She pats my hand. "You'll figure something out."

She's getting weaker. We chat for a few more minutes, mainly so Blythe can apologize for not understanding me. I tell her she had every right to feel the way she felt, but she doesn't want to hear it. "I want you to accept my apology," she says.

"I do," I whisper. "And I thank you for loving me as long as you did. Loving you and Morgan . . . it's my whole life."

"I love you, too." Her voice is barely a whisper. "Always."

Her eyes close and she goes silent. For an instant, I think she has passed, but one hand twitches and she takes a deep breath. Her eyes open. "I'd like to say goodbye to everyone now," she whispers.

I call Morgan and Virginia back to her bedside. Blythe reaches her hands out, one to Morgan, the other to Virginia. I stand behind Morgan, my hands on her shoulders. Blythe's eyes close and her lips form a contented smile. Minutes elapse. At times, I think she has passed, then I see her chest expand ever so slightly to take in air. Morgan glances at her grandmother with a questioning look on her face. Virginia smiles ever so gently, as if to say, *we're doing the right thing*. More minutes pass. Blythe is motionless. There are no more inhalations. I realize she has passed, but I sense that Morgan and Virginia need this time with her so I remain still and silent. Eventually, Virginia checks Blythe's pulse. She stands and kisses Blythe, then pulls Morgan to her. "Your mother is gone," she says.

"Your grandmother needs you today," I say to Morgan as we sip coffee in Virginia's kitchen. Virginia has given us time for a private conversation, retiring to her room to get ready for the hard day ahead. I ramble for a few minutes about the soul-deadening labors of making funeral arrangements, and how her grandmother will need moral support and maybe some clear thinking at times.

"But it's not forever, right?" Morgan's words are matter-of-fact, but her face is pleading. I feel a tinge of pride, that my daughter needs me, but it's wiped out by a tsunami of responsibility. How can I ever fulfill her faith in me? I have an enemy who could be waiting to kill me as soon as I walk out the door. And even if I dodge him, he could target Morgan any time he felt like it. And even if I had killed him and gotten away with it, I have a mutiny taking shape at the café, and I don't know anything about the high school that serves my neighborhood, but I know it's nothing close to Winnetka's finishing school for young aristocrats.

"Let's talk about it after your mother's funeral," I say. It's a weak, phony dodge and she picks up on it right away.

"You don't want me," she says.

"I do. You're everything to me," I say. "But even more than I want you, I want you safe."

"I can't lose you, too," she says in her little girl voice.

I hold her hand. "You won't lose me. I promise, no matter what, I'll be here for you."

She nods and smiles and accepts my promise. I have no idea how I can make good on it. Guilt floods my body and soul. I leave for the train station feeling burdened and pathetic.

30

Vernon I. Gibbs is thirty minutes late and I know as soon as he walks in, this is a waste of time. When he came calling a few short weeks ago, he was early, and he greeted me with a beaming smile and the round-eyed wonder of a vassal greeting his queen. Now, he enters the BeatNikki's office with a weasel smile on his thin face, and his crazy-preacher eyes gleam with a predatory intensity, a tiger closing in on a lamb. He shakes hands with me like I'm a man, just like the first time we met. I force my negative impressions of him out of my mind. He's here. I don't have to like him to do business with him. And if he still wants to make me rich, I might be able to disappear from the Nazi's view and let things cool off for a while.

"You look as beautiful as ever," he says as we sit down. The one thing I like about him is, he doesn't throw out a bullshit line like that with the greasy ease of a slick Romeo who thinks all women will quiver and quail under such flattery. Of course, he recites the line like it's something in his playbook—say hello, utter a ridiculous compliment, then go for the jugular.

"You look very dapper yourself, Mr. Gibbs." It's a lie of the same magnitude as his. He looks like an undertaker in a horror movie, his expensive suit sagging on his gaunt frame like an old shirt on a scarecrow, his hair thin and oily with sweat from the muggy day.

I thank him for coming and repeat what I told him on the phone: I'm thinking of selling my building and I'm listening to offers for it.

Gibbs flashes his weasel smile again. "Things change in this world of ours, don't they? One minute, everything's perfect, the next, everything falls apart."

"Nothing has fallen apart for me," I reply. "I've just decided I want to explore the possibility of selling. You indicated before that you could make me rich buying my building, so I want to give you a chance to bid."

Gibbs locks eyes with me and I know before he says anything he thinks I'm a stupid woman and he's going to play me.

"I'm so glad, Nikki," he says. "I'll have my inspector come by as soon as possible, but I have to forewarn you, the market has changed, too. You changed your mind. Everything changes, right? The real estate market's really cooling off in this area. All the money's moving to the suburbs."

It's pure manure, but I play along. "Does that mean you aren't interested?" I ask.

"I'm interested," he says. "I like the location. But I would have paid a lot more for it three weeks ago than I would today. I'm sorry to say that. I'd love to do business with you. I know you're one of the pioneers in this neighborhood and people think the world of you and I'd love to make you rich—and I will, but not quite as rich as you would have been a few weeks ago."

I sit back and cross my legs. "Has there been an outbreak of some exotic disease?"

He forces a smile. "No. But, you know, the attraction of this neighborhood is its eclectic shops and arty people, but people like me and your friend Mr. Campbell are buying up properties and we're not going to retain that ambience. We're going to build modern buildings, ten, twelve, fifteen floors, steel and concrete and glass. The charm value of your property is declining."

I shake my head and flash him a sarcastic smile. "So, as soon as you buy, your property becomes trash? Mr. Gibbs, that's the worst justification for low-balling I've ever heard."

"Oh, don't kid yourself, Ms. Finch," he says. "I'll do just fine with my properties. For me, the ground floor is just where you get on the elevator. I'm building up. I'll be selling luxury condos to upwardly mobile professionals too smart to buy into the overpriced, over-taxed Lincoln Park market, not when they can have the best of both worlds just across the street."

He continues for another ten minutes, a brilliant professor lecturing a dim-witted student. When I can't stand it anymore, I press him for a ballpark figure. He hedges. It's bad business giving ballpark numbers, then finding out the place has hidden problems. I insist.

"Well," he says finally, "I'm guessing our evaluation will come in between $500,000 and $800,000." He presents the numbers with great fanfare, like I've just won the lottery.

"That's a far cry from the millions you were talking about before," I say.

He denies ever mentioning millions.

"You said you were going to make me rich beyond my wildest dreams," I say. "A half million for this building isn't a wild dream, it's a nightmare. I can get that kind of money by putting a 'For Sale' sign in the window."

Gibbs raises his eyebrows and shakes his head, like I've just made a terrible mistake. He lectures me on current property values in the area, and how he has capital reserves so he can close right away, and he starts imaging all the things I can do with the money. He talks about the beautiful clothes I can buy, the cruises I can take, the fine automobiles I can purchase. I shut him down.

"Let's stop right here," I say. "I won't sell to you. Period.

Thanks for your time." I stand and gesture to the door. Genuine surprise transforms his face. Apparently his hooey usually works, though it's hard to imagine.

"Do you know what you're doing?" he objects.

"Of course," I say, motioning for him to go out the door.

"This is a negotiation," he says. "You're supposed to counteroffer."

"If I wanted to do business with you, I would have countered," I say. "But I don't want to do business with anyone who thinks I'm an idiot."

He tries to object but I'm walking him to the exit and as we near the door his rap turns to threats. I'll never get such a good offer again. He's well known and respected in the real estate business and when word gets out about this meeting, no one will want to do business with me.

"Mr. Gibbs," I say when we step onto the sidewalk, "that's the silliest thing you've said yet. Capitalists go where the money is, just as surely as flies gather on shit."

I close the door behind him and Little John is standing there, his face angry.

"What's going on here, Nikki?" he demands. "Are you selling? Without talking to me?"

I motion for Little John to come into the office. After I close the door, I face him and answer.

"I'm thinking about selling the building," I answer. "The business is a separate entity."

"But, without talking to me?"

Before I can answer, he freezes and stares at me. "It's that Nazi, isn't it?"

I nod.

"You said you'd take care of that. Yesterday. That's what you said." Little John repeats himself, like a child who feels betrayed by a parent.

"It didn't work out the way I planned," I say, when he stops.

"What's that mean?" He says it sarcastically, like I'm keeping secrets.

"It means that man is still alive and he wants to kill me and maybe Morgan, too. I doubt he cares about you one way or the other, but I'm sitting here with a dead wife, a daughter who's in mortal danger living with me, and a business staffed by a bunch of people who are scared shitless and want to leave, starting with you, and I'm saying to myself, really, what's the point? I can sell this building and give you the business and move Morgan and me out to the suburbs so she can go to a good school and live in safety and you can find some other idiot to beg you to come to work each day." As I rant, Little John's eyes flare and his face flushes a deeper red and at one point I think he is coming over the desk at me, but he contains himself, barely, and when I finish I have tears of frustration trickling down my face and that seems to blunt his fury.

"I didn't realize you felt so betrayed," he says. We sit in silence. "You'd give me the business?" he asks. I nod. He shakes his head. "It wouldn't be any good without you, Nikki."

I make a face and wave a hand as if to erase what he said, but truthfully, it's the nicest thing anyone's said to me in ages. "Your creations make this place go, Little John," I say.

"They're important," he says, "but you make the business work. We all know that. You do the money, the discipline, make the hard decisions, so I don't have to. And you're the face of the place. Everyone knows who Nikki is."

I should end the meeting and get moving. This has nothing to do with the problems I have to solve. But I can't bring myself to take action, not for a minute or two more. I have a compulsive need to bask in this moment of glory. It's like getting laid. When the moment passes, I put one hand on Little John's. "Thank you, Little John," I say. "I needed that."

We chat quietly for a few more minutes, friends again. I promise to stay with the business if we move it and we talk about

Boystown as a possible relocation area. "All the businesses are LGBTQ-owned," quips Little John. "We wouldn't stand out at all."

Alan answers on the second ring. "Nikki, I'm so glad you called," he says. There's real enthusiasm in his voice and he'd gush some more but I cut him off.

"Are you still interested in buying my building?" I ask. "I'm collecting bids. You don't even have to fuck me this time."

My little dig flusters him and leaves him groping for words for the first time since I've met him. "The romance was about you and me," he says. "Not business. Why do you want to sell now?"

"That's personal," I snap. "There's only one question on the table: Do you want to buy? And if you do, what's your best offer?"

"Nikki, this really isn't the best way to go about selling," he says. "You want to hire an agent, get an assessment done, provide documentation, have an open house, things like that."

"All I need from you is a number, or a 'not interested,'" I say.

"I can't give you a number without doing some research."

"Please!" I draw the word out sarcastically. "You tried to pressure me to sell. You must have had a number in mind. Give me that one."

"I just wanted you to sell, Nikki," he says. "It would have been for market value."

"Then you gave me some fabulous orgasms, too. You must have figured that was good for a discount of some kind. What's the discount for giving a pathetic transgender woman multiple orgasms these days? Five percent? Ten percent? I mean, I won't fight you on it, Alan. It was the best sex I've ever had."

"Stop it, Nikki," he says. "Robert was a mistake. The actor was a terrible mistake. Insanity. The intimacy was real. I care

255

about you." I laugh sarcastically. He continues, "I'll give you a number when you do this right. Get an agent. If you want some referrals, I'll be glad to give you some good people."

"Thanks, but I'd prefer a more reliable source."

"Okay," he says. "Why are you in such a hurry?"

"None of your business."

"Nikki," he says, "Can we meet somewhere? In person? I don't want you to do something you're going to regret."

"How about one of your model apartments?" I coo. "You could fuck me, then fuck me over." I realize I'm starting to sound like a whining teenager.

"How about your café?" he suggests.

"I'll let you know," I say, and hang up the phone.

A flood of emotions sweeps over me when Virginia Bascomb opens the door to her home. The first is relief. The walk from the train station to this house made me feel like a target in a shooting gallery, knowing the Nazi is still stalking me. My hair felt like it was standing on end each time a new noise sounded: a squeaky brake, an engine roar, a honking horn. One good engine backfire would have induced an immediate, life-ending heart attack.

There are other feelings, too, starting with the surprise from seeing Virginia's face, which seems gently human. I couldn't be more amazed if she were wearing a gorilla suit. Then the image of Blythe rises in my mind, the permanent image, a highly romanticized portrait of her, with loving eyes and radiant skin and perfect lips parted in a gentle smile. And I feel the numbing weight of grief, too.

Virginia ushers me into the kitchen where she and Morgan are preparing a light dinner. Morgan smiles when I enter and we exchange cheek kisses. Her face is solemn and sad, but she manages polite conversation. We dine at the informal table adjacent to the kitchen, looking out on Virginia's flowers, now in full bloom. No one is really hungry. We pick at our food. I mention that Blythe would have loved this scene, her family together, looking out at a fantastic array of flowers in the fading light of day. That starts a gentle flow of shared memories about Blythe and her time with us. We sit together well into the night, talking intermittently, recalling Blythe's life. We go to bed exhausted, but what little sleep I get comes in short, tortured snippets.

The next morning, I get a text from Alan. *Parked out front. Let me drive you to work. Someone's following you.*

I reply, *Go away.* But what I want to know is, what is Alan doing here?

Alan texts again: *Big guy, close-cropped hair, like a Marine. Old SUV, greenish, Jeep. A few houses down from you.*

I flush with anger. *What are you doing here? Go away!* I text. But the truth is, he's described the Nazi to a tee and I know what *he's* doing here.

Alan's reply comes back in a second. *Is this why you're selling? Let me help.*

Right. I can feel the heat of indignation flow through my body. *Go away,* I text back.

My phone chirps. It's Alan, calling this time. "You don't want to mess with this guy yourself," says Alan. "I can help."

"How?" I ask. I should just hang up.

"I have experience—"

I come to my senses and cut him off. "I don't need your help, thanks." I hang up.

I run downstairs and pause in the foyer to look out on the street. I don't see any older vehicles parked at the curb, but I have a limited field of vision. I open the door and step out. Halfway down the block, a squad car sits alongside an elderly Jeep SUV parked at the curb. The officer bends to the window of the SUV.

It looks like he's returning the driver's documents. I can't see the driver, but I know who he is. I wonder if Alan called the police. More likely, it was a neighbor. Millionaires are very touchy about being robbed. I head into the kitchen to make coffee and wonder what reason Mr. Nazi gave the cop for his presence on an elegant street in Winnetka.

31

I've had almost no experience with funerals as an adult, so I'm ill-prepared to share a limo with Virginia and Morgan as we roll slowly from the church to the cemetery. That Virginia Bascomb has included me as family in such a solemn occasion is a shock. I'm so intimidated by her generosity, I literally don't know what to say in the bleak silence of the car. I try to recall movie scenes of moments like this so I can pirate a tasteful line, just to break the dark monotony.

"That was a beautiful service, Virginia," I say to break the oppressive quiet. I don't remember where I heard it, but it's a common line, not that I'd know a beautiful service from a bland one.

Virginia nods. Morgan squeezes my hand. "Blythe would have loved it," I say. The words just pop out. I don't know why I said them.

"Why would she love it?" asks Morgan.

I blush, caught in my own phony rap. Then I think about it. "Because the sun was streaming through the stained-glass windows," I say. "The music was grand, especially the Mozart piece. The readings were poetic. It was all the things she loved, including you and your grandmother."

"No need to flatter me, dear," says Virginia.

"Sorry?" I say, confused.

"Grandmother picked the music and the psalms," explains Morgan.

I blush at my ignorance. I figured the preachers picked all that stuff. Good grief, they seemed to be in charge of everything else. I pause a moment, then say, "You knew your daughter well," I say.

Virginia smiles and thanks me, and Morgan squeezes my hand again. The three of us relax into silence. I let my mind fill with memories of Blythe, the happy ones, recorded in our courtship and early marriage. There must have been times when she was angry or snappy, but all I remember are smiles and soft touches and a woman perpetually filled with gladness.

I've heard that in some circles, funerals are like weddings in that people who attend may not know the deceased, but they know someone in the family and turn out to show loyalty and support. That has to be at play here because Blythe was a mostly private person with a small circle of friends and business acquaintances, yet her service filled the church and the line of cars filing into the cemetery seems to extend for miles. As we wait at the grave for people trekking in from distant parking places, I look upon the long ribbon of cars and shake my head in wonder.

Morgan smiles a little. "I know," she says. "Quite a showing."

"Do you know all these people?" I ask her.

"Not even Grandmother knows them all," says Morgan. "Lots of them are people who knew Grandfather. In business, the country club. And the church people. They're very supportive. And people from town."

The large crowd is quiet, like a rock concert on mute. The priest performs what amounts to another service, with Bible readings, group prayers, and his own recollections of Blythe. At the end of the service, the priest nods to Virginia. She stands up and motions for Morgan to stand, then, to my shock, for me to join them. She leads us to an array of cut flowers lying loose at graveside. She selects one and stands next to Blythe's casket while Morgan selects a flower. I follow their lead. Virginia drops her flower on the casket, crosses herself, and closes her eyes in a brief prayer. Morgan does the same thing, and I follow along, wondering when my daughter became so familiar with this strange ritual. I don't cross myself because that would seem sacrilegious, an atheist aping a religious rite, but I do cast my eyes low to the ground and hold my hands together at my middle and call Blythe's beautiful face into my mind and tell her I love her and I'll miss her. I follow Virginia and Morgan to thank the priest for the service, then stand and watch as friends and well-wishers file by the gravesite, many pausing to pick up a flower and lay it on the casket. It takes forever for everyone to pass by, many stopping to express their condolences to Virginia and Morgan. I position myself behind Morgan and Virginia to avoid confusing their acquaintances, most of whom have no idea who I am.

As the procession wears on, my mind drifts away to my Nazi problem and how to keep Morgan safe. I descend into a trance-like state that's broken when Ophelia steps forward to hug me. We chat briefly, and when she leaves, Little John is waiting to express his condolences. He's sweet and considerate, like always, rising on his tiptoes to kiss me on the cheek, then hugging me tightly.

"Is everything okay?" I ask him. "You're all safe? We're still in business?"

He nods. "Everything's under control," he says. "We've got almost everything ready for your return."

I thank him and admit I still don't know how I'm going to deal with our stalker.

"These things have a way of working themselves out, Nikki," he says. He flashes a radiant smile and hugs me again. He seems to have crossed some kind of threshold, passing from his previous state of fear and irritability to, well, something better.

Alan shows up near the end of the procession. I don't see him until he's almost in front of me. I can't decide whether to hug him or send him away but I'm incapable of words or movement, so I just watch him approach. He embraces me in a tender hug and kisses my cheek, then puts his face next to mine and hugs me again. I feel the warmth of his face and the strength of his body as it presses against mine. I can feel my emotions rising, the hidden sobs and wails I haven't been able to express at Blythe's death, the loneliness, the desperation of facing a hostile world alone. If only he hadn't betrayed me, I could take such comfort in his expressions of love and affection. If only.

"Deep breaths," he says. "You have bright days ahead."

I thank him for coming. I try to sound like Virginia saying the same thing to a distant friend. I don't want to encourage him. He starts to say something, then chokes it back. He nods, smiles, says he'll call me later, and leaves.

By the time we're able to walk back to the car, most of the people from Blythe's funeral have already reached theirs, even the distant ones. Slow-moving vehicles wind along the narrow roadway through the cemetery grounds toward the exit. The sight of so many well-wishers has me briefly contemplating my own funeral which I'm sure would be as small as this one was large. Not that it matters to me. Funerals are for the living. The dead are literally beyond caring.

I stare out the window on our way out of the cemetery. At the gates, I see a stirring of bodies and lights in the parking lot of the office building. It's a stately old structure with stone walls and split-cedar roof shingles, looking for all the world as though it had been built before the Civil War. Three squad cars cordon off a car at the edge of the small lot, their lights flashing; people in uniforms and civilian clothes mill about.

"You don't see that every day," I comment to Morgan and Virginia, gesturing toward the police cars.

"What do you think that's about?" Morgan murmurs, not really that interested.

"Probably not a robbery," I quip.

"Could be body snatchers." Morgan says it with a smile.

Virginia glances out the window. "Probably some poor soul who came here to plan a funeral for a loved one and had a heart attack when they told him how much it would cost."

I've never heard her make a joke before.

Morgan holds her hand. Virginia kisses Morgan's hand and smiles. "I was trying to be funny," she says.

I join my hand with Morgan's and Virginia's for a brief moment, shocked at myself, and even more shocked when Virginia squeezes my hand. We turn onto the highway outside the cemetery and I catch one more glimpse of the activity in the parking lot. The only thing that registers is that the vehicle at the center of the hubbub is kind of a beater, more of a gravedigger's car than something a grave-buying North Shore socialite would be driving.

The morning after the funeral is filled with sunlight pouring in the many windows of Virginia's stately home. Our mood is curiously laid-back, probably because we all went to bed exhausted last night and slept like the dead. I spent the night in a guest room, mainly to be here in the morning so the three of us could talk about Morgan's safety, and where she would go to school in the fall. It's eerie, waking up in this house for the first time in nearly twenty years, and in a world without Blythe in it.

Even when she hated me, I understood, and a small part of me dared to hope she would someday forgive me and love me again, maybe as a sister.

I'm the first one downstairs and have coffee brewing and water for tea on the stove by the time Virginia and Morgan arrive. I serve coffee to Virginia with the self-assurance of a North Shore matron. She thanks me and brushes my arm with her hand. I couldn't be more flattered if Brad Pitt had asked for my hand in marriage

Our breakfast conversation is slow, desultory, and gentle, mostly about the funeral and the people who showed up, and how much we enjoyed the close friends who came to the house after the funeral. I busied myself working with the caterers, keeping food trays stocked, glasses filled and dishes whisked into the dishwasher, trying to look like hired help to avoid questions about who I was. When people asked me how I was connected to the family I just said I'd known Blythe for years and Morgan all her life.

It was Virginia who blew my cover. As I was serving wine she introduced me to a circle of her friends as Nikki, then added, "Before Nikki became a woman, she was Blythe's husband and Morgan's father. We love her very much." I was shocked speechless. The second shock was that the news wasn't a very big deal among Virginia's friends. I made polite conversation with them, mostly just listening as they talked about other trans people they knew, and a few exclaiming they would have never guessed I was trans.

Later, after all the guests had left and Morgan had gone to bed, I thanked Virginia. She said, "Sit down, Nikki," and poured us each a glass of wine. "At the end of her life, Blythe told me her biggest regret was that she never made peace with you. She did love you, you know."

"I loved her, too," I said.

"Well, I don't want that same regret, especially since we have

Morgan's future to consider. I want peace between us."

Now, with the three of us together, I thank her again. "And thank you for yesterday, too," I say. I don't have to explain.

She smiles. "We need to work together," she says. "We have a big job ahead."

We both look at Morgan, who catches the drift right away.

"I want to be a city girl." Morgan says it almost apologetically to her grandmother. They both look at me.

"I'm willing to investigate schools with you," I say, "but I doubt we can get you into anything as good as your school out here."

Virginia is visibly surprised at my largesse. She fully expected me to snatch Morgan from her orbit, and frankly, I would have been eager to do so a couple of weeks ago. Our war has gone on for many years. It seems a sudden end, to both of us. We discuss the merits of various school options in a civilized manner, and the possibility Morgan could weekend with me if she went to school in Winnetka during the week.

"There's one other thing," I say, when the school talk ebbs. I look at Virginia. "I don't know if Morgan's told you, but I've had some trouble with a neo-Nazi type at the café. He's dangerous. He's a danger to Morgan, too. So that's a factor, until I get the situation resolved."

Morgan objects to being coddled.

"We can't go through life afraid of bullies," she says. "I want to work in the café with my friends and I'll take my chances with a city school. Michelle Obama went to a Chicago high school and she's done pretty well, hasn't she?"

I urge caution. Virginia watches the two of us, rapt. Morgan goes into a monologue about her work at our self-defense class, and how she and I practiced using pepper spray like quick-draw artists from the Old West. As she talks, Virginia's eyes get wider. Then Morgan retrieves her purse and demonstrates how quickly she can pluck the can out of her bag, pop off the lid, and have it at arm's length, aimed perfectly away from herself, ready to do damage. Virginia gasps.

"Very impressive," I say. "But, honey, these people aren't morons, especially this one. They're like predators in nature. They strike when it's best for them. You may not see him coming." I suggest he might have been the goon who attacked her and Little John, and I remind her how sudden and violent that was.

"We need to use our wits," I tell her. "Let's just take this a day at a time for now."

As I finish the sentence, the doorbell rings.

Morgan comes back to the kitchen table, a worried look on her face. "There are two policemen at the door," she says to me. "They want to talk to you."

Alarms go off in my head like a Fourth of July fireworks display. Virginia and Morgan follow as I walk to the door, wondering if the café has been bombed, or Little John murdered by the Nazi terrorist I didn't have the courage to put away.

Two men stand at the door, one in a Cook County Sheriff's police uniform, the other in a civilian suit. The suit greets me. "Ms. Nicole Finch?" he asks. I nod. He introduces himself as a Detective Leconde, and the man with him as Patrolman Porter. Leconde wears a tan summer suit that fits him well, and a tie that looks like one of the avant garde paintings Virginia's husband invested so heavily in. He seems a decent enough guy, soft-spoken, direct, a sincere face. He asks if they can come in and talk to me.

"What's this about?" I ask. I can hear Virginia come up behind me to see what's going on.

"It would be better to discuss it inside," Leconde says.

"This isn't my house," I object. "What's this about?"

We circle through the conversation again. Virginia steps

266

forward. "You can take them into the living room, Nikki," she says, gesturing.

It's a large, formal room I've only been in a few times. It's filled with priceless furniture and two area rugs that are probably more valuable than all the furnishings in my apartment. Virginia seats us in a corner of the living room, the two policemen on one couch, me on a facing couch, a priceless black walnut coffee table between us. Morgan sits next to me, but Virginia intercedes, asking Morgan to help her bring coffee.

Leconde gives me a Cook County Investigations Bureau business card.

"Are you here about my café?" I ask. "Is everything all right?"

Instead of answering my question, Leconde asks, "Do you know Dmitri Krill?"

"No." I'm confused, but relieved that the question is so easy to answer.

The detective pulls a photo out of a file folder and shows it to me. It's my Nazi terrorist on a gurney in what looks like the coroner's office. He's been shot in the temple.

"Oh my God." I don't want to say anything but the photo is so horrific in so many ways the words escape me in a reflexive gasp.

"You know him, then?" the detective asks.

"Not by name, but yes, I've encountered him," I say. I ask again what this is about and Leconde takes me on another circular conversation where he answers my questions with questions.

The picture is still sitting on the walnut coffee table when Morgan comes in with a tray of cups and saucers and tea and coffee. She sets the tray on the table as Virginia enters with a smaller tray of pastries. Morgan distributes coasters to each of us and sees the photo.

"Oh my God," she says. "That's that guy!" She takes in a deep breath and holds one hand to her mouth in horror. "My

267

God, he's dead."

"I'm sorry you had to see that, honey," I say.

The detective apologizes and puts the photo back in his file. His apology seems sincere.

"What sort of encounters have you had with him?" the detective asks.

I look away from him. "Morgan," I say, "I don't think you should hear this."

"I want to," she says. "I'm not a child, and that man hated me, too."

She sits next to me, and Virginia sits next to her. I give Virginia a confused look.

"I have an attorney on retainer," Virginia says. "I'll leave if you want, but I can be of help."

I nod gratefully and turn to the detective. "That man, Krill, was terrorizing my staff and me. He was some kind of neo-Nazi and he took exception to me being transgender and my business employing minorities."

"You had a violent encounter with his brother in May?" Leconde asks it, but it's a statement. I'm impressed and filled with dread. He's done his homework.

"Yes. He assaulted my business partner and me," I confess.

"You did quite a number on him according to the arrest report," he says. He's pushing me to elaborate.

"If you know all that, why are you asking me about it?"

"Let me ask the questions, Miss Finch," Leconde says politely.

Virginia intercedes. "Unless you answer her question, I'm going to advise Nikki to stop talking to you until I get my lawyer here."

Smith nods for a minute, as if making a momentous decision. "Okay," he says. "Here's the situation: Mr. Krill was found in his car at Oakwood Memorial Garden yesterday. He had been shot in the head. The time of death coincided with a funeral you attended there. You have an interesting history with Mr. Krill and we want to have a chat with you."

"Am I a suspect?" I ask.

"You're on a very short list of people who had motive and opportunity," says Smith.

I'm speechless. My mind races to find words. There's something crazy about this but I'm so panicky I can't think.

"I hope your list isn't too short," says Virginia, in that patrician voice of hers. "Nikki was in full view of hundreds of people at that funeral and she rode to and from the cemetery with Morgan and me in a car chauffeured by a driver from the funeral home."

"She doesn't own a gun, either," says Morgan. She's angered by the implied accusation. "She didn't use a gun on that other Nazi, did she?"

I pat Morgan's hand.

Smith nods his agreement. We all sit back and sip coffee while Morgan and I tell them about Krill's visits to the café. I leave out the part about Alan's actor and the part about me visiting Krill's apartment to kill him. The actor thing is between me and Alan. My visit to Krill's place opens a door that might take months and hefty lawyer fees to close. I'm sure Krill didn't file a complaint or I'd be in cuffs by now. Still, I'd breathe easier if I'd never made that trip.

32

When the police leave, the three of us begin picking up dishes and straightening up the kitchen and living room. I'm loading the dishwasher as Virginia busies herself cleaning the stove and counters.

"Thank you for your help with those men," I say. "It meant a lot. Legally, of course. But personally, too."

She keeps working, but I wait for her to say something. Finally, she pauses, gives me that smile again, and says, "You're family."

I think about our exchange as I finish loading dishes. What she said is something I've been feeling from her in recent days, but there's still a lot of mystery about why her attitude toward me changed.

"Virginia," I say, facing her and waiting for her to face me. She does. "Why did you tell your friends about me?"

"Why wouldn't I?" She says it casually.

"You didn't have to," I point out. "I was introducing myself as a family friend."

"You're family," she says again. "You're Morgan's surviving

parent. We're going to be seeing a lot of each other, the three of us. It's too late for secrets."

"I hope your friends don't hold it against you, that you have a transgender woman in the family," I say.

She laughs. "Hardly, Nikki. I have new status. I've accepted a transgender woman into my family. That makes me a thoroughly modern woman myself. Really, if I'd known how trendy it was, I'd have trotted you out years ago." She laughs again, a self-deprecating laugh. I smile with her. After a moment, she comes to hug me. It's momentarily awkward. The mismatch in our heights means her face lines up with my boobs. We laugh a little and then I bend my face to hers and we embrace.

Morgan passes the kitchen *en route* to the laundry room, her arms filled with bed linens. Virginia and I break the hug and smile at her.

"What on earth are you doing?" Virginia asks.

"Taking care of our sheets," she says. "Nikki and I are going back to the city today."

I'm not sure which of us is more surprised, Virginia, that her granddaughter is now a person who washes sheets, or me, that my daughter is coming back with me today. Virginia speaks first. "You do laundry now?" she asks.

"I'm learning to be an independent woman of the city," Morgan says, mimicking the words I once used with her. "You should see me take out garbage and scrub toilets."

Virginia glances at me with a bemused look on her face.

"We're getting her ready for Harvard," I explain. She taps me lightly on the wrist and shakes her head as if to say, *Oh you joker.*

Virginia follows Morgan to the laundry room to help her navigate the complicated directions on the washing machine. My phone rings as they leave. It's Alan. For some reason, relief at Krill's passing, I suppose, I answer. Alan is so surprised he stumbles over his greeting, which makes me smile.

"Can we talk?" he asks when he regains his composure. "I feel like there's more to be said. If you're still in Winnetka, I could drive you home, or to BeatNikki's, or wherever you're going."

I start to say no, then think the better of it. "That would give us a chance to talk about the building," I say, thinking out loud. He doesn't try to dissuade me. "Okay."

We arrange a pickup time and I go looking for Morgan. She and Virginia are upstairs, making beds. I snag her for a brief word before they go to the next bedroom.

"I'm riding back to the city with a friend," I say. "We have some business to discuss. You might want to stay another night with your grandmother."

"Is this that Alan guy?" she asks.

"Yes," I say. "How did you know about him?"

Morgan grins. "That's all they talked about in the café when I came back from the hospital," she says. "The staff thought you were having a red-hot affair." She pauses. "Were you? Are you?"

"I was attracted to him," I say, haltingly. "But this is business."

"If you're sleeping with him, you don't have to hide it from me," Morgan says. "I'm not going to rush out and take a lover just because my mom has one."

Morgan calling me Mom in casual conversation jolts me a little, but in a good way. I recover.

"It didn't get far enough for sleepovers," I say. "We had a disagreement. The romance is over. We just have to clear up some business."

"What business?" Morgan asks.

I sigh. I don't want to get into this, but we've gotten this far, Morgan and me, because we've been honest with each other, even when it hurts.

"I asked him to bid on the BeatNikki building," I say. "He's a developer and our neighborhood is hot, apparently."

Morgan reacts like she's been shot. "No! Sell BeatNikki's?" She goes into a riff about how special the place is, and how it's filled with special people. Her face puckers a little, her emotions maybe fueled by the loss of her mom. Her Mom mom.

I hug her.

"Easy, sweetie," I say. "This came up when Krill was stalking us. The building's worth a lot of money. I thought we might sell the building and move the business to a different part of the city, maybe Boystown, where people like me don't stand out so much."

"He's gone now," says Morgan.

"Yes," I agree. "But we have to solve the school issue for you. If I sell, I could get a place out here, so you could finish up at your school. Maybe I could even open the café up here."

Morgan moans. "No, don't do that!"

She goes on and on about how she loves the city and she'd miss her new friends and she recites a list of famous people who graduated from Chicago public high schools and went on to achieve great things in life. She asks me how Little John feels about it and I tell her, he's with her on the subject.

"It's also—," I start, then pause, looking for words. "We're going to need money for college. You're destined for one of the great schools in this country, and that takes money. I don't make enough to pay as we go, so I'm going to have to sell something."

"Grandmother will pay," Morgan insists.

"No. You're not her responsibility, you're mine. And besides, it's time your relationship with her was based on love and respect, not wealth."

"Aren't I inheriting something from Mom?" she asks.

"I imagine so," I say, "but whatever that is, and whatever your grandmother sets aside for you, it'll be waiting for you when you come of age. I want you to understand the value of money and what normal people go through to pay for things."

"What's the difference between me using your money or Mom's or Grandmother's?" Morgan's chin points out, a victory dance of sorts. She knows her logic has overwhelmed mine.

"The difference is, you'll see the pain. It's not just someone writing a check, it's someone sacrificing something."

Morgan shakes her head defiantly. "If you sell BeatNikki's I won't go to college."

"Don't be silly," I say.

"I mean it, Nikki. I'll take a gap year and travel. Maybe I'll go to culinary school or take courses at the Art Institute. I will not be the reason you sell BeatNikki's."

I take her hands in mine and kiss them and suggest we finish the conversation after I talk to Alan. She agrees, but insists on coming along. "I have to get back to the café," she says. "And I miss my room." That last bit rocks me again. Her room here in Virginia's house is worthy of a European princess, a sea of pink and white and soft textures, enough pillows for an entire Girl Scout troop to sleep over, enough stuffed animals to open a day care. My apartment has its charms, and she's done some nice things decorating her bedroom, but it seems an unlikely choice.

As we go back upstairs, she prods me gently with an elbow and smiles wickedly. "You can have him over tonight if you want."

"I don't want," I snap.

"You're in denial," she says.

Alan greets Morgan like she's a visiting head of state. He tells her how pleased he is to finally meet her, and how I was right when I said she was beautiful and smart. Morgan accepts his blather with poise, but her wide smile and dancing eyes tell me she enjoys the attention. As we drive to the café, he fires questions at her. He's brilliant this way. The questions start with the routine stuff about school and how she likes working at the café, but he segues into more thoughtful questions like her ideas about careers and how she might handle conflicts between career demands and child-rearing, then, her thoughts about marriage and marital roles and issues like equal pay.

My daughter's answers to his questions are intelligent and sophisticated. I'm amazed at how articulate she is, and even more, that she obviously has been thinking about all this stuff. What kind of parent am I to have never asked these questions? I wonder if Blythe did? I wonder if Alan is really interested in her thoughts or if he's putting on a show for my benefit. He seems sincere, though, and more curious about Morgan than I've been. There's a lesson in that for me.

When we arrive at the café, I tell Morgan to go in ahead of me. She smiles and hops out of the car with the grace and lightness of a dancer. She peers into the front window to say goodbye to Alan, then says to me, "Why don't you invite him over?" She skips off to the café without waiting for an answer.

Alan smiles at me. "What was that about?"

"She thinks I need to get laid."

"Do you?" He poses the question with a playful smile on his face.

I ignore the question. "What about my building? Are you interested or not?"

His smile widens and there's a twinkle in his eye. "Nikki, you're safe now. There's no reason to sell. Your café belongs right where it is."

There's something in his voice and demeanor that strikes me as different. The merriment, maybe.

"You know about Dimitri Krill, then?" I ask.

"Of course," he says. "It's all over the news. Plus, the police questioned me."

"You? Why?"

"Because I was at the funeral and I'm a friend of yours."

"Seriously?"

"I'm sure they questioned your other friends, too," Alan says.

"Did you tell them you were following me?" A picture is

beginning to form in my mind.

"I told them I was concerned for your safety," he says. "They didn't press the issue. I suppose they'll be back if they don't find a better suspect." He shrugs as he says it, the nonchalance of a man who can afford great legal counsel.

"You could have hired someone to follow me," I say. "Then they wouldn't have any interest in you at all."

He looks deep into my eyes, his face suddenly serious. "I betrayed you once. I can never get that back. What I can do, as long as you'll let me, is make sure you're safe. That's something a man does himself, if he's any kind of man."

The intensity of Alan's voice and body language jolts me. This isn't the voice of a friend looking after a friend. I'm not even sure he's talking about following me. I wonder if he's telling me he shot Krill. I almost ask him point blank, then stop. What would I do with the knowledge?

"Then you don't want to buy my building?" I ask.

He relaxes, smiles and slowly shakes his head. "No. I'm interested in you, not your building." He stares at me with intense eyes. "I want to rebuild your trust so I can court you."

Court me? I almost laugh out loud. None of my fantasies have ever involved being courted. Loved? Yes. Respected? Yes. Physically desired? Oh, yes.

"Alan," I say, "you know, I'm not like other women."

"My point exactly," he says.

BeatNikki's is crackling with energy when I enter the café. The staff is transitioning from the early morning coffee rush to the lounge and lunch trade. Little John has people hopping, clearing tables, sweeping the floor and preparing the midday menu items. This has always been one of the hustle hours in the café, but today seems even more animated than usual. Little John moves through the shop with brisk military erectness, directing staff to chores with a crispness I've never seen before. I pitch in and set up our coffee brewers. While I work, I watch him handle a customer who's been giving a server a hard time.

"Sir," he says to the customer, "do you really think that's an appropriate way to speak to another human being?"

"I just asked for decent service," says the customer, a working-class guy in the uniform of a delivery service.

"Your coffee and roll were delivered hot, a minute or two after you ordered them," says Little John. "What was wrong with the service?"

The customer gives Little John a cocky glare. "Come on, man, that guy's gay. He doesn't even try to hide it. It creeps me out."

"The waiter's a professional," snaps Little John. "You owe him an apology. Otherwise, pay up and don't come back."

I couldn't be more shocked if Little John had come to work in drag. He's always been our gentle soul, the person who *asks* staff to do things, who sits down with an irate customer and patiently listens to them then apologizes and comps them. The epitome of the saying, "the customer is always right."

"What's gotten into Little John?" I ask Morgan when she passes by.

"I don't know," she says. "Everyone's talking about it though."

I watch him through the rest of the morning when I can. He's definitely different. Not obnoxious, not a problem, but different. It's like he took an assertiveness pill or something. I stop him and ask him to have lunch with me.

"You've made a decision about selling?" he guesses.

"Yes, I'm not selling the building," I say. I hear myself say the words, but wonder where they came from. I thought I was still mulling the concept. I shrug, more to myself than Little John. It sounds right. To Little John, I say, "But we have other things to talk about."

Just before I sit down to lunch with Little John, Detective Brooks swaggers into the café like he owns the place. He orders a mocha latte at the bar. When Morgan brings him his drink, he orders her to get me. I consider making him cool his heels out of spite, but in the end I play it straight and join him at the coffee bar.

"To what do I owe the pleasure?" I ask him. I don't offer a handshake and he doesn't either.

His face breaks into a nasty smile, full of sarcasm and scorn. "I understand you took out another Krill brother." His voice is tinged with the usual contempt and maybe a touch of anger, too. "Congratulations."

"You need better informants," I say, trying hard to control my own anger and contempt. "I had nothing to do with his demise."

"You used a gun this time," he says. "You've got a taste for blood now. You can't control it."

"I don't own a gun. I've never shot one in my life, and I never will," I say. My voice is tense. He's lit my fuse.

"Whatever you say," he says with a know-it-all laugh. "You got away with it. Those suburban cops couldn't make a case even if they had a confession. But know this—his brother's getting out someday, and he'll be coming for you. You won't know when or where, but he'll be coming. And you'll pay."

Brook's naked threat throws me off balance. He sounds a lot like Krill. "My God," I say, when words come to me, "are you in that club too?"

The evil grin again. "Makes you think, doesn't it?" He drains his latte and strolls out of the café like an Old West gunslinger who just won a duel.

"Is that guy a Nazi, too?" Morgan asks. She's been standing close enough to hear the conversation.

278

I shake my head. "I don't know, probably not," I say, "but he might be a sympathizer. There are lots of Trumpers on the police force."

"Seriously?" asks Morgan.

"Sure. The president of their union is a big Trump supporter," I say. "Moral of the story—don't start telling stories about our brushes with the Aryans. The walls have ears."

Little John and I find a quiet corner for our lunch. I open by thanking him for coming to Blythe's funeral.

"It was a beautiful service," he says. "I'm sorry for your loss. I know how much she meant to you and Morgan."

Our chat meanders for a while, until Little John calls one of the staff people over and corrects how she was cleaning tables. The exchange is pleasant, but pointed, and pointed in a way I've never seen before in Little John.

"You seem different today, did you know that?" I ask him.

He feigns ignorance. "How?"

"It's like you've read the Napoleon handbook on management," I say. "I'm not objecting, but you seem more forceful now. You're the guy in charge."

He shrugs. "Could be. I mean, I've been thinking about what you said before, about how you have to do all the dirty work. You're always the bad cop and I hand out the gold stars. You're stuck with keeping us safe while I'm in here making fancy drinks and sandwiches. So, I'm trying to step up my game, be a better partner. Take some of the weight off your shoulders. Is that a bad thing?"

I shake my head. "No, not at all."

I turn the conversation to the murder of Dmitri Krill. Little John knows about it. It's been a news headline for the past twenty-four hours: "Neo-Nazi Meets His Maker in a Cemetery." Too juicy for the media to pass up.

"That relieves some of the pressure, I hope," I say to Little John.

279

He shrugs. "I guess." He says it like there was never a Nazi problem and he never threatened to quit.

I fill him in on Brooks' visit. "Brooks has a point," I say at the end. "Krill's brother just might roll around one of these days looking for revenge. How do you feel about that?"

Little John shrugs yet again. It occurs to me, he's been practicing this shrug in the mirror. There's a specific technique for shrugging that tough guys employ to communicate a sort of bravado, like, *bring it on, no problem.* That's the shrug he's using.

"You won't be wishing we'd moved the business?"

"Nikki," he says, "we can take care of whatever comes along."

"We were lucky this time," I say. "We can't count on some mystery assassin intervening next time."

Little John smiles and leans back in his chair and cups his hands behind his head. He looks like a macho dude who just kicked the shit out of an angry mob in a Hollywood movie. "Maybe," he says, "maybe not."

It's the way he says it, equal parts wiseass and testosterone, that makes me focus hard on his face, his cocky expression, his eyes. And for the second time this morning, I find myself wondering if I'm looking at the man who shot Dmitri Krill. I start to ask him about it, then muzzle myself. If I don't hear the confession, I can never betray him. He's still smiling. I smile back.

"Still," I say, "from now on, let's try to work inside the letter of the law. I've got a daughter to raise." Little John nods. "Let's court the police, get them to stop in for a cup of coffee once in a while, maybe comp them a nice spread at the station house. Things like that. And get the other businesses here to do the same thing."

Little John agrees, dropping his tough guy act long enough for me to see the old Little John just beneath the façade, the sweet, gentle man who has conquered the world around him with love and goodness.

AUGUST 2017

33

"But I love being in the city," Morgan says. We're on the train heading out to Winnetka to attend Virginia's afternoon tea and stay the night. The train is lightly populated and we've positioned two seats so we can face each other.

"You'll get the best of both worlds," I counter. I'm trying to sell her on the idea of finishing up at her suburban school, and spending the weekdays with her grandmother and the weekends with me.

Morgan smirks. "You want me out of the way so Alan can stay over."

"I know you're kidding," I say, "but, no. Alan knows you come first. Everyone in my life knows you come first. Besides, I don't kid myself about Alan. I enjoy his company but it could end tomorrow."

"It sounds more serious than that," Morgan says with a knowing look.

I shrug and blush.

"Whatever happened to William?" she asks.

She's toying with me now. This has become a thing with us,

where she kids me about my sex life, like we're friends rather than parent and kid. I'm horribly uncomfortable with this kind of familiarity. I can't imagine that any other parent in the world has such frank exchanges with a daughter about her sex life. And yet, I can't think of a legitimate reason for me to cut her off. For one thing, this has become one of the keys to our ability to converse. The more I treat her as an equal, the more she enjoys our chats.

Besides, I'm in no position to become an imperial parent who issues commandments from the mount about morality and restraint. At least this way we're communicating and I have some chance of influencing her and the choices she makes.

Morgan repeats her question about William, bringing me back to the here and now.

"I haven't thrown away his number," I say, flashing my own sly grin, "but right now I'm putting all my discretionary income into the Harvard fund. If you decide to go to a state school, maybe I'll have William over to celebrate."

Morgan laughs. "Good one, Mom," she says.

I'm getting over my self-consciousness about being called Mom. I still see Blythe's face when Morgan says "Mom," but I no longer feel as though she's being slighted when Morgan calls me that.

We look out the window at the passing suburban landscapes until Morgan asks, "Do you think Krill would have been terrorizing us if you hadn't beat up his brother?"

I've thought about that, too. "I doubt it," I say. "He probably wouldn't have ever heard of us."

"Do you ever wish you hadn't done it?"

I shake my head slowly. "I don't know, honey," I say. "Was it really an answer to let him beat up Little John and me? You saw what one of those people did to Billy from the hair salon. He'll never be the same. Should I have stayed in the café and let him beat Little John while I called the police and watched? If he got away with beating one of us half to death, would he have stayed away, or would he have come back for more? We can't know the answer to any of those questions."

Morgan's eyes widen. "So, if it happened again, you'd do it again?"

"I'd change some things," I say. "We're cultivating personal contacts with the police, so if something like that happens again, I'll make sure someone calls the police before I go out there. Then, knowing they'll be coming soon, I can try to stall the guy until a pro gets there."

"What if they don't get there in time? He starts killing Little John?"

I flash the palms-up gesture. "I do my best to save him," I say. "That's how it is, sometimes. You try to manage your life intelligently, but sometimes fate intercedes and logic goes out the window."

Morgan nods thoughtfully. "Who do you think killed him? Krill?"

"I don't know, Morgan," I sigh. "He was a thug and a bully. I'm sure he had a lot of enemies."

"That day I was with Ophelia, we thought you were going to kill him."

The parklike greenery of the North Shore suburbs flashes past our window. I stare out. I have nothing worthwhile to say in response. Just a lie. Maybe it will drift away.

"We went to the café looking for you," says Morgan. "Little John was beating himself up for not standing by you. He thought you'd kill the guy or die trying, that he'd let you down, that when the Nazis came for him, you were there, but when they came for you, he deserted you."

"He didn't desert me," I say. "He's a good man, the best."

I'd like to say more, but I don't want to keep this conversation going. Morgan's way too smart and way too observant not to figure out everything if I keep talking.

We lapse into silence and I stare out the window, seeing Little John's face in my mind, his real face, then the Little Napoleon face he flashed in the café after Krill was shot. The real Little John walked through life with a saintly innocence befitting a religious leader. I knew how special that was, or at least I sensed it. Now, I wonder if it has been lost to the world in a single act—the murder of a man I could have killed so easily. No one ever talks about how one person's act of moral purity can cause moral compromise in others.

My mind skips to Alan, the love interest I never expected to have. Could he have killed Krill as an act of atonement for betraying me? Was my failure to execute Krill an act of morality or a moment of cowardice that served simply to draw people of conscience into performing unconscionable acts on my behalf?

I'll never know who pulled the trigger, but I know I'm guilty of that murder, partly because of the things I did, and mostly because of the one thing I didn't do. I also know that I'm glad I'm here and that I need to be here for Morgan. It's like Blythe said about raising our daughter, sometimes there's no right answer, but I think she'd agree, some wrong answers work better than others.

ACKNOWLEDGMENTS

Many thanks to my agent, Tina Schwartz, for her wise counsel, hard work, and wonderful friendship.

Thanks too to all my writing colleagues, especially the Novel-in-Progress Bookcamp crew, and the members of Off Campus Writers Workshop. We don't have enough pages to list all the individuals who critiqued and/or edited portions of this book.

And thanks to Michael Nava, the editor of Amble Press. Working with Michael has been a privilege and an opportunity to put forth my best work.

Finally, thanks to Salem West and the staff at Bywater Books. What a great group of people to work with!

ABOUT THE AUTHOR

Renee James is a confessed English major and out transgender author who is also a spouse, parent and grandparent. She is a Vietnam veteran, licensed hairdresser, and wilderness adventurer.

She has long been active in the Chicago transgender community, and has edited the Chicago Gender Society newsletter for many years, and participated in many of the other groups and activities that make the Chicago transgender community one of the most vibrant in the world.

Ms. James took up fiction writing after a long career in magazines. She has published six novels and a biography along with short stories under various bylines. Her novels include the Bobbi Logan trilogy (*Coming Out Can Be Murder, A Kind of Justice,* and *Seven Suspects*) which depicts the life and times of a Chicago transwoman after gender transition.

Amble Press, an imprint of Bywater Books, publishes fiction and narrative nonfiction by LGBTQ writers, with a primary, though not exclusive, focus on LGBTQ writers of color. For more information on our titles, authors, and mission, please visit our website.

www.amblepressbooks.com